Praise for the erotic novels of Evangeline
Anderson . . .

"Kept me up all night . . . sexy and funny and,
hidden beneath the wisecracks, a tender love story.
TAKE TWO hooked me from page one. I literally
could not put it down until I got to the end and it
was well worth the ride. Sadie is charming and
funny, the heroes (yes, there are two!) are handsome and gruff and sweet. You'll be rooting for
all three of them!"

—MaryJanice Davidson

"A terrific book filled with anticipation, danger,
sensuality and surprise."

—*Romantic Times* on **PLANET X**, Top Pick
(4½ stars)

D0064175

Take Two

EVANGELINE ANDERSON

APHRODISIA

KENSINGTON PUBLISHING CORP.

http://www.kensingbooks.com

Boca Raton Public Library, Boca Raton, FL

Aphrodisia Books are published by

Kensington Publishing Corp.
850 Third Avenue
New York, NY 10022

Copyright © 2006 by Evangeline Anderson

All rights reserved. No part of this book may be reproduced in any form or by any means without the prior written consent of the Publisher, excepting brief quotes used in reviews.

All Kensington Titles, Imprints, and Distributed Lines are available at special quantity discounts for bulk purchases for sales promotion, premiums, fund-raising, and educational or institutional use.

Special book excerpts or customized printings can also be created to fit specific needs. For details, write or phone the office of the Kensington special sales manager: Kensington Publishing Corp., 850 Third Avenue, New York, NY 10022, attn: Special Sales Department, Phone: 1-800-221-2647.

Aphrodisia and the A logo are trademarks of Kensington Publishing Corp.

ISBN: 0-7582-1535-5

First Trade Paperback Printing: November 2006

10 9 8 7 6 5 4 3 2 1

Printed in Mexico

Dedicated to my wonderful husband who understands why I need time to write; Treasure, for being my constant reader and cheerleader; and my fabulous editor, Hilary, for giving me a foot in the door.

1

"We'll take that one."

Sadie knew she was in trouble when the dark, curly haired man pointed straight at her, despite her attempt to hide behind the cybernetic prostie-borg in front of her. Pasting a blank look on her face, she tried to remain calm and look like all the other girls in the line-up.

There were prosties with small breasts, some with large, and some sported racks any porn-vid queen would be proud of. Some were so short they were practically dwarf size and some were so tall they could have played for any Zero-G team in the league. Their measurements ranged from anorexically slender to downright Junoesque. They sported skin tones from ebony to golden tan to peaches and cream pale, and hair ran the gamut from blond to redheaded to brunette and every shade in between.

Every face was plastically perfect and completely blank. "A Girl For Every Taste—Cybernetic Sex Made Delightfully Easy" was the motto of the Prostie Palace. Every possible combination of attractive female features and attributes was represented in the silent ranks of the assembled prosties and this joker had to pick *her*.

Hidden inside her outrageous scarlet wig she could feel the bargain Overlook-Me chip flicker for the last time, fizzle, and die. The noninterference field she'd been wearing like a protective halo for the past two weeks faded into nonexistence. Damn it, she'd known it was a bad idea to buy her main protection from Big Bob's Bargain Basement Chips, but what was a girl on a budget supposed to do?

It was hard enough financing the ticket from Io to Titan in the first place. In the end she'd had to ride on an ore transport that was far from luxurious. Insinuating herself into the Pleasure Dome Prostie Palace had required several bribes to the right people, both to get inside in the first place, and to add herself to the database of resident prostie-borgs. Add that to the cost of her outfit, make-up, and wig, and she barely had any credit left at all.

My whole life savings spent paying for this trip and now I'm screwed. Literally and figuratively. She stared blankly, as the man pointed her out to the mechanical madam who nodded in her direction. It was the same panicky feeling she had experienced when she first walked into the Prostie Palace and saw the kind of outrageous sexual practices that went on here. Having been raised on the morally uptight colony of Goshen on Io, the scene at the prostie brothel was an education to Sadie in more than one way.

She had financed the trip on her own for the ultimate payoff, a juicy scoop on the nitty-gritty, hard-boiled life of a prostie-borg in the Outer Rings.

Prostie-borgs were cybernetic organisms grown in flesh tanks on Mars. They were a variation on the more common flesh-bots that were used for manual labor all over the solar system but instead of being fitted for heavy lifting and tasks no human laborer could do, prostie-borgs were crafted specifically for sex. Despite a simple synthetic brain that put them on the mental level of a ten-year-old child, they were very popular, especially with the sex-starved men that mined the outer rings of Saturn. Intellectual stimulation wasn't high on the must-have list of female attributes for most Ring miners, and real women were few and far between at this cold, dark end of the solar system.

Sadie was tired of covering joining ceremonies, baby showers, golden anniversaries, and all the other human interest crap that a junior reporter got saddled with at the *Io Moon Times*. Problem was, her senior editor, a grouchy, chauvinistic man by the name of B. F. Fields, thought that was all she could do. Sadie had set out to prove him wrong.

Taking all of her yearly vacation in one big lump, she had hopped an ore transport to the most notorious prostie-brothel in the System, located on Titan, Saturn's largest moon. There she had planned to spend her free time gathering facts for a blistering tell-all exposé that would blow the top off the barely legal prostie-borg industry. She even had a title for her article all picked out: "Pain and Suffering in the Pleasure Dome: A Prostie-Borg's Daily Life in the Outer Rings."

When she got back to Io, Fields would *have* to recognize her reporting prowess and promote her out of the human interest section once and for all. Hell, she might even go freelance and sell her story to one of the intergalactic news vids.

Her plan had been working like a charm, too, until the bargain Overlook-Me chip began to die. When the other prosties began noticing her, Sadie knew she was in trouble, but she kept hoping the chip would last just one more week until her transport for Io left. Now the chip was good and dead and she didn't even have a repair kit to try and get it working again. She was about to find out first hand exactly what the prosties went through and she was afraid it wasn't going to be a pleasant experience.

At least he looks cleaner than most of the clientele you see around here. Sadie eyed the dark man carefully. He had very tan skin and his hair was the color of bitter chocolate, curly and thick, cut short but not too close to his scalp. Any woman she knew would kill for that kind of natural curl, she thought absently, taking in the indigo eyes fringed thickly with black lashes and the narrow but sensual mouth of the man pointing her out. Broad shoulders covered in a black leather jacket tapered to a narrow waist and powerful legs. There was a heavy bulge outlined by his tight black pants that made Sadie bite her bottom lip nervously as she felt those deep blue eyes sweep over her body.

"That one," he said again, and Sadie had no choice but to step forward. *Maybe it won't be so bad. Maybe it'll add realism to the story,* she thought desperately, trying to nerve herself up for the act. She felt horribly exposed in the tiny gold mesh dress that showed her breasts and sex plainly, but, after all, she'd been wearing it and outfits like it for two weeks. While the Overlook-Me chip had remained functional, no one had really *seen* her in them. From the look in the dark man's eyes, he liked what he saw.

Sadie was suddenly aware that her nipples were erect with fright against the scratchy gold mesh fabric. She squeezed her thighs tightly together, trying to keep her knees from shaking.

"Which one for the other gentleman?" the silver-skinned, mechanical madam asked, giving a jerky nod to the man's right. Standing beside him, hidden partially by the dark man's broad shoulders was another client. He stepped out from behind his friend with a nod to the madam and Sadie could see he was almost the exact opposite of the other man.

Tall and muscular with a runner's build, he had hair the color of beaten metal and the clearest sapphire eyes she had ever seen. The dark man wasn't short, but the blond was at least two inches taller with a full mouth that seemed naturally red against his pale golden skin. He was dressed in the same style as his colleague in tight black pants and a white shirt with the ubiquitous mining company symbol stitched in red on the collar. He was also wearing an identical black leather jacket.

Sadie couldn't help noticing that the bulge outlined by his pants was no less impressive than the dark-haired man's. Did they work for some mining company that only hired well-hung men? What was their motto—*Less than nine inches need not apply?*

These two were so different from the typical grimy, disheveled specimens who usually patronized the Prostie Palace that they might have come from Stud Miners R Us. Sadie felt a hysterical bubble of laughter rise in her throat at the thought and forced it back down. Prostie-borgs did not laugh.

"My friend and I prefer to share," the blond man said, to Sadie's horror. "That one will do fine."

Two at the same time . . . ? She couldn't stop her eyes from widening. Merciful Goddess, she didn't have all that much experience in the first place and she'd never done anything even remotely kinky. Certainly nothing like this.

"I . . ." she began and shut her mouth fast as she felt both sets of blue eyes boring into her. A prostie-borg wasn't supposed to have opinions about the clients she serviced, Sadie reminded herself. She simply went with the men the madam matched her with and did as she was told. But still . . .

"Is there a problem . . . ?" The madam stepped forward and scanned Sadie's ID number which hovered like a small holostar over her right hand with glowing red eyes. "Number 217?"

Sadie shook her head mutely, thankful that she hadn't depended completely on the failed Overlook-Me chip for security. The disguise and the fake ID number had seemed like a luxury, but it was a good thing she had them now.

The madam stared at her closely for a minute, clearly processing her personal data, then the blinking slits of her eyes turned green. Sadie knew she was in the clear—as long as she could take whatever these two men dished out. She shivered involuntarily and tried to contain her dread.

I got myself into this; I'll have to get myself out. That was fine, she was an independent girl, but she couldn't do anything, in front of the madam. One more security check and a supervisor would be dispatched to see to the problem—a *human* supervisor who wouldn't be as easily fooled as the mechanical madam.

"Go with the nice gentlemen, number 217." The madam made a creaky shooing gesture with her silver, tentaclelike arms. "Be sure to give satisfaction."

"Yes, madam," Sadie submissively bowed her head. She followed the two men meekly to one of the many pleasure cubicles that lined the long steel corridor to the left, her heart galloping madly in her chest. Could she really do this? As she was trying to answer that question, they reached the room the madam had indicated and the dark-haired man produced a scanner card and reached down to pull up on the sliding steel door, which disappeared obligingly into the ceiling when he yanked.

"After you." He nodded mockingly to his blond companion and made a flourishing gesture with one arm.

"Ladies first," the tall blond man said quietly, gesturing for Sadie to enter before them.

Sadie looked despairingly at the door. It was solid steel–titanium alloy and once she was locked inside the tiny pleasure cubicle anything at all could be done to her. There was a strict noninterference policy at the Pleasure Dome, which was why the customers had to put up a sizable damage deposit before renting the services of any of the prostie-borgs. The deposit was in case the prostie was rendered nonfunctional. *In other words, killed,* Sadie thought, trying to breathe past the sudden lump in her throat.

Sadie swallowed hard. She looked at both sets of blue eyes,

indigo and sapphire staring expectantly at her and then looked at the monitoring device on the wall to their immediate left. Someone was watching right now, probably a bored guard who would like nothing better than to sound the alarm and add some excitement to his monotonous day. Sweet Goddess, she was going to have to go through with it. She swallowed again and edged reluctantly toward the doorway.

The fear she was feeling must have shown in her own amber-brown eyes because the dark man who had picked her out in the first place stepped forward and took her elbow gently, looking at her intently as he spoke.

"Hey, it's okay, sweetheart," he said gruffly. "We're not gonna hurt ya."

She noticed for the first time that he had a strong New Brooklyn accent and wondered why anyone would come all the way from Old Earth to be a miner in the Outer Rings of Saturn. It was a hell of a long trip to do a dirty and dangerous job even if it did pay fairly well.

"My friend here is correct," the blond man put in quietly, taking her by the other elbow. "We have no interest in hurting you in any way." His voice was softer and more cultured than his friend's, but no less deep and commanding for all of that.

In spite of her fear, Sadie found herself propelled into the tiny steel room. Breaking their hold on her arms with a convulsive effort, she turned around just in time to see the dark-haired man slam the rolling door closed with a muffled bang.

She was trapped.

2

"Look . . ." Sadie backed away from them slowly, her hands out in front of her in a placating gesture. "I'm not what you think I am." Acting as though she was fluffing her hair, she reached carefully under the back of her scarlet wig to retrieve the miniature tickler she had concealed there in case of this sort of emergency.

"It's okay, baby," the dark-haired man soothed again. "We're not who you think we are either." He took a step toward her and Sadie took another step back, the tickler held tight in her sweating palm. She shivered as she felt the cold metal of the far wall of the tiny room touch her bare shoulder blades. There was nowhere left to run. *Trapped!*

"I'm w . . . warning you." She hated the way her voice trembled but seemed helpless to make it stop. "I . . . I'm armed."

"And dangerous, huh?" The tall blond man sounded amused and not the least bit frightened. "Come on, honey, what've you got? A blaster? You couldn't hide a thing in that skimpy little outfit." Sapphire eyes raked her nearly nude body appreciatively, taking in her firm breasts, the nipples hard with fear, and her neatly trimmed sex. He walked forward as he talked, holding one hand out in front of him as though he was intent on soothing a frightened animal.

"I won't tell you again." Sadie felt a cold calm drop over her like an icy blanket and suddenly her voice was steady and her nerves stopped jumping. *So much for going through with it for the veracity of the story,* she thought. She had no idea how she would get out of this room and the Pleasure Dome Complex alive—let alone back to Io—but she did know one thing, she was going to do some serious damage to these two men if they didn't leave her alone. "Back off, buddy," she snarled with the ferocity of a cornered feline.

"Hey, Holt, look at her eyes. I think she means it," the darker man cautioned, taking a step back. But his companion just grinned. He had a nice smile with white, even teeth, Sadie noticed in a detached sort of way. He was lucky she was holding a tickler and not a set of brass knuckles or she would've happily knocked every last one of them down his throat.

"Not gonna hurt you, honey," the blond crooned softly. "Look at her, Blake, she's just scared." He turned to the dark-haired man to talk and that was all the opening Sadie needed. Lunging forward with the tickler in her right hand she pressed it into the blond man's lean flank. She hit him right in the vulnerable junction where the armpit met the ribs, enervating the entire brachial plexus just as she'd been taught in self-defense class. The effect was instantaneous. One moment the tall blond had been creeping toward her speaking in that low, hypnotic voice, and the next he was doubled up on the floor, his long body convulsed with helpless fits of laughter.

"Hey, what the . . ." The dark man closed in on her, but Sadie stood her ground and pointed the tickler in his direction.

"Get away from me." She was amazed at the calm in her voice. "I'm only going to say it once."

"Okay, okay, you convinced me." He held his hands up,

palms facing her as he backed carefully away. "I just wanna check on my partner, is that all right?"

"No funny stuff." Sadie made a short, jerky motion with the hand holding her weapon, indicating he could do as he asked.

"Hey buddy, you okay?" The dark-haired man touched his partner tentatively on the shoulder, causing another outburst of laughter.

"Don't . . . don't touch me, Blake!" the light haired man pleaded. He thrashed on the floor, sliding away from his companion's hand. "Not hurt, just . . ." He was unable to finish the sentence and simply shook his head, chortling and gasping in turns while tears streamed out of his tightly shut eyes. At last the chortles died off to chuckles, then to the occasional giggle and he was able to sit up, wiping his eyes and shaking his head.

"Well, looks like the little lady taught you a lesson you won't soon forget," the dark-haired man remarked with obvious satisfaction. "Told ya to leave her alone." Now that he was certain his partner wasn't injured in any way, he seemed to think the whole thing was a pretty good joke. The blond man, however, was not amused.

"Haven't been hit with a tickler since training at the Academy," he muttered, getting shakily to his feet with a hand up from his friend. "Forgot how much I hated it." The sapphire eyes were like two chips of ice. Sadie's stomach did a big flip-flop at the look on his chiseled features.

"Hey now, she tried to warn you," the dark-haired one reminded him. "Look, sweetheart," he turned his attention to Sadie. "We're gonna sit tight right here on the bed and not come anywhere near you so suppose you tell us your story? I bet we're on the same side." He pulled the blond man down on the rickety metal bed that was shoved to the far side of the room and sat looking at her expectantly. His partner allowed himself to be maneuvered but shrugged off the dark-haired man's hand irritably once they were settled.

"Please enlighten us," he said sarcastically. "My partner and I are eager to hear your story."

"Well, first of all I'm not a prostie." Sadie wanted to make that perfectly clear from the start. "And I'm sorry about the credit you spent; I'll try to see you're repaid, although you'll have to give me some time because I'm flat broke right now . . ." She realized she was babbling. Now that the immediate danger of rape appeared to be over the cool blanket of ice had melted leaving her a bundle of nerves.

"Calm down," the blond man said, a little more gently. "My partner and I didn't come here for sex."

"Y . . . you didn't?" Sadie sank gratefully into the one chair in the room, which was bolted to the far wall. Really, the rooms were more like prison cells than pleasure cubicles, she thought. She cupped her elbows in her palms and crossed her legs tightly, covering herself as well as she could.

"No. We're after information and since you're not a prostie maybe you can help us." The dark-haired man looked at her hopefully. "I'm Detective Sergeant David Blakely and this here," he pointed a thumb at the other man, "is Detective Sergeant Christian Holtstein. But he just goes by Holt. We're a special unit assigned to Old Earth Vice to check into the prostie-borg racket."

"Tell her everything, why don't you?" Holt muttered, giving the dark-haired detective a dirty look.

"Hey, the lady needs a little reassurance, Holt. Quit bein' such a sore-head just 'cause she got you with her tickler." Blakely reached into the inner pocket of his black leather jacket and Sadie tensed but he shook his head. "'S all right, sweetheart, just goin' for my badge," he reassured her. He withdrew a worn leather wallet and tossed it to her. Sadie fumbled it at first but managed to catch it and flip open the leather. Inside was a dull, titanium badge with a small blue and green holo of Old Earth floating above it. On it were printed Blakely's name and rank, Detective First Class.

"Well." Flipping the wallet closed she tossed it back. "It certainly *looks* genuine, although I'm sure you could fake that kind of thing."

"Great," Holt muttered. "The lady's a skeptic. You know who we are, so who are you?" he asked, a little frown on his full lips.

"I'm undercover here," Sadie evasively replied. If they really were cops they would probably be reluctant to deal with the press in any form.

"Oh yeah, what agency?" Blakely looked genuinely interested.

"None of your business. Just don't blow my cover and I won't blow yours." She shivered and rubbed her palms over her bare arms. Did they really have to keep these cells so cold? Holt's face was stony, but Blakely got a sympathetic look in his dark blue eyes. He removed his leather coat, revealing the butt of a deadly looking blaster hooked under his arm in a shoulder holster. Sadie wondered why he hadn't drawn it earlier when she was threatening him with the tickler. *Must not think I'm much of a threat.* She frowned. Making sure the pockets were empty, the detective tossed the jacket across the room to her.

"Here, kid. Warm up a little."

"Thank you." It occurred to her to refuse the generous offer, but when she considered how cold she was and how much skin the mesh dress exposed, she decided the gesture wasn't worth it. She slipped the oversized jacket around her shoulders and snuggled into the body heat still lingering from the dark-haired detective. The faint, comforting scent of sandalwood soap clung to the leather making her want to turn her face into the collar and deeply inhale. She restrained herself and settled more comfortably on the chair.

"I'm collecting information about the prostie-borg industry, too." She nodded at them. "I've been here two weeks and I was scheduled to ship out on the next ore transport but my Overlook-Me chip failed. That's how you were able to see me during the line-up. I've got some inside information I'd be willing to share for the right price."

"What exactly would the price be?" Holt asked sourly. The dim overhead light glinted on his hair, changing it from silver to gold and back again.

"I need a ride back to Io," Sadie said coolly as though it was the simplest thing in the world. "As soon as possible, I might add. I don't want to have to go through this . . . *scenario* again." She gestured to the three of them sitting in the sordid little metal room and shuddered delicately.

"Oh, *just* a ride back to Io. Hear that, Blake?" the blond detective snorted in derision.

"Sure did," the dark-haired man replied shortly. "Don't want much, do ya, sweetheart?"

"I am *not* your sweetheart." She frowned as she snapped at them. "My name is Sadie Thomas, for your information."

"Well for *your* information, Sadie, *we* are not an interstellar taxi service," Holt snapped back. "We've got a lot further to go before we're done with this mess. Titan isn't our last stop by a long shot."

"Why don'tcha call in your back-up?" Blakely asked more reasonably than his partner. "Can't they get you home?"

"I . . . I don't have any back-up." Her lips began to tremble. Resolutely she firmed her mouth. It wouldn't do to show any weakness.

"No back-up?" the blond-haired detective exploded. "What kind of agency sends in an agent without back-up?"

"Well . . . I'm sort of freelance," Sadie admitted. She sighed. "I'm with the *Io Moon Times*, all right?"

"You're a *reporter*?" Blakely groaned out loud. "Oh man, do I ever know how to pick 'em," he muttered under his breath.

"You said it, not me, partner," Holt replied, rolling his eyes.

"Yes, but I can *help* you." Sadie leaned forward in the cold metal chair and tried to look them both in the eye at once. "It's like you said, we're on the same side. We both want to put an end to this kind of sexual servitude." She gestured to the door, thinking of the thousands of prostie-borgs and the sick things they were forced to do on a daily basis. "Think of these poor prosties. Just because they're grown in the flesh tanks and have synthetic brains doesn't mean it's right to enslave them, torture them—even *kill* them," she said hotly, warming to the topic. "They feel pain the same way humans do."

"Ah . . . while I do agree with you, sweetheart, it's not quite that simple." The dark-haired detective sighed and ran a hand through his thick curls. "Ya see, some of these gals might be more human than you think."

"*Blakely*." Holt gave him a warning look, the light blue eyes flashing. "She doesn't need to know all that."

"Why not?" Dark blue eyes looked back at the blond man challengingly. "She said herself that she's been livin' here for the past two weeks. Maybe she can help us spot which prosties are synthetic and which are transplant. Besides, it's not like the BRC can hush it up forever. It'll be all over the news vids pretty soon."

"Transplant? As in illegal mind transplants? Black market brains? *Mind rapes*?" Sadie definitely smelled a story—a much bigger one than she had originally been after. There were always rumors about such things, but so far no one had been able to provide substantial evidence. "I thought the whole mind rape thing was just an urban legend," She tipped her head to the side and raised her eyebrows with skepticism.

Holt sighed and mirrored his partner's behavior, running one large hand through his straight blond hair until it stood up in a golden halo around his square-jawed face. He shook his head as though deciding that he might as well give in and share their information. "Yeah, yeah. Well, three thousand bodies minus their temporal lobes and cerebral cortexes is no legend.

Someone cleaned out a whole colony on Phoebe. And that's just for starters."

"Three thousand . . ." Sadie could barely wrap her mind around the concept. "But why . . . ?" Phoebe was Saturn's smallest and most remote moon and it had only recently been fitted with atmosphere domes and cleared for colonization. Now these two were saying that someone had wiped out an entire colony there—an unheard of crime and possibly the story of the decade. Forget writing this up for the *Io Moon Times*—Sadie smelled a Solar Pulitzer. It made her mouth water.

"For purely financial reasons, kid," Blakely answered her unspoken question.

"Do you know how much a synthetic brain, even a low-end one, costs? Compare that with the average life span of a prostie-borg, especially at some of your rougher establishments and well . . . let's just say when you do the math it ain't pretty." He shifted restlessly on the bed, causing it to bounce and earning himself a dirty look from Holt.

"So you think that some of these prosties . . ." Sadie looked at the partners with wide eyes. "You know, they *did* bring in a fresh batch of them earlier this week. You can tell them from the older prosties by the blue tattoo on the right eyelid. And they seem different somehow. More, I don't know . . . vacant. Not really there." She frowned. "But it seems like a transplant prostie would be *more* emotional than a real one, not less, because a transplant would have more brain power and an actual personality instead of just an emotion chip."

"Appearances can be deceiving," Holt said darkly. "If the new girls were transplant, they'd have to be keeping them under control somehow."

"Well . . ." Sadie thought about it. "Now that you mention it, the new prosties get an injection twice a day and the old ones don't. I thought it was just standard procedure for new prosties, but . . ."

"Syntho-narcotics." Blakely snapped his fingers, indigo eyes narrowing. "Gotta be. Keeps 'em quiet and nobody knows the difference. Listen, kid, can you get us a sample of what they're injectin' the new ones with? If it checks out as an illegal substance we'd have enough evidence to order a full-scale bust on this place."

"Wait a minute, Blake, she's not even . . ." Holt objected but Sadie cut him off.

"I'm sure I can get what you need as long as I get to come along with you and get exclusive coverage on the rest of the bust. Otherwise, no go." She folded her arms and sat back in the chair, tapping one high-heeled foot on the floor.

"Hold on now, lady, you can't just invite yourself in on something like this. It's a federal case." Holt's voice was stern.

"Why not?" his dark-haired partner countered, rounding on the blond detective suddenly.

"Well *because*. The breach in protocol alone . . ."

"Oh c'mon, as if you ever gave a damn for doing things by the book. What's she gonna do if we *don't* take her with us?" Blakely demanded. "Her Overlook-Me chip is blown. We can't just leave her here to be raped or Goddess knows what, Holt."

"You can't just take her along like a stray kitten you found on the side of the road, Blake. Think with your head instead of your heart for once," the blond-haired detective shot back, poking a finger in his partner's chest.

"Yeah, but . . ."

"Excuse me? Would you mind not talking about me like I'm not in the room?" Sadie had to raise her voice to be heard. Both sets of blue eyes turned in her direction. "Look, I can *help* you." She stood and shrugged off the jacket, leaving it on the chair and began pacing as she made her point. "I'm good undercover," she pointed out. "I've survived on my own out here for two weeks and I would've been fine until my transport showed up except for the rotten luck with my chip. I can get you information you couldn't get otherwise. I'm sure you're both very good detectives, but you're *men* and most prostie-borgs are female. And *I* have extensive experience impersonating a prostie; I know what I'm doing." Sadie took a step toward them, hands on her hips and breasts thrust out, showing all her flesh through the golden mesh of her skimpy dress. She knew what she looked like—hot, wild, and wanton. She normally wouldn't act so brazenly but there was a big story on the line. A once-in-a-lifetime chance.

"Hmmm." With the mesh dress back in view and most of her considerable assets on display, the blond detective seemed to be rethinking his position. He exchanged an unreadable look with his dark-haired partner.

"She's got a point, Holt," Blakely murmured. "I bet she'd be real good under the covers."

"Undercover," the blond man corrected him, a sardonic grin curving his full lips.

"That, too," Blakely agreed, smiling back.

The mood in the tiny metal room had changed. Sadie could sense it like a new weather pattern, the heat from both sets of blue eyes raking over her body and pulsing against her nearly naked skin. She blushed from the tips of her toes to the roots of her hair, but she held her ground determinedly. *Think Solar Pulitzer,* she told herself. This kind of story could make or break her career.

Holt looked at her appraisingly. "So you're up for a little *undercover* work, hmm?" The blond man's tone was mocking, but interested.

Sadie felt her cheeks grow hot but refused to drop her eyes. "Absolutely. I won't lie to you; a story like this could make my career. I . . . I'd be willing to do almost anything to get a first hand exclusive."

"*Almost* anything?" Holt drawled, rising with catlike grace from the rickety bed and circling her. He didn't touch her in any way, but he was so close she could smell a faint hint of masculine musk that clung to his big frame. Sadie looked to the dark-haired detective for help because he had been so sympathetic to her earlier; but Blakely seemed content to watch the by-play between herself and his partner without saying a word.

"Y . . . yes." She hated the stupid tremble that came into her voice when she was nervous. She had no doubt what he was implying. Men like Detectives Christian Holt and David Blakely didn't give you a free ride and an exclusive scoop on a story this big for nothing. There was bound to be a price, a mutual exchange of favors involved. *Sexual* favors.

It looked like she was right back where she had started when Blakely picked her out of the prostie line-up.

Trying to control the tremble in her tone and sound sophisticated, maybe even a little bored, Sadie asked, "What do you say, boys?" What would they think of her in Goshen right now if they could see her using her body as a bargaining chip to get an exclusive scoop? She pushed the thought away.

Holt sat back on the bed and looked at Blakely. The look they shared seemed to convey something—some form of nonverbal communication that Sadie couldn't begin to decipher, but at last the blond turned back to her and spoke for both of them.

"Fine. You can come with us on the condition that you *stay out of the way.*"

"And promise to behave yourself." Blakely looked up at her from under the fringe of tangled black lashes and Sadie thought she had never seen a blue so deep.

"I'll be a perfect angel," she promised, trying to regain her composure. "Cross my heart, officer. If I'm not you can put me in cuffs." She held out her slender wrists, miming a set of restraints and then blushed. What had made her say such a thing? She was definitely going too far. From the look in his eyes, Blakely liked the idea.

"I'll have ta keep that in mind, baby," he drawled, obviously enjoying the mental image of Sadie in a pair of handcuffs.

Trying not to think about what she had just let herself in for, Sadie attempted to get back to business. "Well then it's all set. You two bring your ship around by the back of the far dome, I'll palm a sample of the evening injection, and we're home free." She smiled brightly and stepped away to go for the door, but a large, warm hand encircled her wrist, keeping her from completing the motion.

"Wait a minute, sweetheart. Aren't you forgetting somethin'?" Blakely's eyes were a sleepy-hot blue in his dark face, and Holt was looking thoughtfully at her as well.

"W . . . what?" Sadie quavered, all of her self-possession momentarily gone. "You said you weren't here for sex." *At least not yet . . .*

"We're not." Holt's voice was calm and he reached up to hold her other hand in a large palm, pulling her down to sit between them on the squeaky bed. Both men put an arm around her and despite the skimpy mesh dress, or maybe because of it, Sadie felt truly warm for the first time in weeks. In fact, she was beginning to feel distinctly overheated. "But I think what my partner is trying to say is, don't you think we'd better make it look real? I mean, you've been in here for over half an hour, supposedly with two sex-starved miners who haven't seen female flesh for a lunar year. Don't you think you'd be a little . . . shall we say, *roughed up* if that were really the case?"

"Oh, well . . ." Sadie flashed on the usual appearances of post-clientele prosties, *the ones that were able to walk out under their own power that is*, and swallowed hard. "I guess you're right. I could, um, mess up my hair." She ruffled the scarlet wig with one hand and looked hopefully from sapphire to indigo eyes.

"Not quite what I had in mind." Blakely's voice rumbled in his chest and Sadie noticed that with his jacket off, she could see a hint of black, curling hair peeking from the neckline of his plain white shirt. The scent of sandalwood soap was stronger and Holt also gave off that appealingly masculine scent of musk and something else she couldn't quite name. Something fresh and sharp . . . The scents seemed to mix in her brain making her dizzy.

"What did you have in mind?" She kept her voice steady by force of will.

"Just this." Blakely leaned toward her and Sadie drew back until she realized it almost put her in the blond detective's lap. She turned to look up at Holt and he was smiling, a look of cool condescension in his ice-blue eyes. On the whole, she thought she preferred the dark-haired detective's openly predatory attitude to his partner's sarcastic one.

"Don't worry, sweetheart. I'll keep my hands to myself. Just gonna give you a little love mark on the side of your neck, okay?" Blakely raised his hands, palms up to show his intentions were honorable.

"Well . . . I guess, as long as that's *all* you do. Make it quick." Tilting her head, she offered him the side of her throat and gave an involuntary sigh when the sensual mouth descended, licking delicately along her slender neck before settling in the sensitive area beneath her ear to mark her. Blakely's breath smelled like cinnamon. "Mmmm," she moaned involuntarily, feeling the brush of his coarse curls against her tender flesh as he worked. *What's wrong with me?* she wondered, even as she responded to the searing mouth on her throat. *I shouldn't be acting like this.* Blakely did something hot with his tongue that made her gasp, but she didn't try to pull away.

"Like that, huh?" he whispered. Raising his head for a moment, he looked over at Holt. "You joinin' the party, babe?" he asked his partner, his voice low and sensual.

"One for each side?" The fair-haired detective raised a silvery-blond eyebrow. "How does the lady feel about that?" He looked at Sadie and the sapphire eyes were filled with the same sleepy sensuality that lit Blakely's.

"Well, I . . ." To tell the truth, Sadie was pretty far gone. It was obviously wrong to be enjoying something that was simply a necessity, but she couldn't quite seem to help herself.

"Good for your cover," Blakely explained reasonably, his hot breath blowing against her ear. When she turned to look at him, the indigo eyes were dark and intense, and Sadie got the distinct feeling that he wanted his partner to do this with him. To *share* this with him for some reason. She wondered why, but somehow it didn't seem important. He was right, after all—it was important that she look the part of a recently rented prostie and another love mark could only help that impression. She decided not to worry about it . . . for now.

"Well, when you put it that way . . . I guess so," she heard herself saying.

With a low laugh, Blakely returned to the spot under her ear and then she felt another hot mouth—Holt's—kissing lightly along the heavy pulse on the other side of her throat until he stopped to suck gently at the sensitive place where her neck met her shoulder.

At that moment, something strange happened. When Holt's mouth opened and his tongue touched her flesh it was as though the sensation from both sides had not just been doubled, but infinitely multiplied. Sadie stiffened between them and then melted helplessly into the embrace. Her nipples felt like two hard pebbles at the tips of her breasts and she pressed her thighs together tightly, trying to deny the heat and moisture that was gathering between them. It was hard to believe that this simple act when the two men weren't touching her in any other way that was remotely sexual could make her respond so blatantly, but her arousal was undeniable.

"Goddess . . ." she breathed softly, drowning in the hot sensation of both mouths tasting her, sucking her, marking her.

Involuntarily she reached out and gripped their legs, one in each hand, feeling the bunching of heavy thigh muscles under her palms as she did. Both men were excited, as excited as herself if not moreso; she could feel it in the tension that thrummed through the big bodies on either side of her like an electric current. *And I'm the conductor between them,* she thought faintly. The strange thought was enough to bring her back to herself and she pushed suddenly, convulsively away from them, using their legs as a prop to propel herself off the rickety bed.

"I think that's enough, gentlemen." Her voice shook as she stood in front of them and tried to catch her breath. She placed her hands on either side of her neck protectively, feeling how tender the flesh was.

"I guess." Blakely looked disappointed, but Holt still looked amused.

"You look fairly *roughed up* now, I would say," the blond detective drawled, annoying Sadie even as he agreed with her.

Sadie felt herself flush and forced herself to speak calmly. "Take me back to the common room now and I'll meet you with the injection the new prosties are receiving at the back of the far dome at eight tonight. Be sure you're on time."

"We'll be there, sweetheart," Blakely assured her, rising from the rumpled bed and retrieving his jacket.

"Wouldn't miss it." Holt agreed.

3

"I still say it's a bad idea. We may have to go all over the Outer System to crack this case and it's federal business. The last thing we need is a nosy reporter hanging around us every step of the way." Holt glared at his partner, knowing that it was too late to do anything about it now. He tried to pace, but the inside of the boxy little landing craft was too cramped for his long strides.

"Will ya shut up already, Holt? I think she's gonna be a real asset to the mission."

Blakely glared back at him and continued his surveillance of the nearest dome. A light methane mist was drizzling outside and it cut down on the visibility considerably.

Just another beautiful day on Titan—at least it has an atmosphere, even if it is mostly nitrogen, Holt thought. He waited for his partner of seven years to continue his thought; he already knew how Blakely *felt*—the T-link between them made that a given.

"'Sides," the curly haired detective said smugly. "You're just jealous 'cause she went for me more than you. Those blond good looks can't always getcha everything you want, ya know."

The blond detective snorted. "Oh please, she played us *both* for suckers, Blake. The minute she took off your jacket and stood up in that tiny little dress I knew exactly what she was doing."

"Yeah, so? Worked didn't it?" Blakely grinned. "Anyway, we turned the tables on her pretty quick. She wanted us to think she's used to this kinda thing, but you can always tell. She's a nice girl, Holt. You see how she blushed after we . . . uh, roughed her up? She's not used to it, but she liked it. And I know you felt the way the T-link opened when we both touched her. Who knows, she could even be the one, like Professor Klinefelder said." He licked his lips thoughtfully. "She tasted like some kinda flowers, ya know?"

"Oh come off it," the blond detective protested. "Don't start that again."

"Start what?" Blakely sounded defensive. "You don't know—it could happen." Indigo eyes narrowing, he resumed watching the dome. If everything went according to plan the newest addition to their team should be coming out the plexi-tube leading from the fat gray half-globe at any moment. Sadie didn't have a protective suit, but their landing craft was nestled snugly against the tube's opening, locked tighter than a lover's embrace, so it didn't matter. "Any minute now," he muttered to himself.

Holt sighed and put a hand on the leather clad arm to get Blakely's attention. "Look, partner, it's not that I want to rain on your parade, but you might as well face it, most women don't want what we have to offer. Even if they do, only one in a thousand can handle it. And the chances of us finding a perfect match . . . well, I don't have to tell you what the odds against that are. I'm sorry because I know what you want. Hell, I want the same thing—a girl who completes us and who can accept us for who and what we are. But you better face facts—it's probably not gonna happen."

"It might." Blakely gave up watching the dome and turned

to face his partner instead. The classical features of Holt's face were drawn into a dour expression. "She doesn't necessarily have to be a perfect match, ya know. There's bound to be *somebody* out there for us, Holt. The right girl, one who's got a high sensory tolerance. Understanding, beautiful . . ."

"Both morally and physically flexible. Come on, Blake, get real," the blond demanded.

"If by 'get real' you mean abandon hope, then you can shove it, pal." Blakely shrugged his partner's hand off and poked him in the chest. "Ya know, I think you're still angry about Gillian, and that was *months* ago. I'm sorry she couldn't handle it, but I offered to do the detandemizing. Don't forget, *you* were the one who said *no*."

"Ah, buddy . . ." Holt sighed heavily and looked down at the accusing finger pointed at his chest until Blakely removed it. "You know I couldn't do that. It'd be easier to cut off my arm than lose you that way. How many years have we been together? How many times have we saved each other's asses? I couldn't let it all go just because Gillian couldn't handle the linking. I just . . . I hate to see you get your hopes up all over the place and then have them come crashing down on your head. You got too much heart, you know that?"

"Yeah," Blakely's mobile features softened and he grinned a little at his partner. "Well, somebody's gotta have it and you're always claimin' to be the brains of this outfit. Just don't let our new friend know it. We gonna keep up the act for her benefit? See how far she's willing to go?"

Holt couldn't stop himself from laughing. His partner always knew how to cheer him up. "You're a mean son of a bitch."

Blakely grinned even wider. "And you were just sayin' I had too much heart. I'm not saying we should hurt her, ya know. I'm just sayin' . . ."

"Call her bluff. Maybe teach her a lesson about trying to

manipulate officers of the law. I'm up for it, I guess. Should be interesting to see her reaction to our good cop–bad cop routine. Although in this case I guess we're both playing bad cop."

"The worst," Blakely agreed. "Hey." He turned back to the dome. "Here she comes and it looks like she's in a hurry. Get ready, Holt."

Holt watched the lithe, curvy figure of the woman who'd barged her way into their lives as she scurried out of the dome and down the plexi-tube. The gold mesh dress didn't hide much and everything jiggled as she ran. He had to agree with his partner on one thing at least—she was very attractive. With those big, honey-brown eyes and those luscious curves . . . no doubt about it, she was Holt's type to a T. Blakely's, too, for that matter, although there was no use hoping she might be "the one" for whom his partner kept wishing.

Professor Klinefelder, the neurobiologist who had implanted their tandem chips, had made it clear that the odds against finding a girl who was both able to withstand the sensory overload caused by their connection and who could also join in the T-link and form a Life-bond with them both were about a million to one, but that didn't keep his dark-haired partner from hoping. Holt sighed. Well, it would still be fun to teach the manipulative little reporter a lesson. At the very least it would make their trip more interesting.

"Wonder what color her hair is under that wig?" Blakely muttered, watching the rapidly approaching figure.

"Hard to tell. Maybe we can get her to take it off . . . among other things." Holt raised his eyebrows at his partner and the dark-haired detective shook his head.

"Enough about that for now, Holt. She's here." Blakely threw open the hatch and allowed the shivering figure to enter the landing craft.

"H . . . hurry," Sadie gasped as she threw herself into the cabin. She stumbled and Blakely caught her handily, setting her reluctantly back on her feet. She didn't even seem to notice. "Right behind me." She gestured and now Holt, who was already at the controls, saw several figures in bulky, bright orange protective suits running clumsily down the plexi-tube toward the ship. "They only . . ." Sadie took a ragged breath. "Only stopped to put on suits. Hurry!"

"Better buckle up." Holt shifted gears and that produced a high grinding sound somewhere in the engine.

"Since when do you drive?" Blakely bumped him out of the way and Holt let him. The dark-haired detective adjusted the controls and the whining sound stopped. He manipulated them again and the engine purred as the clumsy little craft began to rise smoothly.

"Blake, I think they've got some kind of weapon down there. Maybe a laser cannon." Holt peered apprehensively out the small round port window. A flash of blue light skimmed the side of the ship and he was thrown on his face on top of the girl who was suddenly face-down on the floor. "Yup, that's a laser cannon all right," he remarked.

"Hold on," Blakely barked, banking the ship tightly to avoid another blast.

"Trying to," Holt yelled. *Good thing the ship is so small or we'd be sliding all over the damn place.* Beneath him, Sadie wiggled and squirmed in the most appealing way. Her scarlet wig had gone askew and a few honey-brown tendrils almost the exact same shade as her big eyes were sticking out. *Well that's one question answered,* Holt thought.

"Will you get *off* me, you big lug?" she panted, trying to roll out from under him.

"You heard the lady," Blakely said, without turning around.

"Sorry." Holt took his time about it, enjoying the way her luscious ass was undulating against his groin as she wiggled to get free.

"Yeah, right." Sadie brushed ineffectually at the mesh dress, which was torn beyond repair. Holt couldn't help noticing her full breasts, which were now completely visible through the gaping hole in the gold mesh. Sadie noticed him noticing and, blushing deeply, she hastily wrapped her arms around herself to cover the exposed flesh. Holt just grinned. *Blake doesn't know what he's missing. And he wonders why I let him do most of the navigation.*

"I think we're out of range now," Holt said and his partner grunted a reply from the front of the ship. Sadie was sitting quietly, shivering, with her arms wrapped around herself and her eyes on the floor. Without saying a word Holt took off his jacket and draped it around her shoulders.

4

Sadie took a deep breath and considered her image in the small holo-viewer of the space-needle's fresher. The sonic shower had been exactly what she needed to feel more like herself again. The latex make-up that gave her skin the plastic texture of tank-grown flesh was washed away and her own pale, smooth face stared back. Even though the autodryer was set too high and had turned her long wavy hair into a golden-brown puff ball, she still looked and felt a hundred percent better. Pressing the cold water tap she gathered a small amount of the precious liquid and rubbed it through her hair until the puff lay down obediently in silky waves around her slender shoulders. She surveyed the results with satisfaction. *Now that's more like it.* Her hair was so long it almost hid the two bright red marks on either side of her neck. Almost.

Thinking about the way she had gotten those marks made her cheeks get hot. The feel of both mouths on her at once . . . it was so strange, the electric shock she'd gotten when both Holt and Blakely had touched her skin-to-skin at the same time. Sadie still wasn't exactly sure how she felt about it. *Well, there's nothing you can do about it now so you might as well put it out of your mind, Sadie.* Still, she couldn't help thinking about the two men who were so different in appearance and yet so in sync with each other in every other way. The way they reacted to each other—competitive, pushy, totally at ease—they almost reminded her of brothers. They were clearly very protective of each other, but she supposed that was natural for good partners. They had to be watching each other's backs constantly in their line of work. And yet . . . it was more than that.

Sadie dabbed on a little lip gloss as she considered Detectives Blakely and Holt, glad that she had managed to grab her small make-up bag before she made a break for it. She already knew that she liked Blakely. The dark-haired detective seemed so up front, so open with his feelings and desires, and he appeared to have a good sense of humor, too, which was absolutely essential in a man. There was also an intensity about him . . . *He could definitely be dangerous,* Sadie decided. She had better watch herself around Blakely.

Holt was more difficult to read. He seemed quieter, maybe a little more highly strung than his partner, but no less intense. He had classically handsome features that screamed "vid star." His blond hair and light tan skin made him seem golden all over. He had a beautiful smile that she couldn't help comparing with Blakely's charmingly lopsided grin. Sadie shook her head—*really have to be careful there, Sadie.* She turned her thoughts back to Holt. He was, at least so far, more cautious than Blakely . . . more withdrawn. Harder to know. *As if you could really know either of them after three hours . . .* She frowned at the blushing face in the viewer. She'd be getting to know them both much better very shortly, she was sure. *Goddess, what have I gotten myself into?*

For the first time, Sadie wondered if she'd made a mistake. Maybe she should have stayed at the Prostie Palace and just tried to keep out of the way until her transport showed instead of making this crazy deal, but there was the story to think of, a possible Solar Pulitzer even—her career could be taking off. Surely a few . . . favors . . . was a small price to pay for that. She just wished she had a little more experience . . .

Slut, a disapproving little voice whispered inside her head. Sadie recognized that voice—it belonged to her ex-fiancé, Gerald. They'd been together for almost three years and had a bad break up not six months before she had come up with her wild scheme to get the inside scoop on the prostie-borg industry. She hadn't seen him in half a year, but still heard that little voice from time to time, critical and unyielding just as Gerald had always been. Shaking her head, she tried to think of something else.

Surveying herself in the holo-viewer Sadie thought that if only she had some decent clothes to wear she might almost look presentable. She hadn't been able to take her original travel outfit before she bolted out of the Pleasure Dome complex because an alarm had gone off the minute she palmed a small vial of the drug being injected into the long line-up of new prosties. Remembering the way they had turned as one to look at her when it sounded, the blue tattoos on their right eyelids blinking at her in perfect, unnatural synch, Sadie shivered. She had barely gotten away with no time to grab her travel clothes. The gold mesh dress she had been wearing was completely ruined, ripped beyond repair by her roll on the floor of the landing craft with Holt. She remembered the feel of his body on top of hers, warm and firm and masculine, and the warmth of his jacket when he had draped it around her shoulders.

The warmth had been the same, but the scent of Holt's jacket had been subtly different, sharper than the sandalwood musk of Blakely's. But the scents had combined on her skin and complemented each other in some strange way. Like two separate notes that together made up a deliciously sensual, utterly masculine cologne. She had wanted to keep wearing Holt's jacket long after she was obliged to give it back. Beside the intriguing scent, it had covered her torn dress.

Sadie shrugged, it wasn't like the dress was any great loss—actually, she never wanted to see the horrible thing again—but it was the only item of clothing she had brought with her in her mad escape aside from the high-heeled gold pumps that matched it. As a result, she was wearing one of Blakely's shirts, which was so long on her that it could be used nicely, as a dress as long as what you wanted was a minidress. It was a deep green that suited her creamy complexion and, like his jacket, it exuded a faint whiff of sandalwood.

The shirt tails hung down to midthigh, doing an adequate job of covering her, but Sadie would have given her right arm for a pair of panties. She would have to be careful how she sat, she supposed. *Get over it, Sadie; it's not like they haven't seen the goods already. How do you think you got invited on this trip anyhow?*

She made a face at herself in the holo-viewer. One step at a time. Right now it was time to stop hogging the fresher and go back out to the main cabin of the needle. Sadie had been impressed by the small but luxurious ship at first, but Blakely had assured her it was on loan to their department from the narcotics division who had confiscated it on a bust.

It was time to quit stalling. She shrugged, patted her hair one last time, took a deep breath, and left the tiny room to go find the two men with whom she was going to be spending most of her foreseeable future.

5

She lit up the whole cabin the moment she stepped through the door, Blakely thought. Her hair was a gorgeous golden brown color that reminded him of melted caramel, and it matched her eyes almost exactly. It fell in a wavy mass nearly to her waist and he wondered how she had managed to hide it all under the ridiculous scarlet wig. He couldn't help admiring the way his shirt looked on her, with the green fabric hugging her luscious full breasts and draping gracefully over her silky thighs. She was still wearing the gold high heels, apparently the only surviving bit of her prostie-borg outfit, and her legs seemed to go on forever.

Holt was apparently having similar thoughts about the new addition to their team because he turned to the dark-haired detective and said, "Well Blake, *you* never looked quite that good in that shirt. I vote you let her keep it."

"I second the motion," Blakely agreed, without taking his eyes off the vision in front of him. Her honey-colored eyes tilted exotically and her full pink mouth looked extremely kissable. He knew Holt was nervous about taking a strange girl along with them on the mission; he could feel his partner's apprehension through the ever present T-link they shared. He couldn't help thinking that it was a stroke of good luck, however, both for them and for Sadie, that he had picked her out of the prostie line-up. Where would she be now if he hadn't, with her Overlook-Me chip blown and the ore transport not due back for a whole week? Of course, she seemed like a girl who could take care of herself. But hell, he liked a girl with some spunk, and it didn't hurt that she was gorgeous.

"Hey, c'mon over and take a load off," he invited her as she hesitated on the edge of the circular room.

"Hi," Sadie said shyly, crossing to sit beside Blakely on the c-gel couch and across from Holt who was sitting in the lounger opposite them, long legs spread out in front of him. The comfort gel obligingly began to conform to the shape of her body and Sadie jumped up and whipped around, glaring accusingly at Blakely.

"Hey, buddy, I don't appreciate . . ."

"It's just the comfort gel, Sadie. It manipulates itself to support you," Holt told her, amusement evident in his deep voice. She flashed an annoyed glance in the blond man's direction.

"I've never seen anything like that before. Or *felt* anything like it either. I thought . . ." She turned back to Blakely.

"You thought I was coppin' a feel." He grinned at her. He was relieved when she smiled tentatively back. "Don't worry about it, sweetheart. I thought the same thing the first time I sat down on this damn gel couch. Nearly punched poor Holt over there for gettin' fresh. C'mon," he gestured to her. "Sit back down; it won't bite. Feels kinda nice once you get used to it."

"Well . . ." She sank reluctantly back onto the couch and sighed involuntarily as the gel molded around her shape. "It *is* kind of nice," she admitted after a moment. "Firm, but giving." If Blakely had been alone with his partner he could have thought of several choice things to say about *that* comment, but one glance from the blond detective was enough to make him bite his tongue. He couldn't help smiling, though, and was glad to see an answering smile from Holt in return. *It's all gonna work out, buddy, you'll see,* he thought, wishing his partner would relax about having Sadie along for the ride.

"Try taking off your shoes," he suggested. Sadie looked at him uncertainly.

"Why?"

"The carpeting's semi-sentient synthi-wilk," Holt explained. "Kind of like a cross between wool and silk that wants to rub your feet."

"Try it—'S better than a foot massage," Blakely promised her.

Sadie looked uncertainly from one man to the other and finally slipped off the gold spiked heels and let her bare soles rest on the plush maroon carpeting. Blakely saw the ripple in the deep nap as the semi-sentient carpet went to work on her dainty feet. Her toenails were painted a pale, innocent pink, he noted.

Sadie sat quietly for a moment, a strange expression growing on her face. She pulled up her feet and crossed them under her, madly giggling. "Sorry . . ." she gasped at last as the two men gave her puzzled looks. "St . . . stood it as long as I could but it just tickles too much!" She smoothed the tails of the shirt down modestly, being sure she was covered, still helplessly giggling. Blakely grinned as he studied her, cheeks flushed from laughing and eyes bright. She looked so innocent—like a little girl.

It was an unguarded moment, definitely not in keeping with her projected image of a tough, self-sufficient reporter willing to do whatever it took to get the story. Despite her wanton display and unspoken but definite promise of sexual favors in the pleasure cubicle at the Prostie Palace, Blakely got the feeling that she was a lot more inexperienced than she wanted them to believe. *Probably not a virgin, but innocent just the same*, he thought, his detective's instincts kicking into drive. He couldn't wait to get Holt alone and compare notes. He just hoped his partner wouldn't start telling him not to get his hopes up again. Blakely hated it when Holt got in one of his down moods, which had become a lot more frequent since Gillian had dumped him. *Dumped him because of me—because of us.* It was an unhappy thought, but not an unfamiliar one. Why was it so damn hard to find a woman who could understand and accept the reality of their lives? One who could handle all they had to offer *together*?

"Hey partner, the lady asked you a question." Holt's voice cut into his reverie and Blakely looked up to see Sadie looking at him expectantly.

"Sorry, kid. Guess I was daydreamin'," he said.

"I think I can guess about what." Holt gave him a significant glance. Blakely looked back at him neutrally.

"Later for that, blondie," he said casually, knowing he was playing his part to a T. Sadie flushed as she looked back and forth between them and Blakely's heart gave a little lurch. The poor kid was scared to death about what they were going to do to her. He didn't mind teaching her a lesson, but still . . .

"I just wanted to know where we're going," Sadie explained, looking up at him out of those big, honey-colored eyes. She still had her feet tucked under her and the posture made her look very young. "And what's going to happen to the prostieborgs that aren't really prosties?"

"Well," Blakely said. "We'll send the sample you swiped for us off to the lab. A full-scale bust should reveal which prosties have synthetic brains and which are black market transplants. Unfortunately for the transplants, even if we rescue them they'll be stuck in the prostie-bodies. The mind rapers left the original human bodies to rot on Phoebe when they cleaned out the colony."

"Well, with good treatment a body grown in the flesh tanks should last as long as the original body they lost," Sadie said. "And a prostie body has no inherent genetic defects, so at least they'll be healthy."

"*Physically*, yes." Holt's voice was sharp, and he sat up from his lounging position and leaned forward, steepling his long fingers. "But what about mentally or emotionally? Think what they've been subjected to, most of them over and over again. And don't forget that only half of the colonists who were mind-raped were women—the other half were men who were shoved into female prostie-bodies. The BRC is going to have the mother of all gender identity crises on their hands when we finally get them off the syntho-narcotics. Thank the Goddess that at least they were all adults."

Sadie's small hand stole up to her red mouth. "I . . . I didn't think about that. What *will* the men do? Having to live in the body of the opposite sex for the rest of your life . . . how *horrible*." She shivered, wrapping her arms around herself which caused the V-neck of the green shirt to gape interestingly.

"That's gonna be an issue for the Body Reclamation Council that's being formed on Old Earth, kid." Blakely grimaced. "Poor bastards." He meant both the colonists and the people that would have to deal with the messy issue of body reclamation.

"I think they got a sample of everybody's DNA before they cremated the originals, so theoretically it should be possible to re-grow all the lost bodies in the tanks," Holt said.

"Theoretically? Why not just do it?"

"Think of the price tag, sweetheart," Blakely ran a hand through his hair "Who's gonna pick up the tab? Your average Joe Taxpayer ain't too eager to spring for a whole new body for some colonist from the back-side of the galaxy he doesn't know from Adam. So the BRC is gonna have a hell of a time getting funds for that particular project. Unless . . ."

"Unless we can find the scum who mind-raped the colonists in the first place," Holt continued the narrative seamlessly to Sadie's obvious interest. Blakely saw her noticing the easy interaction between his partner and himself and wondered if she had any suspicions about their situation. *If she's a halfway decent reporter she'll have a clue,* he thought.

"If we can find the bastard who's responsible for this, the BRC can order him to pay punitive damages to the tune of three thousand brand new bodies for the people he wronged, not to mention some other pretty nasty penalties. That's our job now—to track down the person or organization behind this whole operation." Blakely picked up the narrative from Holt again. "Besides the colonists missing bodies, we wanna keep it from happening again. Whoever did this in the first place isn't gonna stop. It's too damn lucrative."

"I assume you have some leads and this isn't just some wild goose chase." Sadie looked back and forth between them, as though trying to catch them in some nonverbal communication that would give her a clue

"We have a few information sources we're going to check out." Holt's words were cautious, not giving too much away.

"And where are these *information sources* located?" She raised a delicate eyebrow in Blakely's direction. *Hmm, catches on quick.* The dark-haired detective smiled at her with approval.

"Iapetus for starters."

Sadie made a face. "Iapetus? What's there except a lot of drunk miners and whore hous . . . uh, bars?" She blushed, not quite catching herself in time.

"Now Sadie, what's wrong with whore houses?" Holt teased her, a sardonic glint in his sapphire eyes. "We found *you* in one."

"That's not the same thing." She turned on the blond-haired detective angrily, clearly embarrassed. "I was there undercover and I never once . . ." Stopping short, she bit her tongue.

"Not even once?" Blakely's voice was dangerously soft. "Thought all you hot-shot reporters were into realism."

"Blake is right," Holt said. "I personally can't think of a better way to get a down and dirty story than to experience what the prosties have to go through on a daily basis. Didn't the thought even cross your mind, Sadie?"

"Yes, all right?" she burst out angrily, glaring at them both. "It crossed my mind the minute you and your partner picked me out of the line-up. It crossed it again when I made the bargain I had to make to get you two to let me in on this story. Look, I know what this is about." She stood up, heedless of the carpet tickling her bare feet and began unbuttoning the green shirt with swift, jerky motions.

"What are you doin', sweetheart?" Blakely asked carefully as the green shirt parted, revealing the creamy swells of her breasts, topped with ripe, berry colored nipples and the tiny strip of curly thatch that decorated her sex. He stood and put a restraining hand on her arm but Sadie shrugged him off. Holt was hovering on her other side, clearly afraid to touch her for fear of upsetting her further.

"I'm getting ready to pay." Her voice came out small and constricted as though a hand was squeezing her throat. She took a deep breath and her full breasts heaved enticingly. Blakely drifted closer, unable to help himself. On the other side he noticed that Holt was also getting nearer, as though drawn by some invisible magnetic field.

"Pay for what?" Holt asked carefully and Blakely was relieved to hear that his partner's voice was still the calm, even tone of reason despite the situation at hand. Holt was always better than him at handling emotional crises.

"You made it clear enough back at the Prostie Palace exactly what you expected of me if you let me come along," Sadie took a step back so she could look at them both. The shirt hung open on either side, framing her luscious nakedness. Blakely noticed her honey-colored eyes blazed, but her full lips slightly trembled She was a lot more upset at the prospect of trading sexual favors for exclusive rights to the story than she wanted to admit, even to herself, he thought. It obviously wasn't something she did on a regular basis. He opened his mouth to tell her not to worry about it, that everything was going to be okay and she didn't owe them anything, but a sharp look from his partner stopped him. Blakely realized Holt wanted to teach her a lesson she wouldn't forget. His partner despised being manipulated and they had been burned by the press before.

"What did we make clear, Sadie?" Holt asked her, still in that calm, neutral voice.

"Don't play dumb with me," she flared at the blond detective. "I thought at the time that coming along with you two was the best choice. Thought it was better than staying at that damn brothel and being raped and maybe murdered if I was found out. Now I'm beginning to wonder."

Blakely couldn't keep silent any longer. "Sadie, sweetheart . . ." he began, stepping toward her, but she didn't let him finish.

"Which one of you?" She looked from him to Holt defiantly. Putting her hands on her hips she thrust out her naked, ripe breasts, a deliberate gesture, a come-on that had Blakely's cock hardening in his pants like a bar of lead. He could tell Holt was in a similar state of discomfort.

"Which one of us what?" Blakely asked, as gently as he could. Her nipples looked achingly hard and he longed to lean over and suck one into his mouth while Holt sucked the other.

"Come *on*. I want to get this over with." Sadie tried to look bored and worldly, and failed miserably. *Poor kid is scared to death,* Blakely thought again. It did a lot to take the edge off his desire, but her lush body was still on display and his rampant hard-on wouldn't die completely.

"Which one of you wants to go first?" Sadie demanded.

Holt stepped up to her side and ran one long finger down her throat from the love mark he had made earlier to the ripe, pouting nipple of her left breast. He let his fingertip circle lazily for a moment before giving the tight pink bud a gentle tweak that made Sadie gasp. Blakely watched, mesmerized, until his partner nodded at him. *Oh right, bad cop, bad cop*, he remembered. He followed Holt's lead and stepped up beside the girl. Capturing her other nipple between his thumb and forefinger he gave it a tender squeeze.

"What if I told you both of us?" Holt's voice was low and dangerous, the long fingers never leaving the nipple he was toying with so casually. Blakely looked up sharply, but the sapphire eyes were trained on the girl between them. Holt was intent on making a point. The dark-haired detective looked away from his partner and observed Sadie's reaction to the question.

"At . . . at the same time?" Sadie's voice was choked, disbelieving. "I've never . . . I mean, I couldn't . . ."

"Sure ya could, sweetheart." Blakely leaned in close to whisper in the little pink shell of her ear, never relinquishing the nipple he had claimed as his own. There was terror in her voice, disbelief but not disgust, he thought. He suddenly longed to reach between her legs and test the tender V of her sex to see if she was getting hot while they toyed with her this way. Would his fingers part the plump folds of her pussy and find her wet and ready for them—*both* of them—if he touched her there? Abruptly he released the nipple he had been torturing so sweetly and he saw Holt do the same.

Moving at the same time they circled her, Holt taking the back and Blakely taking the front. Blakely moved forward, backing her up until she was pressed against his partner's broad chest and her ripe breasts were pressed against the flat plane of his own chest. She was breathing rapidly, nearly hyperventilating with fear and titillation as he cupped her flushed cheek in his palm.

"It wouldn't be so bad, baby," he whispered in her ear, caressing her heated cheek with his thumb. "Holt and I know how to treat a lady." Her skin was silky soft, and a faint, feminine scent that was indefinably delicious perfumed the air between them.

His partner leaned forward and whispered in her other ear, "Think how it would feel, Sadie. Both of us at once, filling you up . . ." Holt's long fingers caressed her shoulders, pulling gently at the green shirt until it dropped away and she was naked between them. "We could make it so good for you." He licked gently at her ear, sucking the lobe into his mouth.

Blakely kept petting her cheek as he stepped forward again, pressing the rock-hard cock threatening to burst through the too-tight pants he wore against the soft juncture between her legs. He could feel her heat, even through the fabric he was wearing. He pressed harder, nudging between the pouting lips of her pussy to rub against her tender inner folds with his hardness, making her gasp. He felt an answering pressure from the other side and knew that Holt was pressing his own erection into the lush cleft of her ass, pinning her tightly between them.

Then the T-link between Blakely and his tall blond partner suddenly opened. The sizzle of connection between them was like a tangible thing, a high-voltage current that flowed through all three bodies, lighting nerve endings on fire and electrifying the pleasure centers of all three brains. Blakely felt the sense of *almost*-wholeness as the link widened from a narrow ribbon to a highway of pleasure and interconnection, weaving three nervous systems into one. *This is the way it's supposed to be,* he thought, feeling Holt's hands on the girl's naked skin as though they were his own and knowing his partner was feeling the same. *This is what we need . . .*

He wanted desperately to take her then, to share her with Holt and finish the connection the T-link was begging for. He could lower his zipper and slip his throbbing cock into the tight, slippery wetness rubbing against his shaft while Holt did the same from behind, filling her . . . fucking her . . . The sense of wholeness, of total completion was so damn *close* and Sadie's body was responding to the link. She was picking up on the energy they generated and feeding it back to them both in a closed loop unlike anything he had ever felt before.

"Is this what you want?" Blakely wasn't sure which of them had said it or whose hands were filled with her ripe breasts, whose hands were gliding over her softly curving sides, caressing the silky skin of her inner thighs so wet and hot and ready . . .

Then he felt Sadie stiffen between them, her body going rigid as a board. She had been unprepared for any of this, he realized; they might be overloading her system. Blakely looked at her anxiously, he didn't detect any of the usual symptoms of sensory overload and she hadn't fainted, but the flushed face still cupped in his palm trembled and her delicate features were tense with the overwhelming sensations.

"Oh . . . Goddess," she whispered brokenly, her honey-brown eyes huge with fear and pleasure. "I don't understand but please . . . *Please* don't. I've never . . . I can't . . . Please . . ." A tear leaked from the corner of her eye and ran over Blakely's thumb as he caressed her cheek and her breath hitched unevenly in her chest. Her body might be responding to the link, but it was obvious that emotionally she was unprepared.

Cursing himself and his partner for going too far, Blakely stepped back abruptly, giving her space and narrowing the link to its previous dimensions, feeling the loss like a suddenly amputated limb. He saw Holt wince and knew his partner felt it, too. Caught off balance, Sadie almost fell, but Holt grabbed her roughly from behind and held her until she regained her balance. When it was obvious she wouldn't fall, the blond man came around to stand shoulder to shoulder with Blakely and look her in the face.

"We won't ask you for that kind of payment, Sadie." Holt's voice was cold and precise. "But Blakely and I don't like being manipulated. We took you along to insure your safety, not for our own sexual gratification. Although we appreciate the offer," the sapphire eyes took in all of her luscious curves naked before them, "neither one of us gets off on forcing anybody to sleep with us against their will." Blakely nodded his agreement, not trusting himself to speak. If he did, it would be to reassure the girl and he would undo everything his partner had been trying to accomplish. Besides, the sense of loss was still so fresh. The link between him and Holt throbbed like an empty socket, needing a third to complete them, but he tried to ignore it and concentrate on the girl.

"But, I thought . . . the way you . . . what you said . . ." Sadie was clearly taken aback at her sudden reprieve. She dried her cheeks with her fingers using quick, jerky motions, and crossed her arms over her bare breasts, trying to regain her composure.

"No, it was what *you* said," Blakely reminded her gently. Leaning toward her, he kissed her softly on the side of her neck, over the spot where he had made his mark on her creamy flesh earlier. He was glad she wasn't going into some kind of hysterics, but sad too—she had proven what Holt had been saying earlier. Sadie might possibly be able to handle the physical aspect of the T-linking, which was rare, but she definitely wasn't receptive emotionally to what he and his partner had to offer. He tried to shrug off the melancholy mood. "It's time for bed, kid. You can have Holt's half of the bed tonight and he can sleep on the couch."

"I was going to offer her *your* half of the bed," Holt mildly protested. He smiled lazily at Sadie and leaned in to give her a slow, lingering kiss near the corner of her mouth, as though the

T-link wasn't throbbing like an empty socket in his chest the way it was in Blakely's. Holt had always been better at hiding his emotions—at hiding his pain, the dark-haired detective reflected.

"Forget it, both of you." Sadie put one small hand on either broad chest and pushed as forcefully as she could. Then, obviously remembering that she was still naked, she scooped the shirt off the floor and put it on, buttoning it as rapidly as she had unbuttoned it earlier. "*I'm* taking the couch." Her voice still trembled slightly. "I don't know what's going on with you two, but I'm not interested in being anywhere *near* either one of you in bed." She turned her back on them and tapped one small foot on the carpet, obviously waiting for them to leave. She wasn't up for a discussion of the strange reaction she'd felt when she was sandwiched between the two of them yet.

Blakely wondered if she would ask or try to find out on her own. Knowing what he did of reporters he was betting on the latter. *Good luck, sweetheart.* She would never guess. Looking at his partner he raised an eyebrow. "Holt, I think we've been dismissed." He grinned and the blond man grinned lazily back. They had certainly made their point. It wouldn't hurt to let Sadie have her way now.

"Guess we'd better get to bed, partner," Holt replied. He nodded to Blakely and winked, no discussion was necessary. "Breakfast is at seven sharp," the blond man told Sadie, or rather, her slender back held rigidly stiff. "If you're not up you miss out."

"You snooze, you lose," Blakely clarified, snagging a thermal wrap from the storage area and tossing it onto the couch which promptly began to melt around it.

"Fine, whatever," she muttered, hunching her shoulders. It was obvious she wanted to be alone. Taking pity on her, Blakely headed for the tiny cubical which was barely big enough to hold the king-sized gelafoam-bed where he and Holt slept. The designer of the ship had apparently been big on outer luxuries, like the well-appointed living area, and more frugal with such inner areas as the fresher and sleeping spaces. Personally, he wished the designer had included at least one more bedroom. Holt had a tendency to snore.

6

No matter which way she twisted on the c-gel couch, Sadie couldn't fall asleep. The couch accommodated her every move, cushioning her beautifully. It was certainly much softer than the steel storage locker she'd been sleeping in while playing the part of a prostie-borg, but sleep continued to elude her. Sadie knew why, too. Her discomfort wasn't physical—it was mental.

What the hell is going on with those two? she wondered for the hundredth time. *And why do I react that way when they put me between them?* She shivered and remembered the sensation of the two strong, muscular bodies pressing hard against her, two sets of hands caressing her, two mouths kissing, licking, whispering what they would do . . . Just thinking about it made her breath come short and shallow in her chest and her cheeks flush a dull red with shame when she remembered her reaction. When she had felt that connection, that electricity between them flowing through her like a conductor, she had been almost ready to do anything they wanted. The words, *take me,* had been trembling on her lips and Sadie had never felt so hot and wet in her life.

What's wrong with me? I barely know them and I'm not that kind of girl . . . Slutty, Gerald's voice whispered in her head. Sadie frowned, studying the gently curved ceiling above her in the gloom. Yes, she had agreed, or *thought* she had agreed, to trade sexual favors for a chance at the story of the century, but it wasn't something she had ever done before or ever imagined herself doing in her wildest dreams or fantasies. Then Holt had made it clear they were just teaching her a lesson, getting her back for trying to use sex as a weapon and manipulate her way into their case. Well, she *had* been to some degree, although he didn't have to make such a humiliating display . . . Sadie felt her cheeks get even redder. *It still doesn't explain why I reacted so strongly to them . . . to their hands on my body . . .*

She thought of Gerald, her ex-fiancé back on Io. Sadie's parents had died when she was very young and she was taken in by a strict elderly aunt who barely tolerated her. Despite being raised in Goshen Land, which was Io's most conservative colony, Sadie had always been lively and curious. *Her Aunt Minnie called it nosy,* which was probably why she became a reporter in the first place. Gerald had been the first real boyfriend she'd had after going off to college and getting out from under Aunt Minnie's thumb.

Sadie really hadn't been with anyone else, and Gerald's idea of a kinky sexual escapade was to leave the fresher light on with the door cracked so they could just barely make out each other's outlines in the darkened bedroom while they made love. Like everyone else in Goshen, he was extremely conservative sexually, and when Sadie had dared to ask for more, the relationship crumbled under the weight of his disapproval. Sadie could almost hear him, remembering the way he had reacted to the "unnatural" requests she'd whispered in his ear one night as they were preparing to make love . . .

*   *   *

Rolling up on his side and staring down at her in the semi-darkness, Gerald's thin hair had been in a tangle of fuzz at the top of his egg-shaped head. Even in the gloom of the bedroom, Sadie could see the look of distaste on his narrow, pinched face.

"Honestly, Sadie, I don't understand this sudden obsession with trying strange things." Gerald had what Sadie thought of as a "prissy" tone that he used whenever he was uncomfortable or unhappy. It made the register of his speaking voice jump nearly half an octave turning his usually pleasant tenor into a mosquito-like whine. When she heard that tone in his voice, Sadie knew she wasn't going to win whatever argument they were currently having.

"I just want to try something new once in a while," she'd said defensively. "What's wrong with trying to spice up our love life a little, Gerald?"

"If it isn't broke, why try to fix it?" he had countered. "Look, darling," Gerald had always called her that when he was making a point. Near the end of their relationship when everything was falling apart, Sadie had come to actively hate that particular endearment. "I'm sorry, but I'm just not comfortable with what you're asking. I don't know where you got those ideas but some of what you're saying is just, well, disgusting.*"*

Sadie had apologized, feeling about an inch tall, and they had done their usual routine, which consisted of her lying in the dark under Gerald while he grunted on top of her until he was satisfied, and then rolled off, already half asleep. The whole incident had made Sadie feel dirty and terrible although she didn't think she had been asking for such outrageous things. It didn't help of course that Gerald's remarks echoed her aunt's words on sexual misconduct. Aunt Minnie's entire lecture about the birds and the bees had consisted of three words: "Nice girls don't."

*   *   *

Sadie had gradually realized that she wanted more, although she really wasn't sure how much more. She had secretly dreamed of having wild and amazing sex with the man of her dreams, if she ever found him, but her fantasies were vague and unfocused. She mostly just wanted to get out on her own and try something new for a change. Well, disguising herself as a prostie-borg to break the most scandalous story the Solar System had ever heard certainly qualified as something new. Sadie had decided to throw herself into becoming an excellent reporter and put the idea of finding Mr. Right on hold for a while.

Breaking up with Gerald had been difficult, and getting rid of that disapproving little voice in her head was harder still. It sometimes sounded like her ex-fiancé, sometimes like her Aunt Minnie, but it was always loaded with guilt and shame. It was amazing, Sadie thought, that she had able to overcome her upbringing enough to make the deal she'd thought she was making with Blakely and Holt to come along on this mission at all.

"All I wanted was to try something different once in a while," Sadie grumbled to herself in the darkness, turning over and forcing the couch to readjust again, which it did immediately. That had been the sum of her sexual ambition, although she had always felt there was more out there . . . something else she wanted and couldn't put into words. But it certainly wasn't this . . . this *scenario* that Holt and Blakely seemed to be offering. *Both of them . . . at the same time.* The very thought was shocking, horrifying . . . intriguing? No, certainly not! So then why did she feel the way she did, react the way she did when they touched her at the same time? She hadn't felt that tingling burst of near-orgasmic pleasure when either one of them touched her separately so why . . . Could it be all in her head? Did she have some latent desire to be with two men at once? Or was there something else going on?

I should just come right out and ask. Of the two Blakely was the more approachable, whereas Holt seemed colder and more forbidding . . . But no, never mind how damn embarrassing it would be to ask in the first place, what if the dark, curly haired detective just looked at her blankly? What if the truth was some part of her desired this so much it was making her behave like a feline in heat the moment they both touched her? Did she really want to walk on the wild side that badly? Sadie could hardly believe it. *I know myself—I'm not like this.* Something *had* to be going on.

Sadie sat up in the dark and punched the side of the innocent couch; it sighed faintly, molding around her small fist. "Something's going on with those two and I'm going to find out what it is," she said in a low, decisive voice. Just saying it out loud made her feel better. She had never been the kind of girl to lay back and take whatever life dished out. She was going to get to the bottom of this if it killed her . . . and she was going to get an exclusive scoop on the biggest story to hit the news vids in years while she was at it!

Pulitzer Prize, here I come!

7

In the two week trip from Titan, which was at the far end of its elliptical orbit around Saturn, to Iapetus, Sadie got to know the two men quite well. Holt was quieter and more introspective, with a dry sense of humor that Sadie had come to appreciate, although it could turn to biting sarcasm if he was angry. He also tended to be inflexible. Once the tall blond detective made up his mind about something it stayed made up. He had an air of breeding and refinement that the earthy Blakely lacked. Sadie learned that Holt had been raised in a very wealthy family on the first moon colony and his parents had disowned him when he decided to join the Old Earth Peace Keeping Force instead of becoming an officer in the Interstellar Fleet. Despite being cut out of his father's will, Holt retained an air of privilege and tended to look at the world in a cool and analytical manner. Coupled with his golden good looks that sometimes made him seem stand-offish and unapproachable. He was beginning to let down his guard, however, and inside the cool blond shell, Sadie had seen a vulnerable man with a heart that was more easily touched than Holt wanted to admit.

The blond man was often moody and troubled. Blakely had confided to Sadie that Holt had recently had some romantic difficulties and she privately wondered if his love life was in any way complicated by the strange bond that seemed to exist between the two partners.

Blakely, Sadie learned, was almost as different from his tall blond partner as it was possible to be both in background and temperament. The dark, curly haired detective had been raised on the mean streets of New Brooklyn on Old Earth. He had told Sadie candidly that Holt was the brains of their partnership and he was the brawn. Watching them interact Sadie realized that even though Holt might be the more educated one of the two, Blakely was more intuitive. He was also more laid back than his cool blond partner, almost childlike at times in his enthusiasm for life and simple enjoyments, and he could always make Sadie laugh. He was always brimming over with energy and had cat-quick reflexes that were almost scary. He had once caught a cup full of nutra-shake that Sadie had knocked off the table in midair, though he had been half-way across the room when she did it. He had set it back down, without spilling a drop, and neither he nor Holt seemed to think anything of it. There was a natural athleticism about him—a bounce in his step and a gleam in his eye—that was instantly attractive. Although he didn't have the perfect bone structure of his tall blond partner, Sadie found his lopsided grin charming. She had yet to see him angry or upset, but she suspected there was more to him than met the eye. There was a dark intensity about Blakely that was as intriguing as Holt's aloof vulnerability.

The more time she spent with Blakely and Holt, the more Sadie liked them. They were the most unlikely set of partners imaginable, but they seemed to complement each other perfectly. It was obvious despite their good-natured bickering that the caring between them was profound. The confines of the space needle were small, but as Holt tended to be a morning person and Blakely was more of a night-owl, Sadie found time to talk to them both separately on occasion.

Sex with either or both of them hadn't been mentioned again after the disastrous first night. In time Sadie got over her embarrassment and almost forgot that she had been willing to trade sexual favors for a chance at the story of the century. She was both relieved and strangely disappointed that the subject had been dropped so thoroughly, though that didn't make any sense—did it?

Holt was charming and a perfect gentleman and Blakely flirted with her outrageously, but he didn't seem to mean any harm by it. According to Holt the dark-haired detective would flirt with anyone—it was just his exuberant personality coming out. Sadie enjoyed the attention and liked spending time with both partners. To pass the time she often played chess with Holt or cards with Blakely, who was an expert at every possible means of cheating. He taught her several tricks and they ganged up on Holt when all three played together until the blond detective quit, grumbling that there were more aces up either of their sleeves than in the actual deck.

The two-week trip was so genial and pleasant after the initial awkwardness of the first night that it would have been like spending time with two older brothers if not for the slight edge of tension that still existed between them. Sadie didn't notice it so much when she was alone with either Blakely or Holt, but whenever all three were in any kind of close proximity it gave every word spoken, every gesture made, a special significance that she found impossible to ignore.

Somehow she kept finding herself between them, sitting on the couch, at the table, or just standing in the food prep area. It took her a while to notice that, but when she did, she wondered if it was a conscious effort on Blakely's and Holt's part or if they were completely unaware of it. Whether it was on purpose or purely accidental, Sadie took care that no matter how close they got, she was never directly touching both of them skin-to-skin at the same time. It just seemed . . . safer that way.

She wasn't able to find out anymore about the mysterious bond between them, but it was daily in evidence. It was there in the way the two men finished each other's sentences, knew each other's whereabouts at any given time, and sometimes seemed to communicate volumes with only a look.

Sadie had almost given up on understanding whatever it was that bound them so closely together, but then something particularly strange happened the night before they reached orbit around Iapetus.

Sadie had found a small chip repair kit and was sitting in the middle of the couch, working with a light stylus to try and bring her Overlook-Me chip back from the dead. The kit's components were out of date, but she thought with just a little tweaking she could make it work. She was concentrating fiercely, the tip of her tongue caught between her teeth as she worked, thinking that she was pretty certain she would be able to coax at least a few more hours of life out of the chip when her grip on the slick barrel of the stylus slipped and the micron-thin beam of pure radiance that powered the instrument sliced neatly through the flesh of her palm leaving a deep gash.

She sucked in a deep breath, almost a gasp as the searing, white-hot pain screamed along her nerve-endings, insisting that her hand was on fire. The injury was so sudden and sharp that she could only stare at the wound, her palm rapidly filling with blood, and think distantly that it looked like she had a handful of her favorite nail polish. The name of the polish, she remembered, was *Hot Blooded.*

"Hey, you all right, kid?" Blakely was there immediately, he had been close by in the food prep area and obviously heard the noise she made. He sat down on the couch beside her and took the hurt hand between his own. "Damn, that's nasty," he commented, looking at the scorched edges of the cut. "Hey, Holt," he called. "C'mere and bring the . . ."

"Got it." The tall blond man suddenly appeared on her other side with a flat metal box that had a large red cross on the cover in his hands. Sadie spared a moment to wonder how in the Solar System Holt could have known what was happening and what was needed. He had been in the Navicom chamber, which was at the far end of the ship and soundproof as well, for the past hour. Before she could frame a question, Holt sat on the other side of her on the c-gel couch and opened the box.

While Blakely held her steady, Holt cleaned and bandaged the wound and wrapped her hand in a flexi-seal designed to reduce movement and promote healing.

"You'd better be careful with that for a while," the blond man said, still holding her hand gently. "Bad cut like that will take a while to heal."

"I . . . thank you." Sadie looked gratefully from one set of blue eyes to the other and realized that, yet again, she was directly between them. They were all sitting so close together on the couch that she could feel their warm breath caressing her cheeks and they both still held her wounded hand, Blakely touching her forearm to steady her and Holt holding her fingertips. *They were both touching her.*

As the realization hit Sadie, it was like a switch was thrown somewhere in the region of her solar plexus and a surge of strange, sensual energy poured through her as it had on the two other occasions when she had been making skin-to-skin contact with both of the men at once.

"Oh . . ." The sigh was torn from her throat as the comfortable atmosphere between the three of them was suddenly charged with a hot current of need. She became aware that Blakely was kissing her throat while Holt leaned over her and took her mouth with an intensity she had never felt in any kiss before.

"Goddess, you're sweet," growled a low voice in her ear that Sadie recognized as Blakely's.

"Mmm," Holt affirmed, too busy kissing her to make a more verbal agreement. Sadie felt like she was drowning in the sensations assaulting her and the feeling of four strong hands roaming over her body. She was wearing another one of the men's shirts, Holt's this time, and she was suddenly aware that someone had unbuttoned the front of it to bare her breasts. Fingers were idly twisting her aching nipples and someone's hand was sliding between her unresisting thighs to caress the sudden wetness there.

She knew she had to stop what was happening between the three of them, but her brain and her body were on two completely different wavelengths. All she could think as strong hands parted her thighs and two long fingers slid deep into her hot sex was how good, how utterly *right* it all felt. She was drowning in sweet sensation, no longer sure which man was doing what to her and not caring either. Blakely was kissing her now, having taken over for his partner so that Holt could suck her sensitive nipples into his mouth and nip them, rolling a talented tongue over each aching bud. The strong fingers continued to fuck her, slow and deep. A broad thumb brushed roughly over her swollen clit making her cry out softly. Sadie felt herself building toward a shattering climax. She was gasping and moaning into Blakely's mouth and he swallowed her cries eagerly as she writhed between the two, large masculine bodies on the couch.

Goddess . . . going to come. Going to come so hard . . . Sadie was thinking, arching her hips to meet the thrusting of the fingers within her. She still didn't know whether they belonged to Blakely or Holt, but it didn't seem to matter—they were equally welcome in her body, she realized. She only wished she could have *more*. The image of the three of them naked in bed together, Blakely taking her from the front and Holt from behind swam deliriously before her mind's eye and wouldn't go away. To be sandwiched between them like that . . . to be filled so utterly and completely . . . a part of her knew she would regret it, would feel like the Solar System's biggest slut if she let that happen, but the desire was so strong, burning inside her like a white-hot star that couldn't be quenched in any other way.

I'm not like this. Not that kind of girl, part of her mind screamed desperately, but, again, Sadie's body wasn't prepared to notice anything other than the current of desire and the deliciously dizzying sensations to which the two men were subjecting her. Sadie had to bite her tongue to keep from begging them to take her . . . to fuck her. She was close . . . so *close* . . .

Oddly enough, it was the itching sensation in her wounded hand that brought her back from the edge of no return. It started as a slight tingle that she hardly noticed, mainly because she was tingling everywhere as the two men touched and fondled her, but then it grew. The tingling became itching, and the itching became a burning sensation that became impossible to ignore.

"Wait . . . wait!" She struggled away from Blakely and Holt, pushing out from between them with some difficulty. As she slithered off the couch, breaking contact with them she saw a look of almost pain pass over both faces, light and dark. *Hurt them somehow,* she thought vaguely, but the pain in her palm was distracting her too much to think of anything else.

"Sorry." Holt was the first to find his voice. "Didn't mean to . . ."

"Yeah, it's just . . ." Blakely trailed off, apparently unable or unwilling to finish the sentence. They were both looking at her with a raw hunger, almost a need, still burning in their eyes, both sapphire and indigo alight with it. Sadie shivered at the intensity of emotion that still quivered in the air between the three of them like a volatile charge of static electricity.

"That's not it." She blushed and realized the shirt she wore was still hanging open. Snatching it closed with her free hand she backed up a step. "I mean . . . I'm not happy about . . . about what just happened, but there's something else." She held out her hurt hand, wincing as another flare of itching pain lanced through it. "I think something's wrong with my hand. It's itching and burning."

"Let me see." Holt was suddenly all business, but Sadie stood where she was, looking at him uncertainly. This was how all this had started in the first place. What if he and Blakely pulled her down on the couch between them again? What if she couldn't say *no* this time? Between her legs her sex was still hot and slippery and her nipples ached from the attention both men had been paying them. *What's happening to me? How did I turn into such a slut?* she wondered unhappily. *Why am I acting this way?*

"He won't hurt ya, kid," Blakely saw her hesitation to approach the couch. "We're both real sorry about what happened."

"What *did* happen?" Sadie asked but the dark, curly haired man just shook his head, a look of pain crossing swiftly over his mobile features.

"Nothing we need to talk about right now," Holt said sternly. He had pasted a look of blank concentration over his own chiseled features and he held out his hand a touch impatiently, waiting for Sadie to let him examine her. Reluctantly, Sadie held out her still tingling palm to the blond man. Quickly but gently he stripped away the flexi-seal. Sadie was afraid to look, the pain was fading now but it had been almost as intense as when she had first been wounded—what could possibly be wrong? She braced herself to see something awful and looked down quickly. What she saw was so surprising that she couldn't comprehend it at first.

"What the . . . ?" she heard Blakely mutter in a low voice but a look from his blond partner cut him off quickly.

"I . . . I don't understand." She flexed her hand experimentally. The evil-looking wound that Holt had bandaged so carefully not ten minutes before was almost entirely gone, leaving only a thin, white line in its place. As she watched, even that disappeared leaving her palm as smooth and whole as though she had never been injured at all. "It's gone," Sadie breathed softly, opening and closing her hand gently at first and then with more force. "The pain and the cut, too. Both gone. But that's not *possible*."

"No, it shouldn't be." Holt looked grim. "Come on." He grabbed Blakely by the shoulder and pulled him away to the bedroom, slamming the door behind them. Sadie could hear them muttering in there, but she couldn't make out anything they were saying. She sank back onto the c-gel couch, everything but her newly healed hand forgotten.

What was going on?

8

"We healed her, Holt. Do you realize what that means?" Blakely demanded in an excited tone that Holt hoped Sadie couldn't hear from her spot on the couch.

"It doesn't have to mean anything," he answered, frowning. "And keep your voice down, damn it!"

"All right, all right," Blakely muttered. "It's just that . . . I never saw anything like that before. And I never felt the T-link open so wide. It was almost like . . ."

"Like having three bodies at once. Like merging into each other," Holt finished for him. It had been stronger than anything he had ever felt before . . . a melting into each other that was different from any other time he and Blakely had shared a woman. So intense and yet they had only been *touching* Sadie, not even actually making love with her. How could the T-link be so strong without the double penetration it usually required to come to life at all? What would it be like if they actually *did* make love? Holt wondered if any of their nervous systems could withstand the intensity.

The strange sensation had reminded Holt of when he and

Blakely were first linked. It had taken a while to get used to feeling his best friend's emotions and occasionally catching his thoughts. It was jarring, at first, having someone else inside your head and hooked into your nervous system. Knowing that nothing you ever did or felt would ever be completely private again.

He and Blakely had gotten used to it in time and now the tall blond man couldn't imagine what life would be like without the constant feedback and support from his dark-haired partner. Without Blakely he would feel like only half a man, and he knew his partner felt the same, but they had never expected to add another person to that equation.

Holt looked carefully at the excitement shining from his partner's indigo eyes and corrected himself. *He* had never expected to add another person to the equation. Had never expected to find the perfect match for both of them—the woman who could both handle the physical and emotional aspects of the T-link and who could also join in it and bond with them, becoming a part of it as much as he and Blakely were. Someone with whom they could form a Life-bond.

"She's the one—she has to be. We healed her, Holt. It's like the Professor said—if we ever found a woman with the exact right brain chemistry to complement us both the T-chips could have all kinds of hidden benefits. If we form a Life-bond with her . . ." Blakely said excitedly, echoing his thoughts.

"You can forget about that right now," Holt said, more harshly than he had intended.

"You've seen the way she acts every time we touch her. She might be physically able to handle the link, might even have the exact right brain chemistry, although Goddess knows the chances against that are astronomical, but she's not up to it *emotionally*, Blake. Not a lot of nice girls are."

"But Holt, we *healed* her. We could be on the edge of something big—*huge*. Remember Professor Klinefelder said . . ."

"Will you stop talking about him?" Holt snapped. It had taken a long time to get over his anger at the professor of neurobiology who had invented the T-chips they both wore, and there were still a lot of latent feelings that he kept buried. "What did he know? He's the one who screwed us up in the first place."

"That's not fair and you know it, Holt. How many times has bein' linked saved our asses? I think a little emotional trauma is a small price to pay for our lives," Blakely said, frowning. "Now I like Sadie—like her a lot and you're lyin' if you say you don't feel the same. She's smart and funny and she's got a lotta spunk. I know we haven't known her long, but I think we should take a chance and tell her about us—let her make up her own mind."

"No, absolutely not." Holt couldn't imagine a worse idea. "Blake, we're on a mission here or have you forgotten? We can't afford to get involved in an emotional mess with this girl when we're supposed to be concentrating on doing our jobs. Besides, we hardly know her."

"I've known her long enough to know I really like her . . . to know that I could love her if I gave myself a chance. And you could too, Holt, don't try to deny it." Blakely's voice was quiet but his indigo eyes snapped with intensity.

He really means it, Holt thought sadly. *He's falling in love with this girl and he wants me to join him.*

"Blake," he said with rough tenderness, laying a hand on his partner's shoulder and squeezing tightly to convey his emotion. "You've got to stop thinking like this. I know you want happily ever after and the fairy tale ending, but just think about it—have you ever read a fairy tale where the beautiful princess goes off with *two* Prince Charmings in the end? Face facts, partner, every time we touch her and the T-link does its thing she gets more and more freaked out. Didn't you look at her eyes a couple of minutes ago? She was scared to death to come near enough for me to look at her hand again even though it was really hurting her."

"She was just in shock," Blakely protested, shrugging Holt's hand off his shoulder impatiently.

"No, Blake—she was upset about what almost happened between the three of us. She was raised in Goshen, for Goddess's sake, and you know how conservative they are there. I know why you like her; she's a genuinely nice girl. Not like the ones who usually agree to try what we have to offer. And that's *precisely* why she's not going to be interested if you start proposing three-way matrimony."

"I'm just sayin' we should give her a chance," Blakely muttered, black brows drawn low over his deep blue eyes. He crossed his arms restlessly and looked at Holt. "I think you're underestimating her, Holt. Forget 'three-way matrimony,' what are we gonna tell her about what just happened to her hand? She's a reporter; she's gonna want to know."

"We don't tell her anything right now. We'll be entering orbit around Iapetus in a couple of hours and we've got to keep our focus on this mission. After we wrap this one up we can make a *joint* decision on what to tell her and what to ask her. But right now the mission has got to take precedence over everything." Holt looked at Blakely, whose arms were still wrapped tightly around his compact frame, and ached for the man who was so much more than his partner—more even than his best friend. David Blakely was the other half of his soul, and the darker man completed him as much as was possible despite the aching need in both of them for a third to fill the void in their lives.

"Blake," he said, cupping the dark, brooding face in one palm and looking earnestly into his partner's troubled indigo eyes. "I'm not saying we'll never tell her. I'm just asking you to wait for a while until we get everything settled. Can you do that for me?"

Blakely sighed deeply and relaxed, letting the tension leak

out of his posture as he looked up into the familiar sapphire eyes of his partner. "Okay," he said at last. "We'll keep her in the dark for now, Holt. But I want your word that once this is all over and done with we'll tell her the truth and at least see how she feels about the idea."

"Done," Holt said, breathing a private sigh of relief. Blakely was usually even tempered enough to agree with him in most things, but he could be stubborn when he felt strongly about something. Or someone. *You really like her, don't you, partner? Well what's not to like? She's intelligent, funny, and gorgeous. Okay, I admit it, I like her, too.*

He wondered if he could fall in love with Sadie, the way Blakely seemed to be doing, if only he didn't guard his heart so closely, but they had been disappointed so many times in the past. And the hurt from Gillian was still so fresh in his mind. It was almost impossible to believe there could ever be a fairy tale ending for their partnership.

Oh, Blake, Holt thought sadly, watching as his dark-haired partner got ready for bed. *I want happily ever after, too, but I'm afraid it just isn't in the cards for us.*

"What do you mean I can't come with you?" Sadie looked angrily from one set of blue eyes to another. Holt kept his cold and Blakely's looked tired, as though he hadn't gotten much sleep, but both sapphire and indigo eyes were utterly impenetrable—presenting a united front. They were sitting in the tiny food prep area with Sadie between them, and Blakely was bitching good-naturedly about the quality of the concentrates they were eating for breakfast when the argument started.

"It means what I said it means." Holt wondered why he always had to be the heavy. Blakely had indicated he would support him in the decision to keep Sadie in the dark and out of danger, but he wouldn't say much to back Holt up. "You can't come with us onto Iapetus and that's final."

"How am I supposed to get a first-hand account if you two cowboys go riding off on your own and leave me here on the ship?" Sadie demanded sarcastically, putting down her spoon.

"Look, we took you along to keep you safe, not put you in more danger," Holt shot back. "I thought I made that clear."

"Nothing about you two is clear." She glared at the tall blond detective. "I'm still wondering what the hell happened to my hand after what we . . ." she broke off, a deep blush staining her delicate features.

"We don't have time to discuss it right now," Holt said, more firmly than he felt. "Blake and I have to get down to the surface and see what we can turn up. We have to find out who's behind the mind rapes and keep what happened on Phoebe from happening again. That's our job."

"I could help you," Sadie argued, recovering from her embarrassment. "I'm good at getting information."

"Information on Iapetus isn't cheap, Sadie. How do you plan to pay for it? Maybe the same way you offered to pay us to take you along in the first place." Holt knew he shouldn't have said it. He regretted the cruel words the moment they were out of his mouth, but he was getting damn tired of arguing with her; Blakely wasn't the only one who'd had a sleepless night.

Sadie blushed again but this time she held her ground and looked him in the eye. "Look, when you agreed to take me with you nobody said anything about . . . that." She flipped her mane of honey-colored hair over her shoulder with a defiant little toss of her head.

"About takin' us both on at the same time?" Blakely spoke for the first time. The words were incendiary, but his tone was mild and the look on his mobile face was neutral.

Sadie looked like she might drop through the floor in mortification. "I . . . I'm not like that. Not that kind of a girl." She lowered her gaze. Holt couldn't miss the disappointment coming from his partner loud and clear through the T-link and it made him angry.

"But you *are* the kind who doesn't mind fucking us separately?" Holt's tone matched his harsh words and the sapphire eyes flashed fire. "Is *that* the kind of girl you are, Sadie? Is that something you usually do—trade sex for information?" He was letting this get to him more than he ought to, saying things he didn't mean, but he couldn't seem to help himself.

"No," she flashed back. "At the time it seemed to be the only way to get you to take me along. But it's not something I usually do, damn it! Not something I've ever done before," she added in a lower voice.

"I don't think you've done much of anything, have you, sweetheart?" Blakely asked her quietly.

"I'm not a virgin if that's what you mean." Sadie toyed with the plate in front of her so she wouldn't have to look into either set of blue eyes as she talked. "Not that it's any of your Goddess-damned business. I'm just not up for anything . . . rough or kinky."

"Nobody said anything about rough, baby. Holt and I know how to be gentle." Blakely's voice was low and he reached out and stroked her cheek lightly. Sadie flinched away from the gentle touch and Holt saw the quick flicker of sorrow in his partner's deep blue eyes, but it was quickly suppressed. Blakely straightened his shoulders, sighed, and went back to the previous topic of conversation. "Iapetus is a dangerous place for a lady. We're gonna have to go to some pretty rough joints and if we had you with us we'd have to be worried about protecting you too much to do our job."

"I can take care of myself," Sadie protested. Holt snorted cynically and she turned on the blond detective angrily. "I put *you* on the floor fast enough," she pointed out, lifting her chin defiantly and glaring at him. "Or have you conveniently forgotten? You were packing a blaster, but you let me put you down with a measly little tickler because you underestimated me. Don't make the same mistake twice, Holt."

"I am not having this discussion." Holt pinched the bridge of his nose between his thumb and forefinger and wrinkled his forehead; he could feel the beginnings of a pounding headache coming on. "I'm taking a sonic shower and then we're leaving for Iapetus. Just the two of us," he emphasized, pointing to Blakely and himself. Feeling angry for letting himself get so upset, he left the table and shut himself in the fresher, slamming the door perhaps a little louder than necessary.

When he came out, Blakely was waiting quietly on the couch, dressed in his roughest clothing for the trip topside. It didn't do to look too conspicuous on Iapetus, and Holt had dressed much the same as his partner in faded pants and a ragged shirt, his usual jacket covering the butt of his blaster.

"You ready, Holt?" the dark-haired man inquired.

"Sure—you?" Blakely nodded. "Where's Sadie?" Holt asked, knowing she was pissed off at him, wanting to say goodbye before they left, maybe apologize if he could find a way to do it unobtrusively.

"Went in the bedroom. Said she wanted some privacy," Blakely stood up. "You better let her alone for a while, Holt. She really had her heart set on getting this story first hand. I don't think she's gonna get over bein' left behind right away."

Holt looked at his partner, incredulous. "You think we should let her come, don't you?"

"I don't see how it could hurt. I'da kept an eye on her." Blakely straightened the lapels of his leather jacket, checking to make sure his blaster was hidden.

"Look, I thought we agreed . . ."

"I don't wanna fight about this, Holt," Blakely cut him off with a dangerous glint in his indigo eyes. "I backed you up like you wanted me to—helped you present, what did you call it?

Oh yeah, a 'unified front.' But that doesn't mean I have to agree with you all the time when it's just us. Personally, I think it wouldn't hurt to have her tag along. 'S long as we kept her close and made it clear she was spoken for nobody woulda bothered her. But you were so dead set against it—so dead set against *her*—I didn't think it was worth the fight."

"It's not about fighting," Holt protested.

"No, it's about a lot more than that," Blakely growled, turning on him. "It's about the way you won't give her a chance."

Holt knew by his tone that the dark-haired man was talking about giving Sadie a chance in more ways than letting her come topside with them. "Will you just stop it?" he nearly shouted at his partner. "Stop talking about giving her a chance to choose when you know damn well what her choice would be. You heard what she said at the table—she's not that kind of girl."

"Yeah, and you talkin' nasty to her the way you did isn't gonna change her mind any time soon, either," Blakely flared right back. "You had no right to say some of the things you did to her."

Holt could hardly believe what he was hearing. Had Blakely gone crazy over this girl or what? In all the years of their partnership they had never had a serious falling-out over a woman. Sure, they bickered from time to time but no female had ever been able to divide them like this. It frightened the blond detective deeply to see what was happening between them.

"Blake," he began. "Look, I'm sorry but . . ."

"You could be a little nicer to her, Holt." His tone was suddenly quieter but no less intense. "Try to let yourself be a little more open. I know Gillian hurt you, but Sadie's not Gillian."

"Blake," Holt started again, but his partner turned away from him and headed for the Navicom where the entrance to the landing craft was located.

"That's all I got to say, Holt. Now can we please get going?" Blakely threw over his shoulder.

Holt frowned—they would have to sit down and talk about this, really *talk*, not just yell, later. He strapped himself into one of the passenger seats and watched as Blakely maneuvered the controls, sliding the little craft smoothly from the docking bay and out into the blackness of space.

Neither one of them noticed the small form crouching quietly at the rear of the craft.

9

Sadie waited a good ten minutes after Blakely and Holt had left the craft to disembark herself. She pulled the oversized shirt and sweatpants she had pilfered from Blakely's pack close around her and clutched the shardi-knife she had also found hard in one hand, a slightly more effective weapon than her tickler. Securely fastened in the scarlet wig once more, the Overlook-Me chip sizzled warningly and she estimated she had only a few hours before it died again, but she hoped that was all she would need. Her plan was to tail the two detectives and find out as much dirt as she could for her mind rape story. She thought it wouldn't hurt to try and get a little personal dirt as well. Maybe if they thought they were unobserved the two men might drop some hints as to the strange bond between them and the mystery of how her hand had healed so quickly. Both their mouths were shut tighter than a Venusian virgin's legs on that subject, but Sadie knew it had something to do with the strange, almost electrical current of desire and pleasure she felt every time they both touched her at once. The memory of their mouths on her, the long, strong fingers inside her, thrusting so sweetly made her blush all over again. What was it about them that made them want—no, *need*—to share a woman?

Sadie shook her head. *Later for that.* Right now her job was tailing Detectives Holt and Blakely and finding out everything there was to find out. A Solar Pulitzer didn't just fall in your lap for the asking; she had better get going.

As she stepped out onto the crowded, dusty street, and began to make her way cautiously after the broad, retreating backs of her men, Sadie mentally reviewed everything she knew about Iapetus. It was one of Saturn's bigger moons, she knew, and it was tidally locked in its orbit around the ringed planet. That meant the same face of the moon was constantly facing Saturn because the immense gravitational pull from the planet it orbited didn't allow Iapetus to rotate on its axis the way Old Earth and the rest of the planets did on their path around the Sun. As a result, the side of Iapetus facing away from Saturn was constantly bright, while the side facing toward the ringed planet was in constant darkness. Sadie shivered at the thought—there were stories about the things that lived on the dark side of Iapetus—creatures that preyed on anyone stupid enough to cross the boundary from bright into dark. She knew that the main atmosphere dome where they had landed was located mainly on the light half of the moon, but a tiny section of it straddled the line into the eternal night of the other side. She only hoped Blakely and Holt had more business on the light side.

As she walked down the crowded street, trying to keep a discreet distance between herself and the detectives and hoping her chip would hold up, Sadie looked around at the dingy town. New Gomorrah was a dirty, hopeless-looking place, even by Outer Rings standards. Wobbly, jack-leg structures stood crowded together everywhere, like drunks leaning against each other to keep upright. They were mostly made of flimsy sheets of green semi-opaque stay-gel because of the prohibitive cost of importing building materials. The result was that all the buildings appeared to be made of half-melted lime-flavored gelatin. The main streets were paved, but the side streets and alleys looked like they might be hard-packed dirt. Sadie didn't want to find out for sure, preferring to keep to the cracked sidewalk on one side of the main thoroughfare.

Sadie followed the occasional glimpse of Blakely and Holt's leather jackets through the slow press of people, none of which paid any attention to her, thanks to the noninterference field her Overlook-Me chip cast around her. The atmosphere dome overhead was supposed to simulate day and night, but she couldn't tell if the grimy gloom that seemed to pervade the city meant it was getting toward evening on Iapetus or if the air was just too polluted with haze from the passing dust-crawlers to look bright at any time.

Looking around her, Sadie noticed that the population was mostly male, which wasn't unusual in the Outer Rings. Not many women wanted to come this far from the more civilized inner planets to the backwoods of the Solar System. The ones that made the journey mostly came with a man who was looking for work. Miners, trawler pilots, and star-diggers all came seeking the outrageous salaries offered by the interstellar mining companies to those who didn't mind risking their necks in deep space. All too often, however, it was a gamble they lost. The women who came with them then had to make it on their own, and there weren't many jobs for women in the Outer Rings. Well, Sadie amended to herself, not many *respectable* jobs, anyway.

Everywhere she looked, on either side of the road were large, neon signs. "Real Pussy" read one. "Tired of pumping Prosties? Try some Genuine Old Earth Vag," read another. Beside it, a large crimson neon vagina flashed. Sadie thought it looked like an ad for pulsating VD, and there were endless variations on the same. A few of the nicer looking establishments had signs that offered both human and cybernetic prostitutes, but the all-human brothels had them beat about three to one. Prostie brothels apparently weren't as big a business here on Iapetus as they were on the other inhabited moons, Sadie thought. She wondered what Blakely and Holt expected to find in this place.

Just as she was passing by another house of ill-repute, this one with a huge sign that read, "Male/ Female/ Prostie/ Human/ & Large Mammal Encounters. No Taste 2 Perverse," she noticed that Blakely and Holt had stopped walking. They conferred for a moment, the blond head and the dark close in intense conversation and Sadie wished she was close enough to hear what they were saying. She dared to edge a little nearer but only caught the end.

"... careful, Holt." Blakely had a hand on his blond partner's shoulder and was looking into the sapphire eyes intently. "The Slice is a rough place. I don't like you goin' in without back-up."

"I'll be fine, Blake," Holt replied, but he reached up and squeezed the hand that rested on his shoulder. "We'll never get everything done if we don't split up. You talk to Sheila and see if you can get those things you wanted and I'll try to catch Snuggly before he goes off shift."

Snuggly? They have an informant named Snuggly? Sadie thought in disbelief. And he worked in a place called "The Slice"? This she had to see. When the two men parted after one last intense look, she marked the large, bulging green doorway that Blakely entered and then turned and followed Holt through the crowd.

Holt was easy to follow; he was nearly a head taller than everyone else in the grimy press of bodies and his blond hair shone like a beacon in the gloom. Sadie was still angry with him, both for underestimating her abilities and for the nasty things he had said at breakfast. Still, she reflected, Holt was a man of deep loyalties, and she had gotten the distinct impression that he was angry on his partner's behalf more than his own when he made his hasty accusations, but what had she done to offend Blakely that made his blond partner so irate? Sadie shook her head. It was maddening to be so close to the mystery and yet be unable to figure it out.

She was mad at Holt at the moment, but more and more she found herself caring for both men in a way that she found a little frightening. The emotion she had for them was certainly stronger than anything she'd had for her ex-fiancé Gerald, and she had been with him for three years, whereas she had only known Blakely and Holt for two weeks. To be honest, she was falling more than a little bit in love with the two detectives, Sadie admitted to herself. If it had been one man only that she was having feelings like this for, she might have considered going to bed with him, but she liked *both* of them and there was no way . . . *I'm not that kind of girl,* she insisted to herself, trying to ignore the disapproving little voice in the back of her mind that insisted she'd certainly been *acting* like that kind of girl lately.

Still, the feel of their hands and mouths on her body and those long fingers sliding wetly into her . . . Sadie pushed the memory out of her head and made herself pay attention; she had almost lost Holt as he pushed his way into a sinister looking building made of black concrete block instead of stay-gel. The flickering neon sign overhead read, "Slice of Night," and it was located near the very edge of the atmosphere dome. She stopped in front of the bar, letting the crowd pass around her in either direction and considered her options.

She could hear the Overlook-Me chip sizzling with alarming regularity now and she realized she might have less time than she'd thought. If she went inside and her chip failed where Holt could see her she was screwed, but she hadn't come all this way just to hang around outside and wonder what was happening. She would have to take her chances and try to keep to the shadows, out of the blond detective's line of vision. Somehow, Sadie didn't think that would be a problem; The Slice looked like it had shadows to spare in its gloomy interior.

Taking a deep breath, she marched bravely through the entry-way and into the bar.

10

The first thing she saw when she entered the crowded, smoky bar was the most enormous Garon she'd ever laid eyes on. It was rare to see an ET at this end of the System, and Sadie took a moment to stare at the odd creature. He was slumped behind the bar, hulking shoulders bowed inward with a morose expression on his flat, scaly face, polishing shot glasses with a limp towel. There was a tiny, frilly white apron cinched around his thick waist and Holt was leaning on the bar, drinking a shot of what looked like Venusian tequila and talking to him.

The rest of the clientele were scattered throughout the bar at rickety tables, drinking like there was no tomorrow, which, Sadie thought, for some of them there probably wouldn't be. Ring miners had a high mortality rate. They were drunk enough and rowdy enough for her to be very glad her Overlook-Me chip was still in working order. She wouldn't stand a chance in a place like this without the protective noninterference field the chip generated. Edging carefully around the crowd at the bar, Sadie was able to find a dark corner by one wall that was close enough to hear the conversation between Holt and the huge bartender over the heavy thump of Jovian Jazz that poured from the speaker grills.

"... anything about it, Snug?" she heard Holt say. So the monstrous Garon must be Snuggly, Sadie mused to herself. Interesting.

"I hear nothing," the Garon replied in a voice like someone gargling with gravel, cutting his one large purple and green eye evasively to one side. Even Sadie could tell he was lying. Holt apparently could as well.

"Come on, Snuggly, don't give me that. If there's anything illegal within a million miles it comes through your bar. The Slice sees more action in one night than the rest of this Goddess-forsaken end of the Solar System does in a year." Holt drained his glass and shook his head when the Garon made as if to pour him another.

"Why you always bother me, Holtstein? I got enough problems without you and your partner come around squeezing my balls." The Garon set down the glass he'd been cleaning daintily and picked up another. "Where is your better half, anyway?" he asked.

"Working the other end of town," Holt answered shortly. He fished in the pocket of the beat-up work pants he was wearing and withdrew a fifty credit chip. "I know you know something, Snug. Maybe this will jog your memory."

The Garon eyed the chip thoughtfully for a moment, then slid it off the bar and made it disappear into one of the embroidered pockets of his frilly apron. Sadie wondered if he wore it on purpose or if he was so big that no one had the nerve to tell him it was a tad girlie for his massive physique. After pouring a round of shots for a rowdy crew of star-hoppers that had just walked in he went back to Holt, who was leaning against the counter waiting patiently.

"Okay, Holtstein, I tell you what I know. Only because I like you, though. You and Blakely never fuck me yet. Better not start now." He glared warningly at the blond detective, his eye going completely purple for a moment.

"Don't worry, Snuggly. You're not exactly our type," Holt said dryly. "What do you know? It better be good."

"Is good." Snuggly nodded his massive bald head. "Or bad, depending on how you are seeing it." Holt just raised one blond eyebrow and waited for the Garon to continue. "About a month ago a prostie trader is coming into my bar," Snuggly said. "And he is how you say? Slick Willie—very smooth talking. He is saying he is representing a new company just set up right here on Iapetus. New kind of prostie-borg that is extra good. Extra cheap."

"Did you get a name?" Holt asked casually, although Sadie saw the tension in the set of his well-defined shoulders. They could definitely be onto something here. The Garon shook his massive bald head.

"No names. He says he is only passing through town, but he will like to make me a bargain before he leaves to sell his borgs on Titan. He says he had extra, would I like to buy."

"Did you?" Holt asked, leaning forward on the bar. Sadie found herself leaning forward as well. If the Garon was telling the truth, there was an illegal prostie-borg plant right here on Iapetus. Because the delicate synthetic brains that powered legal prosties couldn't be shipped off planet until they were hardwired into a tank-grown body, the only legal flesh tanks were located on Mars, where Synthenex, the main manufacturer of the brains, was located. If someone had set up flesh tanks here, they must either have their own synthetic brain manufacturing facility, which was highly unlikely, or they were using black market transplant brains. Real human brains that had been ripped from their living hosts and forced to occupy a body grown in the flesh tanks made for sex. Sadie was so excited by the implications that she nearly missed the huge Garon's reply to Holt's question.

"I am buying," Snuggly said stolidly. "I am thinking it is good for business, yes? But after Slick Willie leaves, prostie goes bad after only two days. Is rip-off."

"Goes bad? What do you mean?" Holt asked. "Did she stop functioning or what?"

"Stop functioning, you could say this, yes," Snuggly replied morosely. "She is refusing to service customers, is punching, kicking, screaming, making a scene. I try to throw her out but she won't go."

Looking at his hulking form, Sadie had a hard time imagining any sort of prostie-borg the Garon would have difficulty evicting from his bar. Maybe they were making them super-size now?

"What happened to her? Where is she now?" Holt stood up straight and looked around.

"Is in the back room drinking a bottle of my best Flare juice and teasing the daemon." The Garon cast a morose glance toward the back of the bar.

Holt whistled under his breath. "Goddess, Snuggly, you still have that thing? Aren't you afraid it'll get loose someday and kill you or one of the customers?"

The huge shoulders shrugged. "Daemon is never leaving dark side of back room and is very good for business. Stupid drunks like to see how brave they are, how long they can stay before they have to run. Slice is the only bar on Iapetus to be having a daemon on the premises." The Garon sounded almost proud of the fact.

"Yeah, because you're the only bar that straddles the dark side line," Holt said. "How long has the prostie been in there?"

Garon shrugged again. "Don't know. Long time. Is very much rip-off. Worst prostie I ever have."

"Thanks, Snuggly. I'm going back." Holt slapped the bar with one hand and turned to make his way through the drunken miners.

"You are being careful, Holtstein," the huge Garon called. "Prostie is there a long time. Daemon is getting strong."

"Yeah, yeah. Thanks." Holt waved over his shoulder and continued to press through the crowd. Sadie had no choice but to follow him.

At the back of the bar there was a long, dim corridor. Holt stepped into it without hesitation but Sadie stopped for a moment to read the warning scrolling tiredly across the holo-loop in twelve languages above her head. ENTER AT YOUR OWN RISK, MANAGEMENT ASSUMES NO RESPONSIBILITY. Could they really be keeping an Iapetion daemon back here, she wondered, clutching the shardi-knife tightly. Shivering, she remembered the chilling stories she'd heard about the creatures that lived solely on the dark side of Iapetus. How much of what she had heard was true?

Sadie looked from the holo-loop to the hallway. Holt's golden head was disappearing down the gloom of the long corridor, his wide shoulders clad in the black leather jacket barely visible now. She had followed him to get information, but now he was going into danger. Going alone. No—not alone. Squaring her shoulders and raising her chin in a little gesture of defiance, Sadie took a deep breath and plunged into the gloom after him. She would have done the same for Blakely.

Walking quietly so as not to let Holt hear her, Sadie crept down the hallway. Just as she thought it was about to end she saw him make an abrupt left and disappear. She followed him so quickly that she barely saved herself from running into him and for a moment all she could see was his broad, leather-clad back. Then he moved out of her line of vision and Sadie could see that the hallway opened out into a room—the strangest room she had ever seen.

It was shaped like a dome, perfectly round with a high, curving ceiling that was made of some transparent material that let light pour in from above. But the light filled only half the room,

Sadie saw. There was a definite demarcation, a line almost directly down the center of the round room, and the light that poured from the ceiling remained on one side of the line like a curtain of brilliance. On the other side was a blackness more complete than any Sadie had ever seen. She frowned, the light should have illuminated the entire room with radiance, but it didn't. Instead, the brightness on one half of the room only served to make the darkness of the other half more impenetrable. What could keep the light that filled one side of the room from spreading to the other side as well?

As if to answer her question, she heard a muffled thump that drew her eyes to the pitch-black half of the room. It was like a pit filled with midnight and it hurt her eyes to look at it. She looked anyway, at first seeing nothing. Then, as her eyes adjusted to the strange duality of the room, Sadie felt her skin trying to crawl right off her body. Something was moving in the blackness. She couldn't see much, but there was a suggestion of power in its coiled form and a sound like a heavy weight dragging across the floor when it moved. Crimson gashes glittered in the blackness and she realized those must be its eyes and it was looking right at her. An Overlook-Me chip apparently had no power to effect the vision of an Iapetion daemon.

Sadie felt her heart pounding as though it was trying to get out of her chest. The red eyes seemed to pin her in place as with an unspeakable, low slithering sound, the thing dragged its bulk closer to where she was standing, still half hidden behind Holt's large frame as he stood in the doorway. Sadie tried to remember everything she had heard. Could the creature really feed on emotions? If so, her fear must be a banquet to it. With a huge effort she dragged her eyes from the midnight blackness of the daemon's side of the room and concentrated on the other side.

The half of the room that was bathed in light was bare except for a rough plexi-table and some form molded chairs. In one of them slumped a tiny, stunningly beautiful woman with long, tangled blond hair and a bottle of Flare juice clutched in one hand. No, not a woman, Sadie saw after studying her a moment. A prostie-borg. Her skin had the slightly plastic tone and marked lack of flexibility that denoted tank-grown flesh. It was an effect Sadie herself had achieved through latex make-up when she had posed as a prostie at the Pleasure Dome complex.

Just then the blond prostie looked up, blinking, and Sadie saw the strange, intricate blue design on her right eyelid. It was the exact same tattoo that all the new prosties—the ones that were receiving injections—had been wearing at the Pleasure Dome Prostie Palace. She wished fervently for a moment that she had brought something with her to take notes.

"Hey." Holt entered the room with seeming nonchalance although Sadie noticed he was careful to stay far to the light side of it. The woman looked up at him without much interest.

"What the hell do you want?" she returned in a high, feminine voice. Then, as though the sound of her own voice had upset her, she raised the bottle and took a huge swallow, her delicate, pixielike features twisting in a grimace as the liquor burned down her throat. She belched and wiped her rosebud of a mouth carelessly across the back of her arm, then just sat staring at Holt.

"You want to take it easy with that stuff, honey," Holt cautioned her, walking across to take a seat at the table beside her. The brilliant light pouring down from above made his hair look like molten gold. Sadie, still standing in the doorway, noticed that he deliberately put his back to the daemon. Was he ignoring it so it couldn't feed off him?

"The fuck I will." The prostie took another hit off the bottle. The words seemed doubly crude, somehow, coming from such a pretty, pouting mouth, Sadie thought.

"Suit yourself but you're gonna have one hell of a hangover, lady," Holt stared at her intently.

"I c'n hold my liquor," the prostie protested, making an effort to sit up a little straighter in the crooked chair. "Used to drink two, three of these a night and still be up for a morning raid."

"Excuse me?" Holt looked interested and he was still paying no attention to the malevolent blackness barely three feet behind him. Even if ignoring them was the preferred method of dealing with Iapetion daemons, it still made Sadie distinctly nervous to watch those hungry crimson eyes caress Holt's back with obvious greed. She crouched in the doorway, the shardi-knife held so tight it was making a groove in the center of her palm and waited.

"If you don't mind me saying so, you don't act like a normal prostie," Holt said to the pixie-faced cyborg.

"That's 'cause I ain't one." She slouched in the chair, legs spread in a most unladylike display and scratched her crotch with the hand that wasn't holding the bottle. "And don't get any ideas 'bout fuckin' me neither, bub. I don't care how long you been in space or how horny you are, it ain't gonna happen. I don't care what that son-of-a-space-whore at the front of the bar told you."

"Who, Snuggly? He's okay," Holt said casually, leaning back in his chair a little in a way that made Sadie even more nervous for him. "He thought he was buying a real prostie. Bet he paid a lot of credit for a beauty like you."

"Well if he did he made it back in the first forty-eight hours before the drugs wore off," the blond-haired prostie snarled. She took another huge gulp from the bottle and banged it down on the table sharply, making Sadie jump. "Karma," she muttered, slurring her words, the long, tangled blond tendrils hanging in her eyes. "'S fuckin' karma's what it is. But swear to Goddess, if I find that red-headed bastard who did this to me I'll fuck 'im up."

"Who did what to you?" Holt asked gently. He raised a

hand and Sadie thought he might have wanted to lay it on the prostie's shoulder to offer comfort. It was the same way he and Blakely often touched each other when either of them was blue or upset, she thought. But Holt's hand wavered and then dropped back to the table—probably a wise choice.

"Did what? Turned me into *this*, 's what he did." The prostie gestured with the bottle at her tiny, voluptuous form and managed to spill the bright orange Flare juice all over herself. Judging from the state of her clothes it wasn't the first time. She cocked her head and fixed Holt with big brown eyes that looked like they belonged in a children's vid about nature. "D'you know who I am?" she asked. "A month ago if I'da sat down beside you at the bar you'da pissed your pants, blondie." She nodded her head in big, exaggerated movements. "Pissed your pants," she repeated to herself apparently liking the sound of the words.

"Who are you then?" Holt asked, apparently losing patience. Sadie knew *she* was; she just wanted him to finish his questions and get the hell out of the back room. Without noticing, Holt had shifted his chair backward an inch or two and the glowing red eyes pinned on his back got noticeably brighter.

"You ready for this?" Without waiting for a reply, the prostie took another swig from the bottle and continued, enunciating carefully. "I, my blond friend, am none other than Bjorn Xavier, terror of deep space for the past fifteen years. I raped, robbed, pillaged, leveled whole colonies, and nobody could stop me. Nobody till my double-crossing right-hand-man Red Mike decided to screw me on our last deal."

Sadie drew in a quick breath and hoped she hadn't been heard. If the prostie was who she claimed she was, she or he was responsible for more raids and attacks on underdeveloped colonies than any other person in recent history. Xavier was known for his ruthlessness and cunning; no one had ever been able to catch the notorious pirate. And now he was trapped in a prostie-borg body. The delicious irony of it would make amazing copy, Sadie thought. She listened more closely, trying to commit every detail to memory, and forgetting to keep an eye on the daemon crouched in the blackness behind Holt.

"You were behind the mind rapes on Phoebe," Holt said flatly.

The prostie who was actually a stellar pirate looked surprised. "How'd you know about that? We figured it'd take longer'n a month for anybody to notice we cleaned out that little shit hole." She shook her head and sighed as with deep nostalgia. "Was our best take ever," she said, her big brown eyes beginning to fill with easy tears. "We had it all planned—we were gonna drop the brains off to Van Heusen and split the profits fifty-fifty."

"Roald Van Heusen?" Holt asked, leaning forward to stare at the prostie space pirate. Sadie could scarcely contain her glee. Van Heusen was known throughout the system for his illegal operations. Like Xavier, he had never been caught. What a story this was going to make! "*The* Roald Van Heusen?" Holt repeated like he couldn't believe it.

"You know of another one?" the prostie asked dryly. "Man's a fuckin' institution, even more than me and Mike were."

"You got that right," Holt murmured, shaking his head. "So you mind raped the Phoebe colonists to sell to Van Heusen who, I suppose, has set up shop somewhere here on Iapetus. Probably on the dark side since nobody in their right mind would go there . . ." He mused silently for a moment, leaning back in his chair. "So how'd you end up here?" he asked at last.

"Fuckin' Mike," the prostie snarled morosely, the high, musical voice sounding bitter. "Decided he wanted it all. Waited 'till I was sleepin', I guess, and mind raped me just like those damn sheep on Phoebe. When I woke up I looked like *this* and there was a line of miners out the door of this place waitin' for their turn. Miners are horny fucks," she said sourly. "Have ta stay back here with the Goddess-damned daemon to keep 'em off me."

The prostie took another drink out of the bottle and slammed it back on the table. "Guess you'll say I'm getting' some of my own back," she said, staring defiantly up into Holt's stony face. "And maybe I am, but I don't give a shit. I just know that I'm gonna kill that bastard Red Mike when I find 'im. And believe me, I'll find 'im."

"Well, you don't appear to be searching too hard at the moment," Holt pointed out. He was slouched comfortably in his chair, one hand tucked out of sight inside his jacket, seemingly completely unaware of the growing darkness behind him. Because, Sadie saw with a start, it *was* growing.

When they had first come down the long hall, the room had been divided straight down the center, equal halves of light and dark like a surreal yin–yang. Now she saw that while she had been engrossed with the prostie's confession, the darkness had steadily but surely begun to creep, encroaching on the half-circle of brilliance, nibbling away at the light. When Holt had sat down at the table, the daemon was a good three feet behind him. Suddenly, the distance was less than two feet and shrinking rapidly.

Sadie wanted to scream a warning, wanted to shout his name but it was as though a cold hand was gripping her throat, freezing her vocal chords with black ice. The red eyes flashed malevolently at her from the growing darkness and she knew it was the daemon somehow keeping her from making a sound.

"Oh, I'll find 'im," the blond prostie assured Holt with a sneer. "See, I made a deal. I gotta friend who's gonna help."

"The only help you're going to get is a one-way ticket to a federal prison, Xavier." Holt drew his hand from beneath his jacket and Sadie saw that he was holding a pair of silver restraints and his badge. "You're under arrest. But first you're going to tell me exactly where Van Heusen's keeping the illegal tanks."

The prostie grinned nastily. "That's what you think, bub. Knew you had to be some kinda cop. You're the first guy who's come back here that didn't try to grab me."

"You're not my type," Holt said dryly. The darkness was only inches behind him now, the glowing crimson eyes longing to devour. Sadie tried to move but her entire body was frozen. She realized in horror that she was going to watch Holt die without being able to do anything about it.

"You're not mine either." The prostie laughed, an evil tinkling sound like fairy music played off-key. "But I know somebody who'd like you just fine." She leaned forward suddenly, moving much more quickly than anyone who'd drunk nearly a fifth of Flare juice should have been able. Planting her delicate, flowerlike hands against Holt's broad chest she gave a tremendous shove, tilting his chair and pitching him backward into the waiting blackness.

When the daemon's attention shifted entirely to the blond detective, Sadie suddenly found she was free. Without hesitating an instant or considering how suicidal her action was, she lunged forward into the room, crossing the line from light to darkness almost instantly, screaming Holt's name.

11

Blakely whistled as he left the private office of Sheila Blex, madam of the biggest mixed-bag brothel on Iapetus and one of his and Holt's best informants. When they had first met Sweet Sheila, she was simply another working girl on the streets of New Brooklyn, Blakely's old stomping grounds. She had given them sound information more than once, mainly, Blakely figured, because she had a huge crush on his blond partner. Sheila had told them time and again that her intention was to get to the Outer Rings and make her fortune and damned if she hadn't done it despite the fact that Blakely and Holt had both tried to warn her off.

Blakely grinned to himself as he looked around the plush interior of the whore house, taking in the choices available to the well-heeled miners eager to spend their credit for a night of companionship. The room was decorated in shades of crimson and black and there was a wide selection of humans and prosties both male and female lolling on the many plush couches in the waiting area. Luscious, ripe flesh was on display everywhere. Firm, naked breasts topped with pouting nipples, silky thighs, and hot, wet pussies surrounded him. There were also plenty of thick cocks if that was your cup of joe, and from a gilt-edged crate in the corner a forlorn "baa" could be heard. Blakely shook his head; no taste too perverse indeed.

A pheromone blower at the door ensured that every man who walked in was instantly horny, as Blakely could attest because his own cock had been stiff from the moment he'd come through the door.

"See anything you like?" The voice purring in his ear made him turn around to see Sheila standing right behind him, her curvy hips cocked in a sexy pose. "You forgot these." She thrust a bundle at him.

"Oh, thanks. Guess I was a little distracted." He glanced around the room again. "Hey, do some guys really go for that?" He nodded at the cage in the corner where the baaing had gotten louder.

"Millie? She's one of our local favorites. Makes me more credit than any two prosties put together. You wanna give her a try? It's a wild and wooly ride." Sheila's green eyes danced with laughter and Blakely shivered and shook his head.

"No thanks, Sheila. I'm not into barnyard porn like some of the sick bastards around here."

She elbowed him in the ribs. "I know that, Blake, I'm just yankin' your chain. But maybe I could set you up with something a little more appealing." She gestured to the couches full of lounging sex workers.

"Thanks but no thanks, Sheila. I've gotta meet up with Holt. He went to The Slice without me." Blakely felt a twinge of unease as he spoke of his partner and, unconsciously, he rubbed the back of his neck.

"Oh yeah, I don't know how I could have forgotten that you two are a team when it comes to sex." Sheila grinned at him, teasingly. "You shouldn't go making fun of poor Millie's

Johns when you and Holt are so kinky you always have to share. Listen, come on back after you pick your gorgeous blond partner up from The Slice. I'll do you together myself for free." She ran one blood-red beautifully manicured nail along the bulge in his pants, causing the dark-haired detective to jump guiltily.

"Don't think I don't appreciate the offer, but no can do, hon." In the past, he and Holt would have certainly taken her up on her invitation. It had been a long, lonely time since they had made love to anyone. His cock throbbed in his pants at the memory of fucking the gorgeous, curvy woman in front of him, of burying his cock to the hilt in her tight pussy while Holt rammed into her from behind and feeling the T-link widen to a river of pleasure, if only for a little while. Sheila was one of the few women able to handle the sensory overload caused by the T-link during their double penetration, although she didn't have the correct brain chemistry to bond with them. Being a working girl and a friend, she was also one of the few women who wasn't shocked and offended when she learned of Blakely and Holt's unusual sexual needs.

"Ah," Sheila pouted prettily. "But I *like* being the filling in a Holt and Blakely sandwich. I can't believe you came all the way to New Gomorrah and you don't want to hook up."

Blakely could scarcely believe it either. They weren't often offered the chance for guilt-free, no holds barred sex, but things were different now. He looked around the room at all the flesh on display and then back at Sheila herself, with her wide green eyes and lush body. As hard as he looked, all he could see was a pair of honey-colored eyes and a long mane of hair to match. That sweet face he had picked out of a prostie line-up two weeks ago, the slender curvy form and the hot, addictive feel of her pressed tight between him and Holt. All he could see, all he could think of was Sadie. He knew Holt thought he was being foolish, that the little reporter from Io would never come around, but the dark-haired detective couldn't help it; he was in love.

"We just don't have time, Sheila," he said, trying to make a plausible excuse. He needed to get back to Holt. "If what you've told me is right, we've got less than twenty-four hours to get to the dark side." He hitched the bundle she had given him up under one arm and tried to ignore his throbbing cock. "I'd better get goin'." He rubbed the back of his neck again.

"All right then, Blake, be that way. But come on back if you get a chance when you wrap up your business."

"Yeah, maybe we wi . . ." Blakely stopped in midword, frozen in place. Anyone who had been watching the dark-haired detective would have thought he had suddenly received terrible news somehow. His vivid indigo eyes widened and his mouth narrowed to a bloodless slit. "Goddess, no," he muttered, half to himself

"Blake, honey, what's wrong? You look *terrible* all of a sudden." Sheila's voice was filled with genuine concern, but Blakely barely heard her or felt her light grip on his tense bicep.

"I gotta go." Abruptly he shrugged off the well-manicured hand.

"Blake, what . . . ?"

"Trouble." He elbowed his way past customers and prosties alike and rushed out of the building, leaving Sheila to stare after him in disbelief.

"Holt. Oh, Goddess, Holt," Blakely muttered aloud, not caring that he was attracting attention and ignoring the threatening stares of the rough men around him as he pushed through the crowded sidewalk. Night had come to Iapetus, courtesy of the atmosphere dome, and he felt like he was stuck in a bad dream, struggling though the noisy, stinking darkness to reach his partner in time.

He had, of course, felt the twinge along the T-link between them when Holt stepped into the daemon's lair. It was a wrenching feeling, a jangling along his nerves that made the hair on the back of his neck stand up, but he could also feel Holt's calm, like a cool hand on the back of his neck. Holt believed he was in no real danger and they had been partnered long enough for Blakely to trust his judgment. The blond detective knew what he was doing.

Then, when he was talking to Sheila, the feeling had grown stronger, like an itch in the back of his brain, making him restless to get back to his partner, to be by Holt's side, backing him up. And there was something else that bothered him, the feeling in his brain was different than any he had felt before. There was a strange . . . *duality* about it, a faint echo to the signal that disturbed him. Almost as though he was receiving danger signals from two minds instead of one, but that wasn't possible. Was it? He still felt Holt's certainty that everything was fine, but it was less calming than it had been.

At last, when he was saying goodbye to Sheila and turning down her offer of a friendly fuck, he had felt the sharp, almost physical pain, like a stabbing at the base of his skull, where the Tandem chip that created the T-link between him and Holt was housed. It was Trouble with a capital T and Blakely knew it. He had never felt such an intense warning through the link he shared with Holt and it meant that his blond partner was not only in a dangerous situation, but that his life was in jeopardy. Again, the sensation was doubled somehow, making it that much more urgent. Blakely didn't know what was going on, but he didn't have time to stop and think about it.

"Hang on, Holt," he muttered to himself, quickening his pace as The Slice came into view. "Just hang on, partner. I'm on my way."

He burst in the door and headed directly to the back room,

knowing by the chip's spatial resolution feature exactly where his partner was located.

"Blakely!" he heard Snuggly bellowing at him, but paid no attention. Holt was in the back room and he was in trouble—that was all that mattered. Running down the dim, threatening hallway with the chip's warning stabbing at his brain, Blakely had to force himself to stop for a moment and drop the bundle he had been clutching and grab his blaster. It wouldn't do to go charging in before he knew what was going on. Blaster in hand, he edged carefully around the corner of the hall to face the back room.

A grim, nearly silent struggle was taking place in the roiling darkness that filled the room like poison smoke. Blakely caught sight of red, glaring eyes and white teeth like knives. Then his partner came into view, his blond hair gleaming in the blackness like a star in space, struggling with the thing that seemed to be made of shadows and scales. Blakely raised his blaster, but they were too close.

"Holt," he shouted hoarsely, trying to get the blond's attention. "Holt, stand clear so I can get a shot." *In the head,* he was thinking. *In the head, right between those fuckin' red eyes—it's the only way . . .*

"I can't," Holt shouted back, not daring to take his eyes from the daemon's leering face. "It's got her . . . it's got her and it won't let go, Blake!"

For the first time, Blakely became aware of a faint sizzling sound by his feet. Looking down, he saw a familiar scarlet wig—Sadie's wig. *Oh, Goddess no—no!* he thought. *Not Sadie!* The idea made him crazy. Lowering his head and charging like a bull, Blakely entered the fray, ready to save his partner and the woman he loved or die trying.

It was a confusing mixed up mess, like trying to fight blindfolded at midnight in the middle of an ice-cold river with a strong current. The daemon's presence had filled the small back room the way water fills a container and Blakely fought to get a deep breath, feeling the muscular coils of blackness snake around his body, pushing him in different directions as he struggled to find Holt's blond head in the gloom.

"Blake, over here!" He heard the shout and turned to find his partner struggling grimly with a smoky tentacle that was wrapped around his torso, pinning his arms to his sides.

"Holt?" he gasped, taking in the pale features suddenly swimming in front of his own. "Where is she?"

"Feeding on her," Holt's voice was breathless, "Won't last long. Shoot it, Blake! Shoot the fucker!"

"Where . . . ?" Blakely started to ask in frustration and then his half-formed question was answered when the daemon's face swam into view, leering and hateful, a predatory grin on its filthy alien face.

Blakely just had time to register that it had Sadie clutched to itself, her head lolling unconsciously to one side, her long honey-brown hair flowing over the thing's midnight-black skin when it opened its jaws, lined like a shark's in multiple rows of razor-sharp teeth and clamped down on the pale skin of her exposed neck.

"*No!*" Blakely heard the scream, but didn't understand that it was coming from his own throat. The unspeakable sound of sucking filled the air and he felt a part of himself dying, dwindling to nothing right along with her fading life force. It all happened in a fraction of an instant. Then Sadie's eyes fluttered briefly and her lips moved; she seemed to be trying to say a name.

The small sign of life seemed to break his paralysis and Blakely felt an icy calm envelop his nerves as he dragged his gaze from her sweet face to the twisted features of the daemon. "Eat this you fucker," he said in a cold, dead voice and, pressing the muzzle of his blaster between the slitted crimson eyes, he pulled the trigger again and again.

* * *

The next thing he knew Holt was shaking him. "Wha . . . ?" he tried to say. "No time, Blake, we've gotta move." The tall blond was scooping something off the floor and to Blake's horror, he saw it was the limp figure of a girl. *Not just any girl— that's Sadie.* Sluggish trickles of blood were running from her torn throat and if she was breathing at all, Blakely couldn't tell it.

"How the fuck?" He staggered to his feet and went to help Holt carry her.

"Got her damn chip working again and followed us, I guess," Holt's voice was grim.

"We've got to get her out of here, Blake. You put the daemon down but it's not completely out, I don't think. Takes a lot to kill those bastards." He jerked his head at the rear of the small round room. Following his gesture, Blakely saw a boiling cloud of blackness still twitching feebly near a slender blond girl splayed carelessly on the floor. As he watched, the cloud moved to cover her face, obscuring the delicate features in a roil of black.

"Who's that?" Blakely pointed at the girl, or was it a prostie-borg? He couldn't be sure.

"You wouldn't believe me if I told you," Holt said grimly. "Just leave him—he's getting what he deserves."

"He?" Blakely stared blankly at the feminine curves on the floor, but Holt's urgency throbbed in the back of his brain like a drum beat and he followed his partner without question down the long hallway.

"No blood vessels torn although I don't know how they weren't if what you're telling me is correct." The Medi-tech sighed and finished sponging off Sadie's neck, which didn't look nearly as bad as Blakely had expected it to. A neat row of double puncture marks decorated her slender white throat like a sideways necklace, but otherwise the flesh was intact.

"So she'll be okay then?" he asked hopefully. "I mean, if she didn't lose too much blood and nothin's torn. Right?"

"I'm afraid not." The Medi-tech looked grave. "I'm sorry gentlemen. If you're not from this area then maybe you don't understand. When a daemon attacks someone, when it feeds, it's not blood that it's taking. It's . . ." he seemed to be searching for the right word. "Emotion . . . the will to live. We don't really understand how it's done, what exactly the daemon does to its victims. We only see the results." He gestured in Sadie's direction and turned away from them, tidying the contents of his small, sterile exam room as though the discussion was closed.

"Wait a minute!" Blakely grabbed the narrow shoulders and turned the man around, forcing a confrontation. "What are you talking about?" He gestured to Sadie's limp form lying cold and quiet on the exam table. "She's gonna be fine, go on, *say* it. I wanna hear you say she's gonna be fine."

"Blake . . ." He felt a strong hand grip his arm and Holt's sorrow and certainty flowed through him. "She's dying, partner," Holt said.

"I'm sorry," the Medi-tech said again, blinking watery brown eyes rapidly. "But I've seen many, many daemon attacks. I wish I could help her, but there's no known cure. Once the victim loses consciousness, well . . . My best advice it to take her somewhere and make her comfortable. It won't be long." He left, shutting the door behind him, leaving them in the room that smelled of alcohol and death.

"Nonono," Blakely was shaking his head, vaguely aware of Holt's arm around his shoulders, trying to comfort. "She can't die, I won't *let* her."

"You can't help it. Nobody can." Holt's voice was rough with unshed tears. "Look at me, partner, you think I don't feel the same way? What happened to her—she was trying to save me. She came at that thing with a pocket knife when it grabbed me. Your little shardi—the one you keep to open wine units, you know? She must have gotten it from your pack before she followed us."

For the first time Blakely registered that Sadie was wearing his clothes, an old shirt and a pair of sweatpants he wore on days off. Her slender, pale form swam in the oversized clothing and he suddenly remembered the bundle of new clothes he had gotten from Sheila for her to wear that lay in a glitzy ball of fabric at his feet. He had wanted to surprise her, to make up for not taking her along. She'd never wear them now.

"Fuck," he muttered brokenly, pulling away from Holt as the misery ate at his soul. He felt her going, felt her slipping away and knew his partner was right, there was nothing he could do about it.

"I'm so Goddess-damned sorry, Blake," Holt muttered hoarsely. "I know how you felt about her. I . . . I was beginning to feel the same way, I guess." The familiar sapphire eyes were bright and the blond man's chiseled features were twisted with the same agony Blakely felt inside himself. For the first time, though, sharing the grief didn't make it less.

"You know the worst part?" Blakely turned from his partner to stroke the honey soft hair away from her pale cheeks. "The worst part is that I don't just feel it in here," he pointed to his chest. "I feel it in here, too," he pressed a palm to the back of his neck. "I feel her dyin' like I'd feel *you* dyin' partner. Feel like a part of me is goin' with her." He cupped the cool, lovely face in his hand, remembering how her cheeks had flushed with desire and fear the first time they pinned her between them. Remembering the heat that had flowed like a cord binding her to him and Holt. She should have been the one. He had been certain she was and despite Holt's doubt he knew she would come around and accept them for what they were. Would agree to join with them and make them complete. "Just wish there was somethin' we could do," he whispered, stroking her cheek. "Oh, Sadie . . ."

"Wait a minute, partner." Holt's voice had a funny sound to it that made him look up at the sapphire eyes that were narrowed in concentration. There was a tiny tickle in the back of his brain, something like hope.

"What? What are you thinking?" He grabbed Holt's shoulders and all but shook the taller man. "Tell me, Holt, what?"

"It's a long shot, but . . . Remember how we healed her hand?"

Blake's hopes deflated. "You think I didn't think of that? That was a little cut on her hand, Holt. This is life or death. Probably death." His shoulders slumped.

"But what you said, about feeling her inside, feeling her die. Blake, I do, too. I feel her, too, in here." Holt pressed the back of his neck the same way the dark detective had a moment before. "I think it's the start of a bond, Blake. Not a strong one, not yet since we haven't actually . . . you know. But it's there, inside us, waiting to grow. If we can feel her the way we feel each other then maybe we can heal her. Come on . . ."

12

"She's so cold," Blakely said worriedly as he laid the precious bundle gently on the king-sized gelafoam bed back in their ship.

"First thing to do is warm her up," Holt said with more conviction than he felt. He wasn't sure if what they were about to try was going to work or not. He only knew they had to try. What he had told Blakely in the Medi-tech's station was no lie; he was beginning to feel for Sadie, too. *No, say what you mean, Holt,* he told himself sternly. *I'm beginning to love her. But Goddess, how can I help it?*

He kept reliving that horrific moment when Xavier had pushed him into the roiling blackness, feeling the cold-iron bands of the daemon's tentacles wrap around him and realizing, too late, that he had seriously underestimated its strength. He should have known better; Snuggly had tried to warn him. The daemon had been feeding off of Xavier's pain and shame and hatred for weeks, growing stronger and stronger from the intoxicating brew of extreme emotion. And Holt had simply walked into the room and put his back to it, ignoring it, as he always had in the past.

The back room of The Slice had always been a convenient place to conduct private conversations without fear of being overheard because of the daemon's presence on one side of it. Holt and Blakely had used it before knowing that if you just ignored the malevolent hunger that pervaded the room's atmosphere and the itch of ravenous red eyes on the back of your neck you'd be fine. Only this time it had been different. It wasn't until the daemon wrapped him in its ice-cold coils immobilizing his arms before he could go for his blaster that Holt realized he had made a mistake. Probably the last mistake he would ever make.

He knew that Blakely would feel his danger through the T-link and come for him, but by the time he got to the back room of The Slice it would almost certainly be all over. He'd had time for a last thought, *Sorry, partner,* and then that double row of razor teeth descended over his throat and knew this was it . . .

Then someone had been beside him in the darkness, shouting his name in a clear, high voice. *Blake?* But it couldn't be. He knew instinctively through their link that his partner was still only halfway there, fighting the crowds desperately to get to him. Then there was the odd sensation of another presence in the link, faint at first and then growing stronger; there was an indefinably feminine flavor to it . . . *Sadie!* He'd realized it about the same time he saw her honey-colored hair whip past his face as she plunged the pitifully inadequate shardi-knife into the daemon's bulk.

The daemon had howled, a soul-ripping noise that Holt heard inside his head rather than through his ears, and turned, full of inhuman rage on Sadie. The moment it caught a taste of her fear it dropped him in favor of the sweeter meat. Holt had been surprised and dismayed, but Sadie was scared to death, and terror was a much tastier emotion than shock.

She was terrified and yet she had come after him into the daemon's lair armed only with Blakely's old pocket knife and a determination to save him or die trying. No one else in the whole Solar System—hell, the whole galaxy—would have done that for him. No one but his partner, Blakely, the other half of his soul. And now Holt was wondering if he would have to count his soul in pieces of three instead of halves in the near future. *If we can just pull her through this,* he told himself grimly.

"Help me undress her," he directed Blakely. The dark, curly haired detective nodded shortly and they began stripping the sweatpants and shirt off her slender form. Her skin, Holt thought, was creamy white—too white with the unnatural pallor caused by the daemon's venom coursing through her system. Somehow they had to neutralize the effects of the daemon's bite and bring her back.

"Now what?" Blakely asked, a look of worry still filling his indigo eyes.

"Now we get undressed too and lay on either side of her," Holt directed, hoping he was doing the right thing.

"Holt," Blakely objected even as he stripped off his jacket and shirt and shoved down the ragged work pants. "We're not gonna . . . not gonna do her now, are we? I mean look at her, she's barely breathing."

"No, not unless there's no other way," Holt said, pulling off his own clothing as fast as he could. Sadie's respiration was shallower by the minute, as Blakely had pointed out; there was no time to lose. "First we'll warm her up, then we'll worry about what to do." He got into bed with her, facing the beautiful, still face, and gathered her into his arms, pressing his naked warmth against her cool flesh. Blakely climbed in on the other side and cuddled close to her back, throwing muscular arms around both Sadie and his partner.

"Come back to us, Sadie," Holt heard him whispering in a low, urgent voice. "Come back, baby, we need you . . ."

"Sadie," he whispered himself, looking down at her sweet face so still on the pillow before him. Despite the fact that her body was beginning to warm he could still feel her life-force ebbing away through the weak, barely there bond they had formed with her. Would it be enough to bring her back? Only if they strengthened it somehow, Holt decided. This wasn't the time or the place to bond fully, to form a Life-bond—they would need Sadie's complete cooperation and willingness to be penetrated by them both for that to occur—but there were other ways to strengthen the fledgling bond. Gently, he bent his head and began to press his lips to her cheeks, laying delicate kisses over the golden fans of her eyelashes and the arch of her brows. "Kiss her . . . touch her," he whispered to his partner before going back to work, covering her beautiful face in light, butterfly kisses.

Holt felt Blakely's hands moving over Sadie's sides and his own, caressing, touching, trying to convey a love so deep it couldn't be put into words. He waited anxiously for the T-link to open between them, to widen to a river of pleasure that would carry them all away, but it didn't happen. Sadie was silent and cold in their arms. They were still losing her. *No, not yet . . . you can't go yet. Not when Blakely and I have finally found you. Not when I'm just beginning to love you the way he does.*

"Sadie, please," he begged softly. Then, acting on an impulse he couldn't explain, he dipped his head and took her soft, pliant mouth with his own. Covering the sweet pink lips, he forced his way inside, pressing his tongue in to caress hers, giving her the kiss of life the only way he knew how . . .

Sadie took a soft, shuddering breath and he felt her stir in his arms. Encouraged, he kissed her again, feeling the flesh that had been as still and cold as marble begin to warm and awaken against him, between him and his partner. "Sadie . . . Sadie," he murmured her name like a prayer between kisses. Her eyelids fluttered open at last and Holt looked into the honey-amber depths to see confusion and pain.

"What . . . ?" The question formed slowly and whisper-soft on her lips.

"Hush," Holt said tenderly, tilting her chin to kiss the terrible necklace of bites the daemon had left on her pale throat. He could feel the T-link beginning to stir between them and he knew Blakely was feeling it, too. *Just a little more*, he thought. He knew just what to do now.

Rolling her unresisting body over so that she was lying on her back between them, Holt caressed the ripe mounds of her full, naked breasts and leaned down to suck one berry-colored nipple into his mouth. On her other side, Blakely did the same, petting the silky skin of her arms and sides as he nursed at the tender pink bud beside his partner.

"Oh," Sadie breathed, and Holt at last felt the link begin to open between them, pouring sweet fire through their veins as the electrical charge of their physical joining took over. He heard her gasp, felt her arch her back to press her sensitive breasts upward and get more of the hot wet suction of their mouths on her flesh.

She was healing now, coming back to them, he knew it . . . could feel it through the strengthening bond that had formed between the three of them. Holt drew back for a moment and watched in fascination as Blakely's curly, dark head hovered over Sadie's breasts, watched his partner suck first one and then the other sweet, ripe nipple into his sensual mouth while Sadie moaned and gasped beneath him. Then he knew he had to taste her.

As Blakely continued to suck and nip her aching buds, Holt slipped down the bed to her silky thighs and caressed them apart. They opened willingly, even eagerly for him and he could see how badly she needed him. The soft, pouting lips of her pussy were slick with desire and swollen with need and her feminine, musky fragrance was strong in the air. Holt thought it was the most beautiful perfume he had ever smelled and he lowered his head eagerly to plant a soft, open-mouthed kiss on her pouting lips. Sadie cried out at the press of his mouth and bucked up eagerly, needfully, to meet him.

Blakely stopped sucking her nipples for a moment to look back at him and Holt could see lust and love mingled in his partner's indigo eyes. "Taste her, Holt," Blakely muttered hoarsely. "Eat her sweet pussy, babe. 'S what she needs." Sadie cried out in wordless agreement and Holt nodded, bending his head back between her fragrant thighs as Blakely went back to her breasts.

Using his thumbs, he spread the swollen pink lips of her pussy open to reveal the tender nub of her clit that he knew was aching with desire. He could feel Sadie's pleasure in the back of his mind the same way he could feel Blakely's, could feel her emotions almost as clearly as his partner's now that the T-link was wide open between them. *But not as open as it could be*, he thought, bending his head and licking firmly over the ripe pink bud at the center of her pussy, causing Sadie to arch her back almost violently and cry out in desperate pleasure.

No, a complete opening of the link could only take place when he and Blakely penetrated her at the same time. As he kissed her sweet pussy, sucking her clit into his mouth and savoring her juices on his tongue, Holt allowed himself to imagine thrusting into her, pulling her onto his cock as Blakely did the same. He pushed his tongue deeply inside her tight channel, holding her thighs spread wide with his large hands to open her up for his assault. As she cried and begged and moaned he imagined her crying for a different reason, a deeper pleasure.

Sadie would be pinned between them, both thick cocks thrust into her, spearing her sweet, submissive body as they fucked their way into each other's souls.

"Coming . . . Oh, Goddess . . . coming, I'm coming!" It was Sadie's sweet voice filling his ears like music. She bucked under his tongue and Holt held on and rode it out, tasting the fresh, sweet wetness of her orgasm, watching as Blakely did the same, continuing to suck and nip her heaving breasts and nipples. He knew without looking that the deadly necklace of bite-marks had faded from her throat and the daemon's poison coursing through her system had been neutralized. She was healed. She had come back to them. The bond between them, although nowhere near as strong as the T-link between Blakely and himself, had still been strong enough to save her.

And it was getting stronger every time they touched.

13

Sadie came back from dreams of icy blackness to the soft warmth of someone's mouth on hers. She realized, with a start, that someone was kissing her, was opening her lips and pouring *love* and *need* and *want* and *hunger* into her mouth. Even before her eyes fluttered open she knew it was Holt, could feel him in the back of her mind like a brilliant golden light—his wants, his needs, his desires.

Large warm hands caressed her from behind and she realized Blakely was there, too, petting her, touching her, loving her back to life. *Don't leave us,* he was whispering softly into the bare skin of her neck as he kissed and sucked and licked. And she felt him, too, lodged in her mind like a warm, comforting weight, with his love for her like a solid thing, a rope she could hold onto with both hands and pull herself back from the darkness.

Pressed between them she was frightened at first, but then the warm, electrical glow began to flow between them and she was caught up in the pleasure they were giving her, the healing bliss they were pouring into her body with their hands and mouths.

Looking down she could see Blakely's dark, curly head licking and nipping her sensitive breasts, laving their creamy swells with his tongue before sucking her hard pink nipples into that sensual mouth. She could feel the heat of his long, hard cock pressing against her thigh, and she knew that they were all naked, but she couldn't make herself care.

Further down, Holt was spreading her legs and pressing his face between her thighs, spreading the lips of her sex to open her wide for his hot tongue. Sadie cried out as she felt him lick her clit and then suck it into his mouth, drawing magical figure eights over the sensitive bud until she thought she might go crazy. His golden head moving between her legs while Blakely's darker one still hovered over her breasts seemed to Sadie to be the most beautiful thing she had ever seen or felt. Light and Dark, a study of contrasts, she was being devoured from both ends by her lovers and she was loving every minute of it as the warm, electrical energy flowed through and around them all.

At last, when Holt pressed his tongue inside her, fucking her rhythmically while Blakely sucked her nipples with a fierce passion, Sadie felt herself beginning to tilt over the edge toward orgasm. Not wanting this beautiful dream to end, she clung to the edge of sanity as long as she could before the dual sensations of both hot, male mouths on her body drove her completely over the cliff and she fell crying into pleasure.

Goddess . . . so good, so good . . . she thought, laying spent and quiet on the bed, her eyes closed tiredly in post-orgasmic bliss. After a while she felt both large, male bodies lay down, one on either side of her and she knew Holt and Blakely were there to protect her and pleasure her. To love her forever . . .

Love? Wait a minute . . . Sadie began to come back to herself a little. Now that the intense pleasure was over and the current of electrical desire between them was weakening she began to wonder what was going on. The last thing she remembered was diving into the room where the Iapetion daemon had Holt and then . . . nothing. Just a cold black void that she thought would never end.

Oh Goddess, the daemon, the blackness . . . Sadie shivered convulsively and whimpered low in her throat.

"Shhh, baby, it's all right, we're here." It was Blakely's voice in her ear and then she was enfolded in four warm, muscular arms and held tightly, safe and secure . . . two hard male bodies bracketing her own smaller, softer form.

"Relax, Sadie. It's all over now," Holt whispered from the other side. "Try to sleep, sweetheart."

It was the best suggestion she had heard in a long time. Although part of her wanted to fight the impulse, wanted to wake up and discuss why she was naked in bed with two very naked men on either side of her, Sadie just couldn't. She thought she had never been more tired and drained in her life. The delicious fragrance of Blakely's sandalwood musk and Holt's fresh rain scent mixed in her head and she drifted off to sleep.

In the middle of the night she woke to feel the pleasure again. This time Holt was pressing tender kisses against the slopes of her breasts and Blakely's coarse curls were brushing her inner thighs as the dark man parted her legs and tasted her hot, wet sex. They brought her to orgasm so beautifully that Sadie could only lay in the darkness between them panting at first. Gradually, however, she became aware that two hot, thick cocks were pressed against her, one at each outer thigh. She felt their need in her mind then, Holt's like a golden flare and Blakely's a solid yearning. They needed to be inside her, she knew it, felt it as clearly as she had ever felt anything in her life. And yet . . .

Not that kind of girl. Don't do that kind of thing . . . the little voice in the back of her head whispered. Although she wanted badly to open herself for them, to give both men what they so desperately needed and desired, she just couldn't. Couldn't spread her legs and let them do that, enter her at the same time.

Instead, Sadie ran her hands down her thighs until she came to the moist, blunt heads of their cocks, both weeping freely for release. She heard Holt's sudden gasp and felt Blakely's groan, deep in his chest, as she took the heavy hot shafts in her hands and began to caress the velvety skin covering the iron hardness. She wished she could see them, wished she could compare with more than touch. Holt's shaft felt slightly longer in her seeking right hand, but Blakely's was thicker, she could barely get her fingers all the way around his shaft as he thrust into her left palm.

Suddenly the impulse to taste them the way they had tasted her was on her, too strong to deny. The warm, electrical current was still flowing through her body, and in the velvety darkness, Sadie thought it must all be a dream anyway. And why not give in to the impulse if it was just a dream that would melt away in the morning? She couldn't think of a reason good enough.

Doing what came naturally, she slid down between them, urging them close with pets and touches until they lay on their sides, the rigid shafts rubbing together in front of her. Leaning her head down, Sadie let her silky hair trail over both straining erections drawing a moan and a gasp from her lovers before reaching down to take them both in hand again. Bringing them close she began to lick, tentatively at first and then more boldly, tasting the broad plum-shaped heads and exploring the leaking slits with a curious tongue, wanting to know them better.

"Sadie, oh . . ."

"Goddess, such a sweet mouth on you, baby . . ."

Both men were panting now, trembling beneath her small soft hands and hot mouth. It gave Sadie a sense of power like she had never felt before to have both strong, muscular bodies strung tight and needful, so sensitive to her touch. Experimenting, she took Holt's shaft into her mouth as far as she could without gagging, feeling Blakely's cock rubbing against her cheek as she did so. The tall blond man cried out softly and she felt large, gentle hands petting her hair, urging her to take more if she could. She fondled the tight sack below his shaft and savored his taste, clean and sharp against her tongue.

Then it was Blakely's turn and the dark man moaned low in his throat, almost a growl as Sadie struggled to get his thick, musky shaft between her lips. He was hairier than Holt and she loved the coarse scratch of his tight curls as she pressed her face against his flat belly and sucked him hard and long, savoring his spicy flavor.

"Sadie, baby . . . gonna come," Blakely was gasping and Holt was whispering something similar from the other side. Sadie knew she wanted to feel their hot liquid bathing her flesh. Taking both straining shafts firmly in her hands, she stroked until the darkness was filled with their masculine groans and cries.

Holt came first, pumping his load in hot jets over her full breasts and Blakely was soon to follow, spraying her throat and upper chest with his seed. Sadie felt hot and wild and wanton, freer than she'd ever been while the warm cum ran down between her breasts and over her flat belly to puddle between her thighs. She thought she could feel some of it trickling into the slippery slit of her sex and had a sudden fierce wish to feel it all the way inside her, to feel their seed filling her cunt instead of coating her tits.

The warm, electrical connection was so strong that she would have spread her legs right then and let them have anything they wanted if it had been possible. But both Holt and Blakely were spent now, at least for the present. She would have to think of an alternative.

Sadie lay down in the warm darkness between them, fragrant with the scent of their sex and whispered, "Clean me off, boys." Two hot, wet tongues went to work immediately, fulfilling her request as Sadie moaned and twisted, loving the way Holt and Blakely licked away the seed from the slopes of her breasts, her aching nipples, her soft belly, and, especially, from between her thighs. Holt made sure personally that no cum was left in the soft, slippery cleft of her hot sex while Blakely kissed her mouth, sharing the flavor of all three of them with her. Sadie touched them in the darkness, burying one hand in Blakely's rough curls as he kissed her and fingering the pale, silky gold of Holt's hair as he cleaned tenderly between her legs and pressed two long fingers into her tight channel.

The pleasure was gentler this time, but no less intense and Sadie felt herself riding the crest of a feather-soft orgasm before she fell panting back on the bed and sleep took her at last.

14

Sadie woke up because something was tickling her nose. Stretching languorously, she became aware that she felt deliciously tender around her nipples and between her legs. She thought hazily that it was some dream she had had last night. Blakely and Holt, both at once, licking and sucking in the darkness. The feel of two hard, masculine bodies bracketing her own as they pressed against her . . . Wait a minute.

Coming fully awake, Sadie realized that there *was* a hard masculine body on either side of her. Opening her eyes, she saw that she had her face buried in the wiry mat of black hair that covered Blakely's chest; that was what had been tickling her nose. Holt's smoother chest was pressed against her back and she could feel his warm breath against the back of her neck as she lay in the warm cocoon created by their bodies. Two warm morning erections pressed against her, Holt's nestling between her buttocks and Blakely's between her thighs. Not only was she lying in bed with two men, but all three of them were stark naked.

Oh my merciful Goddess! Sadie jumped out of bed, clumsy

in her attempt to get away from the dream that had turned into a nightmare. Surely the dream images couldn't be true. Surely she hadn't really let them touch her that way, taste her that way . . .

Stumbling into the fresher and slamming the door behind her, Sadie examined her naked body in the holo-viewer anxiously. Her nipples were red and tender and there were passion marks along the creamy swells of her breasts. Worse yet, there were more marks over her belly and between her thighs. The dream flashed through the forefront of her brain again like a pornographic vid show. Both hot mouths on her body, sucking her nipples, parting her thighs, bathing her sex, licking, tasting, pressing inside her . . . No! It couldn't be true. But the image of herself in the holo-viewer didn't lie.

And if that part of the dream is true, then the rest of it must be, too. Sadie cringed in shame as she remembered touching them both, taking both hot, heavy shafts down her throat and sucking for all she was worth, the erotic spray of warm cum coating her body and two wet tongues bathing her, licking her clean . . . *The Solar System's biggest slut, that's what I've become,* she thought miserably. What would her Aunt Minnie or Gerald think of her if they could see her now? No doubt they'd be shocked and disgusted. Sadie shook her head. How had it happened? Somehow she had been sucked into the strange connection that existed between the two partners.

Not knowing what else to do, she turned on the sonic shower full throttle and stood in the buffeting blasts, wishing she could wash the shame from her memory as well as Blakely and Holt's marks from her skin.

When she came out of the fresher the bedroom was empty, for which she was profoundly grateful. She had no idea how she was going to face Blakely and Holt after the things all three of them had done together last night. No idea at all. She looked around for the shirt and pants she had been wearing the day before, but they were nowhere to be found. Instead, lying on the bed was a selection of clothing she had never seen before.

At first Sadie was delighted . . . new clothes! She was damn tired of wearing Blakely and Holt's shirts everywhere. Then she felt ashamed that the prospect of new clothes could make her so happy in the middle of an emotional crisis. But still . . . new clothes were new clothes, right? Wrong, she quickly found out.

"What *is* this stuff?" she muttered, sifting through the glitzy pile of fabric on the bed. It all appeared to be her size, but that was the nicest thing she could say for the bunch of clothes. Barely there baby-doll dresses, cutaway crop-tops with skin-tight hot pants to match, one thing that looked like an evening gown, but had a neck-line that plunged to the navel, demi-bras that didn't cover her nipples and crotch-less panties all met her eyes as she searched. Everything on the bed put the outfits she'd worn while undercover as a prostie-borg to shame, making the gold mesh dress she'd had on the day she met Blakely and Holt look like a nun's habit in comparison. Was this some kind of a sick joke? Or was this the way Blakely and Holt expected her to dress now that they were all on more "intimate" terms?

Sadie could feel herself getting angrier and angrier as she sorted through the skimpy clothing. They wanted her to dress like a slut? Fine, she would. *Might as well,* she thought bitterly. *I've been acting like a slut, might as well dress like one, too.*

Pulling on the skimpiest outfit she could find, a demi-bra that pushed up her full breasts without covering her plump nipples, a pair of crotch-less panties, and a silky, see-though robe made of some gauzy fabric that clung to her skin, she marched out of the bedroom to confront the partners.

Blakely and Holt were sitting in the food prep area, conversing quietly while Holt prepared some concentrates at the counter and Blakely pored over the portable map-screen he had set up at the table. Neither one of them noticed her until she was standing right in front of them, hands on her hips, one toe tapping impatiently.

At last, Blakely looked up from the map-screen and noticed her. "Hey, kid, how are . . ." was as far as he got before he broke off and just stared at her.

Holt turned around and got an eyeful as well. "Sadie, what . . ." he started but then he, too, was unable to finish.

"What's the matter, boys? Don't you like my outfit?" Sadie asked, her mouth twisted into a furious grin that was more like a snarl. "I thought it was appropriate enough after the way we all acted last night."

"Sadie, sweetheart, it wasn't like that," Blakely protested, a look of hurt and distress passing over his dark features. "It's not what you think."

"Oh, no?" Sadie shot back. "Well then please enlighten me, Detective Blakely. What else could it possibly be?"

"You were hurt—*dying*. We had to heal you, Sadie. The same way we healed your hand. If you'll sit down for a minute, I can explain." Holt's voice was quiet but commanding. Although she didn't want to, Sadie found herself remembering the way her cut hand had healed after the passionate three-way touching and kissing they had shared on the couch. Could this be something like that? After all, the last thing she remembered was charging into the daemon's lair. What had happened to her afterward?

"What happened to me yesterday?" she asked, a little faintly, sinking down at the food-prep table, wrapping her arms around herself protectively. She was sitting next to Blakely who looked like he wanted to put an arm around her but didn't quite dare.

"What's the last thing you remember?" Holt asked her, gently, taking the chair on the opposite side of her so that, once again, she was between them.

Sadie shivered. "I remember standing by the door and watching you talk to the prostie-borg who was actually Xavier. And then I realized that the . . . the daemon was getting closer and closer to you and I tried to shout, tried to warn you, but I was frozen, Holt. It had me locked in place somehow. I couldn't do anything but watch and I thought it was going to kill you. It was going to kill you and there was nothing I could do." Her voice was small and dry and when she swallowed, Sadie heard a dry clicking sound in her throat. The horror of the situation, being frozen in place while the daemon got closer and closer to the back of Holt's golden head . . . It had to be one of the worst memories of her life. And it was still so fresh.

"But you *did* do something, Sadie. You saved me—kept the daemon distracted long enough for Blake to get there. I couldn't believe it when I saw you in the middle of that mess, fighting that damn thing with nothing but Blake's old sardi-knife." Holt sighed and ran one large hand through his hair, making it a fine blond rumple that stuck up all over. He took her hand, rubbing along her palm with one thumb as he spoke. "That took guts, Sadie, real guts, and I owe you an apology. I seriously under-estimated your abilities and your courage. I won't do it again."

"But then why, how . . . ?" She looked up into sapphire eyes, trying to get the image of the roiling clouds of blackness that had been the daemon out of her mind.

"The daemon got you, bit you instead of Holt." Blakely continued the narrative in the way she had come to expect. "It . . . it was feeding on you, kid. By the time we got it off you, you looked half dead. We thought we were gonna lose you." The pain in the dark man's indigo eyes was easy to see and he took Sadie's other hand and brought it softly to his lips. "We did the only thing we could think of, baby. And we were so afraid we were too late, that it wasn't gonna work. You were slippin' away so fast."

Sitting between them, with both Holt and Blakely holding one of her hands, Sadie began to feel that strange, seductive energy flowing again. It prickled along her spine and hardened her nipples with aching need. She felt her sex getting wet and hot and ready . . . It felt so good, so right and yet she knew it was wrong. It was this same energy that had seduced her into doing things she never would have dreamed of the night before.

"Stop it!" she cried, yanking her hands away from them as though they were both red-hot and she had been burned. *Breaking the connection,* she thought, wrapping the see-through robe tightly around her body like a shield. She was tired of dancing around the issue and trying to figure it out by herself. It was time to ask outright.

"What is this weird . . . *energy* between you two? And why were you able to heal me in the first place? I don't know much about Iapetion daemons, but I know their bite is utterly lethal. I should be dead right now if what you're telling me is true. Why aren't I?" She looked frantically between both sets of blue eyes, indigo and sapphire, demanding an answer to the mystery that had plagued her almost from the moment she had set eyes on Blakely and Holt. "Well?" she demanded.

They exchanged a brief glance that apparently spoke volumes. Leaning toward her but being careful not to touch her in any way, Holt started. "This is something we should have told you a long time ago, Sadie. I have to apologize because Blake wanted to tell you and I didn't. I know now that it would have been better to be up front about everything but . . . It's just that I recently ended a relationship with someone I cared for a lot because of . . . well, because of the situation between Blake and me, and I guess I was afraid of being hurt again." Holt sighed and looked troubled. He picked up a packet of lactose spread from the table top and began playing with it aimlessly.

"What my partner is tryin' to say is that he hasn't been very lucky in love lately." Blakely picked up the narrative seamlessly. "He had to give up what seemed to be a very good relationship because the lady in question wasn't able to handle certain aspects of his lifestyle."

"What aspects?" Sadie insisted on hearing him say it although she was pretty sure she had a good idea. "Was it . . ." She swallowed hard. "Did he want to . . . to share her with you? Was that why she left him?"

"That was part of it. But it wasn't just that Holt wanted to share Gillian with me—he *needed* to. But she couldn't handle it." Blakely looked up and there was a depth of sadness in the indigo eyes that took Sadie's breath away. "We're a Tandem Unit, Sadie. Understand?"

"No," she shook her head. "Explain it to me."

Blakely sighed again. "Around six years ago when Holt and I came outta blues and made detective there was a new gadget . . . a real innovation that was s'posed to revolutionize police work on Old Earth. A Tandemizer—a chip implanted in the base of the brain—the medulla oblongata—that allowed two partners to work as one. It allows you to sense your partner's whereabouts at all times, to move as a unit and avoid danger. It was a great idea at the time." He sighed again and ran one hand through his thick, curly hair. "Holt and I have been best friends since our Academy days and we were already great partners, but we liked the idea of being even better. We volunteered for the process. But . . . there were side effects."

"Side effects?" Sadie clutched the flimsy robe even closer around her throat and listened intently. Here was the core issue—the answer to the mystery that had been driving her crazy.

"Yeah. The Tandem chips made us *too* close. We can feel each other's emotions. Sometimes we catch each other's stray thoughts. When the T-link between us really opens up it's like nothin' I can describe to you. What Holt touches, tastes, and sees I feel and taste and see, and vice versa. It's like livin' inside two brains and two bodies at once." He shook his head, a far away look in the deep blue eyes. "And it's so good, so *right*—that sense of completion, of wholeness. It's like an addiction neither one of us can ever break unless we undergo a procedure to remove the chips."

"You don't want to have the procedure?" Sadie asked, puzzled.

"We've both thought about it." Blakely shook his head. "But the docs have told us we're too close—we've been tandemized too long. Odds are if we did the detandemizing now one of us would end up dead. It ain't worth the risk." He shrugged. "'Sides, we're pretty comfortable the way we are. We're best friends even though we drive each other crazy sometimes. There's really only one drawback."

"Which is?" Her heart was in her mouth and she was concentrating so hard on what Blakely was saying that the voice on her other side made her jump in surprise. She had almost forgotten that Holt was still there.

"The drawback is that if you take one of us you have to take both," Holt said in her ear. She turned to face the blond detective, who had put down the packet of lactose spread and was concentrating on her again. His hair looked like burnished metal strands against the collar of the black shirt he was wearing. "You see, Sadie, there were a few bugs in the first Tandem chips, the ones Blakely and I received. The T-link caused by the chips acts like a circuit, a conduit for the energy between us. It's almost like a sixth sense in a way; I know where my partner is at all times, how he's feeling, if he's in danger . . . and he knows the same about me. But despite all that the circuit is incomplete."

"We need a third." Blakely was pressing closer to her other side, staring at her intently.

"A third what?" she asked hesitantly, looking from one to the other, Holt tall and shiningly blond and Blakely, muscular, dark and intense. *So different and yet so much alike*, she thought. Both trapped somehow. The two men looked so serious and sad.

"A third person to complete the circuit, to fulfill the T-link's full potential," Holt said matter of factly.

"You mean you want someone else to have a chip implanted?" Sadie asked flatly.

"No, that wouldn't be necessary," Holt said. "There are . . . other ways to link."

Sadie looked back and forth between them. "Sex," she breathed. "So that's what all this is about."

"Yes," Blakely said simply. "It's like an empty space, a hole that needs to be filled. We're only complete when the T-link is completely open."

"And it's only fully open when we're sharing a woman, making love to her, penetrating her at the same time," Holt finished.

"And you chose me. Well thanks a lot." She didn't know whether to laugh or cry. "Why me, guys? Won't any warm body do? All you need is a way to link to each other—a girl who doesn't mind taking . . ." she swallowed. "Taking you both on at once. Why not use a prostie-borg?" She felt the prickle of tears threaten behind her eyelids and tried to blink them back. All along they had just wanted to use her to make contact with each other.

"Sadie, you don't understand." Holt took her by the arm and led her to the couch and Blakely followed. Soon she was sandwiched between them, feeling the comforting masculine warmth radiating from both sides. "Blake and I don't want just any girl to share our lives. We aren't interested in using someone just to fulfill the link. It's true that only about one in a thousand women have the sensory capacity to handle the sensations of a T-link joining, but there's more to it than that."

"Holt and I have been lookin' for a long time for a girl we both care about—both love. Someone we can share our lives with." Blakely said, taking her hand again. "We started to care for you, a long time before we ever figured out we could bond with you."

"*Bond* with me?" Sadie looked back and forth between them. "What do you mean, 'bond with me'?"

"It's how we were able to heal you last night, Sadie," Holt told her earnestly, taking her other hand. "Your brain chemistry matches the composition of ours so perfectly that we've been able to establish a bond, a mental and emotional connection with you. It's not as strong yet as the T-link the Tandem chips make possible between Blake and me, but every time we touch you together like this it gets stronger."

"I . . . I don't believe you," Sadie said weakly. A bond with these two? The two most handsome, fascinating, aggravating men she had ever met? *It's not possible,* she insisted to herself. But was it? She could feel the energy flowing between them and tried to pull her hands away, but they didn't let her. Sadie felt her body reacting to their presence, to their need and hers even though she didn't want it to and wished that she hadn't been so hasty in her choice of clothing. The robe she had on hid nothing and she was sure that Blakely and Holt could see her nipples hardening with desire. *Oh Goddess, their mouths on me, tasting me, touching me, making me come . . .*

"Close your eyes and feel it, sweetheart," Blakely invited her softly. "I can feel you in my mind—taste you on my tongue like honey and I know Holt feels the same. The bond with you isn't as strong as our link yet, but it's there all right or we wouldn't have been able to pull you back last night. Go on— close your eyes and feel."

Realizing that they weren't going to let her go until she complied, Sadie took a deep breath and forced herself to close her eyes. *Concentrate,* she told herself fiercely, determined to prove them wrong—to feel nothing at all.

At first there was nothing but the warm, sensual current flowing between them. Then, in the back of her mind she began to feel a strange sensation, a doubling and trebling of emotions. A bright golden thread of hope and need like a ray of sunshine in her mind—Holt. A solid certainty, an unshakeable love, like a smooth, warm stone she could cup in the palm of her hand— Blakely. *Need, desire, love, lust* all crowded into her brain. A barrage of emotions she had never asked for and could not block out.

"No, *no!* Stop it!" Sadie yanked her hands away from them and stumbled off the couch, nearly falling in her hasty attempt to get away. Too fast, this was all happening *way* too fast. Hell, she had dated Gerald for nearly a year and a half before he proposed to her. Here were these two, wanting her to submit to the most perverted scenarios she could imagine, wanting some sort of commitment when she hadn't even known them a month. No, not just wanting a commitment—*forcing* one. Merciful Goddess, she could feel them both in her *brain.* In her terror she forgot that she had admitted to herself that she was beginning to care deeply for Blakely and Holt, maybe even to love them both. All she could see was that what they were asking was too much too soon.

"Sadie, please, honey . . ." Blakely appealed softly, leaning forward, the pain and need apparent in his vivid indigo eyes. Holt said nothing but Sadie saw the same pain reflected in his light blue gaze—the same need. Worst of all she felt it inside her mind. They wanted her . . . needed her. *I need them too . . .* No! She shook her head to clear away the treacherous thought.

"Look," she said, attempting to remain calm and deal with the situation in a rational manner. "I appreciate you saving my life last night even if you did use . . . some unconventional methods. But I didn't come on this mission to 'bond' with you or complete you or whatever the hell it is you're talking about. I came for a story and that's *all* I came for." She took a shaking breath and hugged herself tightly, staying far back from the couch where the two men sat, light and dark, day and night, watching her. "Now I'm sorry if you got the wrong idea about me, but I'm telling you for the last time that *I'm not like that.* I just . . . I'm sorry but I can't. Can't be what you're looking for."

Feeling her eyes blur with tears she ran back to the bedroom, hitting the door switch so hard that it slammed behind her and threw herself on the bed. Burying her face in a pillow that still smelled like Holt's fine, golden hair she let herself cry all the worry and fear and frustration out until she had nothing left inside.

It was Blakely that came to her, rapping softly on the door to ask for admittance.

"Come in," Sadie said listlessly. She had an idea she'd been sleeping at some point but if so, her nap hadn't refreshed her at all. She had a dull, throbbing headache right behind her eyes that had settled in and promised to stay for a good long time and she felt completely miserable.

She sat up in the large bed the three of them had shared the night before, leaning against the headboard, the prostie-type clothes scattered around the bedspread in a glitzy litter of fabric. She realized she still had on the ridiculous outfit that showed her breasts and sex and considered covering herself, but then decided not to bother. *I've been acting like a slut, might as well dress like one,* she thought bitterly. It wasn't like Blakely hadn't seen it all before. Seen it, licked it, kissed it . . . she shook her head, trying to rid herself of the intensely erotic memory of having that dark, curly head buried between her thighs while Holt took care of her breasts, sucking and nipping so tenderly.

At least Blakely was alone; they must have known that it would be easier for her if only one of them came. Easier and safer than having them both there, ready to start that sensuous, seductive energy flowing with a touch.

"Hi, sweetheart." He seemed subdued and moved slowly without the usual bounce in his step. "Can I . . . do ya mind if I sit down?" He gestured to the other side of the bed.

"Sure, help yourself," Sadie said. "I'm not worried about you sitting by me as long as Holt isn't on the other side."

Blakely winced at her comment but said nothing. Slowly, he cleared the mound of discarded clothing from the other side of the bed. "Sorry about these," he muttered, gesturing with a handful of gaudy fabric. "I just wanted to get ya something new to wear, but, well, the lady I got these from, she's a working girl. Guess she didn't know I wanted them for somebody who didn't . . . who doesn't . . ."

"Fuck for a living?" Sadie said bluntly and he winced again. "It doesn't matter, Blake." She hated the harshness in her own tone but wasn't able to help it. "Why should I care about wearing a prostitute's clothes? That's what I've been acting like ever since I met you and Holt. Offering to trade sex for the chance to get a first-hand scoop on the story. Acting like a cat in heat every time you and Holt get me between you . . ."

"Is that what's botherin' you, baby?" He scooted a little closer and turned to face her.

"Among other things." She looked down at her hands, letting her long hair hide her face. "I know you probably don't believe me after the way I acted last night, but I've only ever been with one other guy—my ex-fiancé Gerald."

"Of course I believe you," Blakely said quietly. "I could tell from the minute I met you all that hard-as-nails reporter bit was a put on. Holt and me know you're a nice girl. And the way you've been feelin' whenever you're between us—well, that isn't your fault. It's a natural reaction to the T-link between Holt and me. I mean, I've never seen it so strong before, but that's definitely all it is."

"Oh, right, because I'm the one perfect girl for you in the universe," Sadie said bitterly, still looking down. "As if my new status as slut of the Solar System wasn't bad enough."

"Sadie, look at me." Blakely tilted her chin until she was staring into the deep blue eyes, full of hurt and concern. "I didn't come in here to pressure you about that, honey. Holt and me don't wanna take anything you don't wanna give and I'm sorry if we upset you since it's the last thing we meant to do." He sighed and ran a hand through his thick, dark curls. "We just wanted to explain our situation and let you make a choice. Now, you've made that choice, and I want you to know we accept it completely and we don't ever have to mention this again. Except," he cleared his throat and looked away from her. "Except to tell you not to worry about the bond. Holt thinks it'll fade in time as long as we keep from touchin' you, both of us at once, I mean. It was never full strength anyway 'cause we never bonded completely."

"After . . ." Sadie felt her face going red but forced herself to continue. "After everything we did last night? But I thought . . ."

"No," Blakely cut her off, in a low voice. "We . . . we were careful not to form a Life-bond with you last night. We didn't want to go too far without knowing how you felt."

"That's very considerate of you," Sadie said sourly. "I suppose you and Holt ask all the girls you 'bond' with if they mind before you go all the way."

"It's not like that," Blakely said softly. "Sadie, until you came along the idea of finding a girl that was a close enough match for us to form a Life-bond with was purely . . ." He searched for a word.

"Theoretical," Holt said from the doorway. He was leaning against the frame, his tall form at an angle to the door, being sure to stay well back from the bed. "The man who implanted the Tandem chips, a neurobiologist by the name of James Klinefelder, told us it was possible, but far from probable. Along about the odds of winning the Mega Credit Solar Lotto."

"And I'm the winning ticket. Well, gentlemen, thanks but no thanks," Sadie said bitterly. They just wanted her for the connection. Wanted to be inside her mind the way they were inside each other's . . . Actually that part wasn't *so* bad—it was the things they had to do to get the connection. Or rather, the things *she* would have to let them do. If only those things didn't feel so good . . .

"We don't look at you like that, sweetheart," Blakely told her quietly, the hurt in his indigo eyes almost silencing the jeering little voice inside her head. "I think Holt's just tryin' to tell you that this is new to us, too. Professor Klinefelder told us it might be possible, but we've never been able to form a Life-bond with anyone before."

"Not for lack of trying, I'll bet," Sadie muttered.

"That's not true," Holt told her, leaving the doorway and moving a little closer. Seeing her distrustful look, he sat at the foot of the bed, still far enough away that he couldn't touch her. "I won't deny that we've shared women before—the T-link makes that a necessity. But there have only been two other occasions since Blake and I have been linked that we asked a lady to share our lives." A look of deep pain passed over the blond man's face. "The first time was right after we were just linked, when we realized what the chips were doing to us. We wanted to do the detandemizing procedure immediately, but even back then they only gave us a fifty–fifty chance of both of us making it out alive."

"Who . . . who was the girl?" Sadie asked hesitantly, intrigued despite herself.

"Her name was Charlotte—Charlie. We, uh, we were gonna get married." Blakely's voice nearly broke and he had to look away for a moment before he could continue. "She was a sweet girl. I loved her; Goddess knows I loved her so much. We had everything planned. She and I had been together about a year before Holt and me got the chips implanted. Then after . . . after we realized what was happening with the chips I went to her and told her. We told her about the detandemizing, explained about the risks and she didn't want to chance it. She said she was willing to try it . . . try being with both of us."

"What happened?" Sadie asked gently. *Why isn't she sitting here with you instead of me?*

"Wrong brain chemistry; her system couldn't handle it. She overloaded with sensation . . . it nearly killed her," Holt said briefly. "But even if she could've handled it, it wouldn't have been right. Charlotte was Blake's girl. She liked me and I liked her, but the feelings were just friendly. There was no need—no real passion."

"We broke it off," Blakely said softly. "It wasn't fair to her, wasn't fair to Holt." His face was a perfect blank now and Sadie could only guess how hard it was not to show the pain he must be feeling, reliving this old memory for her benefit. She wanted to tell them to stop, that she didn't want to hear any more, but Holt was talking again.

"The last time we thought about it was about six months ago. The girl's name was Gillian. I suppose I have myself to blame for that one." He sighed and pinched the bridge of his nose, squeezing his eyes tightly shut for a moment. "I should have told her right away what the situation was between Blake and me. I could've saved us all a lot of pain that way. But I didn't want to scare her off."

"Did you overload her, too?" Sadie remembered the intense rush, the almost electrical feeling when both men touched her at once. It was easy to see how that tingling current might be too much to handle. Too much pleasure, too much sensation . . . just too much.

Holt made a face. "We never got that far," he admitted. "She and I were getting pretty close and she seemed to like Blake pretty well. She was a flirt—the same way he is—so they got along great. I really thought I'd found the one. So after about six months I sat her down and told her the truth—the whole story about us. What we needed and why we needed it. I asked her if she might be willing to try being with both of us at once."

"And . . . ?" Sadie couldn't help asking.

"And . . ." Holt sighed deeply. "And she slapped my face. She came from a fairly uptight background so I guess I should have seen it coming. She said we were . . . disgusting. That she didn't want to have anything else to do with either one of us. That was the end of that."

"Look, I'm sorry that you two have had such rotten luck romantically." She sat up straighter and crossed her arms around herself protectively. "But I just don't think I'm the answer. I mean, we haven't even known each other a month yet, guys. I can't move that fast, emotionally. I don't think anyone can." *Liar*, whispered the little voice in her head but she pushed it away.

"You never heard of love at first sight?" Blakely grinned at her, but it was a sad, tired grin. "Kid, from the minute I picked you out of the line-up at the Prostie Palace I wanted you."

"All I know is that when you were dying, when we thought we were losing you last night . . . Goddess, Sadie. I don't know what I would have done." Holt sighed and shook his head. "But that's neither here nor there. As I'm sure Blake told you, we'll respect any decision you make and we'll try to avoid touching you at the same time so we don't inadvertently strengthen the bond we've already formed."

"Blake said it isn't a complete bond anyway. Isn't a Life-bond," Sadie said in a small voice.

"No. No it isn't," Holt agreed. "Blake and I haven't been inside you, inside your body at the same time, Sadie."

"But . . . But, last night." Sadie was so mortified she could barely go on but she had to finish. "Last night while Blake was kissing me you were . . . you had your tongue."

"Not like that, sweetheart. That strengthened the bond, but that's not how . . ." Blakely started.

"To bond fully with you would require double penetration and ejaculation," Holt finished for his partner in an almost technical tone.

"So it couldn't be done . . . orally," Sadie asked, feeling like she might blush to death. "I mean because last night when I . . . I sucked . . ."

"No, honey, it would have to be below the belt, so to speak," Blakely told her gently.

"But . . . but both of you at the same time . . ." Sadie couldn't finish aloud. *It would hurt! And isn't that what you're really afraid of? Even more than sharing emotions or feeling like the Solar System's biggest slut? That it would hurt?* whispered the little voice in her head. *After all, it's not like either one of them is small* . . . Nope, both Blakely and Holt were definitely above average in the size department. Accommodating both of them at once would be no easy task, especially for someone with as little experience as Sadie.

Blakely must have seen the fear clouding her honey-amber eyes. "Baby," he said tenderly, cupping her cheek in his palm gently. "If there's one thing you need to know about me and Holt it's that we'd never, *never* hurt you. I know you're not interested, but I want you to know that if you ever changed your mind we'd make it good for you. Intense, but good."

"Oh," Sadie said in a small voice, drawing away from the warmth of his hand reluctantly. Behind her eyes a scene played like a porno-loop over and over. She saw herself caught between them, pressed between both large, male bodies, feeling the hot current of desire running between them all, binding them into one. She saw her body opening to them, hot and needful, willing to give up her secrets—her treasures—to their touch. Willing to be penetrated and filled and fucked, to be taken any way they wanted her or needed her. To feel both of those long, thick, hot cocks entering her, pressing deep and hard to fill her completely . . . She wrapped her arms around her mostly bare breasts and pressed her trembling thighs together tightly.

"Sadie, I hope you understand what we're tying to tell you now." Holt broke the spell, scrambling the erotic scene into static behind her eyes. "But that isn't what we need to be talking about right now. Right now we need to be talking about how to stop Van Heusen before he makes another batch of illegal prostie-borgs."

"But . . ." Sadie sat up straighter and struggled to drag her mind onto less X-rated subjects. "But if Xavier is out of the picture . . ."

"But his double-crossin' partner Red Mike is still out there," Blakely pointed out. "And about a hundred other pirates that'd be more than willing to mind rape any innocent colonists they could lay hands on for the prices I'm sure Van Heusen's payin' out for black market brains."

"Blake's right," Holt said, grimly. "Van Heusen's got the only illegal flesh tank operation big enough for mass production in the System. I'd bet my badge on it. We put him out of business, we put the mind rapers out of business. Van Heusen's the key. We've got back up on the way, but we've got to catch him red-handed. The question is how to make the sting."

Sadie began to feel interested. Suddenly, the Solar Pulitzer seemed like a distinct possibility again. "Listen, boys." She looked from Holt to Blakely. "Remember how I told you I'd be willing to do some undercover work when I signed on to this gig? Well, I think I've got an idea . . ."

15

Roald Van Heusen was the most notorious drug lord and prostie-pimp in the Solar System. He somehow always managed to stay one step ahead of the law. He was prosecuted but never convicted, had credit to spare, and his base of operations showed it, Blakely thought. Van Heusen had built himself a pleasure palace on the dark side of Iapetus complete with its own atmosphere dome and mercury flare lighting to keep the daemons at bay. As the landing craft touched down beside it and the modular flexi-seal hugged the dome's entrance, Blakely whistled.

"Hey, Holt, looks like crime *does* pay." He admired the gaudy structure made entirely of costly Old Earth marble imported at unimaginable expense. It sat in the middle of the atmosphere dome looking like a wedding cake lit up from within. The illegal flesh tanks were probably well hidden somewhere under the lavish structure, Blakely speculated. Even on the dark side of Iapetus, Van Heusen wouldn't be bold enough to have them right out in the open.

"Wonder how many colonists he had to mind rape to build this place," Holt said darkly. "Back-up's standing by?"

"Got a crawler over the ridge," Blakely reassured him, nodding at the large, stony outcropping about half a mile to their left. Very faintly, he could see the wink of the vehicle's lights, but the intense glow of the mercury flares around Van Heusen's dome ought to drown them out until the crawler was right on top of the compound. "All we gotta do is make the bust," he assured Holt.

"So . . ." Sadie unbuckled her harness and scooted to the front of the craft. "All we've got to do is to get Van Heusen to show us the flesh tanks and admit they're his?"

"Got it in one, sweetheart," Blakely told her, patting his chest where the tiny voice-activated recording device was secreted. "We just have to get it all on the listen chip and see the tanks. The minute we do that we'll signal the back-up and he's fried."

He was trying unsuccessfully to keep his eyes off her, but it was damn hard to do. Sadie was "undercover" posing as a prostie-borg, and the outfit she had on certainly showed off her considerable assets to the best advantage. A bright red dress made of some soft, gauzy material clung to her full breasts and floated around her softly rounded thighs. The dress scooped low in the front showing the creamy inside curve of her cleavage, and parted alluringly in front to reveal a pair of tiny black satin panties that barely covered the golden strip of hair that decorated her honeyed sex. Blakely, remembering the delicious salty-sweet flavor of her cunt, longed to drop to his knees and bury his face between her thighs. To make her moan and beg for more as he had the other night while Holt tended to her breasts.

But it was not to be, no matter how much he wanted it. Sadie just wasn't into it and Blakely could hardly blame her.

Holt was right, nice girls *didn't* want what they had to offer. He supposed the idea of a three-way commitment was just a little too strange for most women to handle. He just wished he hadn't fallen so hard for her and encouraged his partner to do the same. Still, they had gotten over failed romances before and they would again. It just might take longer this time because of the bond.

Sighing, he popped the latch on the landing craft and said, "Well, everybody out."

Thanks to a vid-call, from a friend of Snuggly's who owed the big Garon a favor, they were expected. An armed squadron of identical male flesh-bots, all bald and with a gold hoop through the right nostril, and led by a mechanical captain, was waiting to escort them to Van Heusen. After a quick but thorough pat down to be sure they were unarmed, Blakely and Holt walked behind the squad, heads up, alert for anything. Sadie, a carefully blank look on her face, trailed behind them. They were supposed to be wealthy research scientists in the field of cyberbiology, and they had dressed the part in synthi-silk clothes and real jizard-skin boots. Holt even had on a cape. Blakely always admired how well his partner played rich and disdainful, but he supposed it came naturally to the blond man considering his background.

They walked through an echoing marble foyer and down a long hall carpeted in real wool, another expensive import, before they came to a real wood door that was twice as high and three times as wide as Blakely was tall. *Mmm,* he thought, *Van Heusen really likes puttin' on the dog.* The cost of importing this door alone was probably more than he saw in a year as a detective on Old Earth.

The mechanical captain pushed a recessed switch and, with a low rumble, the immense door began to slide into the wall, revealing a cavernous room. Blakely half expected to see a golden throne sitting at the end of the huge room, instead, there was an old-fashioned fireplace with some plush, antique-looking couches and chairs scattered in front of it. Blakely wouldn't have been surprised to find out the furniture was imported directly from some fancy French court on Old Earth. There was a bearskin rug on the floor that Blakely hoped was antique; all species of bear had long been on the endangered list. Van Heusen had apparently spared no expense to make himself at home here on Iapetus.

The mechanical captain escorted them across the vast expanse of marble floor to the fireplace. When they got a little nearer Blakely could see a lean shape sitting in one of the high-backed antique chairs.

Roald Van Heusen, an elderly man thin to the point of emaciation, sat beside a fireplace big enough to roast a bull in, sipping a snifter of aged brandy and looking like an ad for the good life. The firelight played across his lean features and his quiet, conservative clothing and finely molded features marked him as a man of good breeding—a man of taste. Only the diamond ring on the thumb of his left hand that was too large and vulgar to be anything but real spoke of his wealth. *Has to be at least six and a half carats. Maybe seven.* Blakely eyed the diamond and wondered how much debilitatingly addictive synthonarc you had to sell to be able to afford such a nice bauble. How many innocent colonists you had to sell into a life of sexual bondage.

"Mister Van Heusen, these are Mr. Night and Mr. Day, the investors you were expecting, sir." The mechanical captain had a surprisingly smooth voice, like an English butler on one of the old culture vids Blakely had watched as a kid.

"Thank you, Parkins. You may go." Van Heusen waved a dismissive hand and the mechanical captain made a well-oiled bow and hovered away. "So," he turned to Blakely and Holt, a sardonic little grin on his thin lips. "Mister 'Night' and Mister

'Day,' eh?" Using such obvious pseudonyms was guaranteed to get Van Heusen's attention and let him know they were as anxious as he was to keep their business dealings quiet.

"I'm Night, he's Day," Blakely said, giving a quick half-nod to Holt. Van Heusen took in Holt's blond good looks to Blakely's dark intensity with an amused glance.

"But of course you are; the names suit you. And who is this lovely creature that I see with you?" he asked courteously, nodding at Sadie who stood perfectly silent and still behind them.

"This, or rather she, is the reason we're here, Mr. Van Heusen." Holt nodded stiffly and gestured for Sadie to come closer. Moving so smoothly it looked like she was gliding on air she came to stand before Van Heusen's chair, a coquettish smile on her full pink lips. Van Heusen looked from Blakely to Holt with raised eyebrows.

"She's a prostie," Blakely said helpfully. "A prototype from our labs on Venus. Look." He turned Sadie around and lifted the silky red gown to show her softly rounded ass. On the left cheek was a small tattoo (removable, of course, although Van Heusen didn't need to know that) of a red capital C in a small blue circle. "Our logo—Century Labs," he explained, turning her back to face them.

"Surely not," Van Heusen muttered, standing to circle Sadie with an interested air. He ran one lean hand over her bare arm. "Her skin is so smooth and pliable, not a bit plastic. And the texture of her hair is terribly real." He rubbed one of Sadie's honey-brown curls between his fingers and turned back to Blakely and Holt. "I must say, gentlemen, this is really quite something. How is it achieved?"

"We use a special epidural conditioner in the tank during a critical stage in growth. The formula, of course, is something of a trade secret, although we wouldn't mind divulging it if our goals appear to be compatible," Holt said smoothly. "You see, we at Century Labs are working to create the perfect prostie.

One that looks and acts like a real woman. We want to expand into the homes of the wealthy and influential of every inhabited planet and moon in the System."

"You have my interest," Van Heusen said, sitting back down in his high-backed chair and steepling his cadaverous fingers beneath his chin. "Go on."

"You see," Holt continued. "The prosties on the market today are good enough to service men who haven't seen a real woman in a while—Ring miners and the like. But to appeal to a rich man's palate, you must present perfection." He gestured at Sadie who smiled vacantly back. "Using chemical processes and drugs I have specially developed at Century Labs, it is possible to make a prostie that is so lifelike it can fool anyone."

"It seems you have achieved your goal," Van Heusen said, giving Sadie another admiring glance. "But why come to me?"

Holt shrugged. "I have just a few flesh tanks at my disposal—for research purposes only, you understand. Mr. Night here," he nodded at Blakely who nodded back. "Is interested in buying a much larger number of my specialized prosties than I have the means to manufacture. Rumor has it, Mr. Van Heusen, that you have the means to mass produce prostie-borgs at a reduced rate. Even incorporating my new drugs and processes, the profit would still be astronomical. You could sell a specialized prostie at ten times what you're charging for a regular one now."

"The scenario you present is most appealing, but I fear the wild rumors of mass-production are greatly overstated." Van Heusen smiled a thin-lipped, insincere smile. "Why, I would have to have thousands of flesh tanks at my disposal and you know that would be completely illegal if I did not also have a government-sanctioned synthetic brain manufacturing plant on my property. Because what use is a tank-grown body without a brain to operate it?"

"Some people think synthetic brains are overrated," Blakely said, carefully keeping a bland look on his face. They had Van Heusen hooked; now to reel him in.

"My friend Mr. Night is correct," Holt put in smoothly. "In fact, the latest trend in laboratory work is to implant the brain of a human subject into the tank-grown body. Naturally we use only donated brains from organ harvestings," he added.

"Naturally." A small smile played around his thin lips.

"There are problems with such transfers, of course," Holt continued, stepping forward to put his arm around Sadie's shoulders. "The most notable one being that the personality of the brain donor still remains in the temporal lobes of the donated brain. It is this lingering trace of the organ's original owner that causes difficulties and resists the sexual subjugation so absolutely necessary in the perfect prostie-borg."

"That is an important element," Van Heusen acknowledged, cautiously.

"It's a problem to which I have devoted a great deal of research," Holt said. "In past studies, the transplant prostie-borg was simply kept quiet with constant doses of syntho-narcotics. Effective? Certainly, but also expensive and unreliable. If the syntho-narc injections are allowed to lapse, you have an angry, peevish prostie-borg in chemical withdrawal that refuses to service your clients."

"And you have a better way?" Van Heusen took an old fashioned tobacco burning pipe from one pocket of his black satin smoking jacket, filled it, lit it with a flare, and began to puff. Blakely thought he looked ridiculous—why not just use a nicotine popper like everyone else? Probably because it didn't look ostentatious enough.

"I have developed a drug release mechanism implanted in the abdomen that is good for the life of the prostie-borg," Holt told the puffing Van Heusen.

"So that you never run out of syntho-narcs." Van Heusen nodded. "The only problem I see with that is how prohibitively expensive syntho-narcs can be. What if your prostie is rendered nonfunctional before the supply runs out? Terrible waste of drugs, you know."

"I said I had developed a release mechanism that never failed. I didn't say I filled it with syntho-narc," Holt corrected him. He pulled Sadie closer, his fingertips caressing her bare shoulder possessively. "I filled it with a drug cocktail of my own concoction—a mild sedative mixed with a powerful aphrodisiac. It's cheap, legal, and the results are more than satisfactory." He leaned over and gave Sadie a lingering, probing kiss and, on cue, she moaned and melted against him. Blakely had to stop himself from joining them, forcibly. *All an act, it's all an act,* he reminded himself, ignoring the persistent erection that insisted he should step up behind Sadie and begin nuzzling the soft back of her neck, bracketing her sweet body between himself and Holt. Instead, he turned his attention back to their target audience.

"Imagine coming home tired after a long day at the corporate free-zone and finding a beauty like this ready, willing, and eager," he said to Van Heusen while Holt and Sadie continued to kiss passionately. "She's gorgeous and she's got just enough personality not to act plastic. She's always ready for action. All the fun of a real live beautiful woman without the hassles. What wealthy CEO wouldn't want one? Mr. Day and I feel the new, specialized prosties will become status symbols—must have items in a very short period of time. And because we'll be selling exclusively to the obscenely wealthy we'll have a cushion of credit between us and the law that isn't there when you're selling to Ring brothels."

Holt broke the embrace with Sadie and pointed sternly at the couch. "Sit down," he commanded.

"My pleasure, Master," Sadie replied in a low, husky tone and sat primly on the edge of the antique sofa to their right.

"Well?" Holt and Blakely looked at Van Heusen expectantly. Personally, Blakely thought they had made an excellent pitch; he almost believed it himself.

Van Heusen puffed on his pipe thoughtfully for a moment. Finally he said, "You make a convincing argument, gentlemen, I must say. But, speaking purely hypothetically, how could I be sure your processes would work with my equipment? Assuming I *have* equipment, of course."

"Nothing could be easier," Holt said, and Blakely felt his partner's cautious elation through the T-link. It was the opportunity for which they had been waiting. "It would only take me a minute to ascertain the suitability of any equipment you might happen to have. I would, of course, have to see it to make the assessment."

"We'd have to ask for a tour anyway," Blakely pointed out when Van Heusen seemed to be wavering. "Mr. Day and I don't do business with anyone until we're sure they have the means to back up their end of the agreement. No offense intended to you, Mr. Van Heusen."

"None taken," Van Heusen said, setting down the pipe. "So, you want a tour of the tanks, eh?" He smiled the thin-lipped smile again. "I think it can be arranged. On one condition, of course."

"Name it," Holt said confidently and Blakely knew his tall blond partner was thinking that they had this bust in the bag. Van Heusen had just admitted to having illegal flesh tanks; now all they had to do was see them and they were home free.

"Well, your prototype there," Van Heusen gestured with a long, thin finger at Sadie who was still sitting quietly on the couch. "The hair, the wonderfully touchable skin—she seems perfect in every respect, but forgive me if I'm cautious. I'm just wondering how your conditioning process affects the life span and durability of the prostie. It wouldn't do to sell a million credit toy and have it break on the first, ah, *usage* . . . Not if you expected to do your advertising through word of mouth."

"I assure you, Mr. Van Heusen . . ." Holt began but Van Heusen cut him off.

"Forgive me, Mr. Day but I don't want reassurances. I haven't gotten to where I am today by listening to reassurances. No—what I want is a *demonstration*." The firelight glinted in his gray eyes, which had suddenly gone steely in the webbing of fine wrinkles surrounding them.

"You mean you want to . . ." Blakely felt a surge of jealous protectiveness climb up his spine and prickle the hair on the back of his neck. How dare this old bastard even *think* of Sadie that way? She belonged to him and Holt! It was a stupid, possessive thought and Blakely knew it wasn't true, but he couldn't shake it all the same.

"Me? Oh no, my dear boy." Van Heusen was laughing pleasantly as though Blakely had made a very fine joke. "No, I'm quite beyond that, I'm afraid. The spirit is willing but the flesh is weak, as they say. Sadly, the infirmity of old age has turned me into something of a *voyeur*. I'd much prefer to watch you and Mr. Day demonstrate your very fine product."

"Is that right," Holt said blandly. Blakely struggled to make his face as blank as his partner's. Van Heusen didn't look *that* frail and sickly to him. *Old pervert has probably always gotten off on watching,* he thought.

"We came here to discuss business, not put on a show for you, Van Heusen," he said darkly.

The old man's hand twitched to the inside pocket of his satin jacket and suddenly they were staring down the bore of a lethal-looking, snub-nosed needler.

"Indulge me," Van Heusen said mildly. "Speaking of new and better drugs as we were, have I mentioned that the needles in my weapon are tipped with the very latest nerve-destruction agent? One little scratch will induce a lengthy, painful, and completely fatal demylinization process for which there is no cure." He shook the needler warningly. "Consider it a test of good faith between us. You show me your product in action and I will personally give you a guided tour of my tanks." He gestured to Sadie with the evil-looking silver snout of the needler. "There's a lovely bearskin rug in front of the fireplace; it cost me a fortune. You can enact your little demonstration there."

Blakely looked at Sadie who sat frozen, a blank look on her face. He exchanged a meaningful glance with Holt, a look that said, *what can we do?* The blond man seemed to be on the edge of violence, but they were unarmed. Even if he'd had a blaster in his pocket, Van Heusen had the drop on them plain and simple. They couldn't even call in the back-up. Van Heusen would shoot them where they stood before the crawler filled with federal agents could get anywhere near the atmosphere dome where his home was located. Even if he didn't shoot them the bust would be, well, a bust. Blakely knew enough about Van Heusen to know that they would never find the hidden flesh tanks without him. They would have to play along.

The set of Holt's shoulders was rigid with tension as he stalked to the plush bearskin rug the old man had indicated. Jerking his head at Sadie he said, "Come," in a strangled voice. Blakely held his breath—would she?

16

Sadie sat rigidly on the couch, unable to believe her ears. It was something she had never considered when she came up with the prototype prostie story and the idea of passing herself off as the prototype—that Van Heusen might want to see the merchandise in action before he committed himself to the deal. She supposed she should have expected this eventuality, but she had been so excited about being right in the middle of the bust, of getting the story first hand that she just hadn't thought. *Stupid, Sadie, really stupid,* she told herself. *Yet another mess you had gotten yourself into by not looking before you leapt.*

The snub-nosed bore of Van Heusen's needler looked as big around as a tube-station tunnel when he gestured at her and Sadie felt like her heart was right up in her mouth, beating against her clenched teeth. Her nipples were hard with fear. She struggled to keep her face utterly calm and emotionless—to look like the perfect prostie in every way. Now more than ever it was vitally important not to give the game away.

From the looks on Holt and Blakely's faces she could tell

she was going to have to go through with it. Despite their promise not to touch her there was no way around this situation, but would Holt be able to do this without his partner? Sadie realized she didn't know the exact limitations of their T-link, but she remembered Holt saying that sharing women was a "necessity." Maybe he could perform but not come to orgasm if Blakely wasn't involved? She was about to find out.

"Come here," Holt said to her again and she realized that all their lives might depend on the performance she was about to give. Van Heusen had the air of a man who killed casually and without remorse.

"Yes, Master," she murmured. Stiffly, she rose to her feet and walked to the brown bearskin rug to stand before Holt. Looking up into his eyes gone ice-blue with anger and remorse, Sadie wished she could tell him that the situation wasn't his fault, that she wasn't going to hold it against him, but all she could do was stare vacantly, a vacuous smile pasted on her face. Out of the corner of her eye, she could see that Van Heusen was getting impatient, but it was obvious that Holt was having a hard time forcing himself to do what he had promised he wouldn't.

"What would Master have me do?" she asked softly, trying to give him a cue that it was all right, that she would play along. She didn't want to strengthen the bond between them, but she had an idea that as long as only one of the partners was involved it would be all right. Blakely was still standing safely to one side, a scowl on his dark face.

Holt gave her one last, apologetic look. "On your knees." His deep voice sounded husky and strangled. Sadie shivered as she knelt before him, feeling the coarse scratch of the rug against her bare knees. The heavy bulge of his cock was very evident in the tight, synthi-silk trousers he wore. Unbidden, the memory of sucking that long, hard shaft flashed through

Sadie's mind. Was that what Holt was thinking about as well? She looked up at him again, waiting for further instructions.

Roughly, Holt unzipped his pants and took out his sizable erection. "Suck me," he commanded. "Make it good."

Sadie leaned forward, mesmerized by the play of firelight along the hardened club of his sex. Holt was achingly hard and a silvery drop of pre-cum was already shimmering at the slit of the large, mushroom-shaped head. She darted out her tongue and lapped it gently away, causing a harsh sigh to come from the man above her. Holt's clean, sharp scent and slightly bitter taste filled her senses as she teased along the length of his shaft with her lips, loving the sound of his half-stifled groans as she did so. *I'm enjoying this,* Sadie realized with a twinge of shame as she sucked the broad head into her mouth, relishing the feel of Holt's large hands buried in her hair, urging her on. *What's wrong with me?*

She told herself she was being forced to perform a degrading act and enjoying it should be the last thing on her mind, but her body wasn't listening. She was taking Holt as far down her throat as she could, humming with pleasure, enjoying his low cries as he fucked her mouth and nothing else mattered. Not the shameless way she was behaving or the deadly needler pointed at her head. Her nipples were hard as she pressed against his legs, and there was a growing warm wetness between her thighs. She could feel a tiny stir of the warm, electrical fire she felt when Holt and Blakely pinned her between them, but it was barely there, a faint echo of the sensation she craved. She knew it was wrong, but she couldn't stop herself from wishing that Blakely could join them on the rug in front of the crackling fire.

"Stop!" It took a moment for the word to penetrate her brain, but finally Sadie realized that Holt was pulling her off his still erect organ. Her lips felt swollen from sucking and licking him so long and thoroughly, but she was well aware that he hadn't come, probably couldn't come because Blakely wasn't involved. She looked up at him questioningly, feeling a dazed expression on her face. There was a look almost of pain on Holt's finely chiseled features and she realized that it must be a kind of torture for him, being endlessly pleasured without reaching completion.

"Mr. Night," the voice belonged to Van Heusen, whom she had completely forgotten about. Now Sadie turned her head to look at him. He was still holding the needler on them, a dark shape sunk so far back in the plush brocade of his chair that only the barrel of his weapon and his coldly glittering gray eyes were visible in the shadows cast by the fire. "Mr. Night," Van Heusen continued, gesturing with the needler. "I don't believe you're enjoying this show quite as much as I am."

"Fuck you, Van Heusen," growled Blakely, the scowl on his dark face deepening. Even from where she knelt on the rug, Sadie could see the look of pain in his indigo eyes, nearly purple in the firelight, and the hardened bulge of his cock straining angrily against his tight trousers. *It's hurting them,* she realized. *Doing this separately, not being together is painful, physically painful for them.* Unconsciously she reached inside herself for the bond they had created with her; she could feel an echo of that pain in her soul.

"Now, Mr. Night, is that any way to speak to a future business associate?" Van Heusen tsked disapprovingly. "Besides, I think you would find fucking your sweet little prototype prostie much more satisfying." He gestured menacingly with the silver barrel of his weapon to Sadie and Holt. "Join them."

Although it was the very thing Sadie had been wishing for she found herself nearly in a panic. *No . . . no!* If they touched her together the bond would get stronger and she'd never be free. It was a frightening thought.

"What if I won't?" Blakely asked defiantly, eyes flashing.

"Then I'll shoot her," Van Heusen said calmly, directing the barrel of the needler straight at Sadie's head. Immediately, Holt pushed her behind him, but Sadie could still hear Van Heusen's chilling words and see his sharklike grin. "The demylinization process works on tank-grown flesh just as well as on humans. It's quite interesting to watch, actually. The entire nervous system begins to unravel, shredding itself, losing the protective myelin sheath that surrounds each nerve and keeps it intact. The victim feels like every inch of his or her body is on fire. I'm sure you can imagine the results." He grinned again, a predatory baring of teeth. "What do you say, Mr. Night?" he asked. "Want to join the party?"

Scowling, Blakely walked stiffly over to them and stood shoulder to shoulder with Holt, adding his body to the protective shield his partner had formed in front of her.

"You'll regret this, Van Heusen," he said evenly. "Mr. Day and I won't forget being forced to perform like trained monkeys for you."

"I find that most people can forget anything when enough money is involved," Van Heusen said airily. "Now," he gestured with the needler. "On your knees, the three of you. I think Mr. Day had had quite enough oral attention for the moment so Mr. Night may take his place by that luscious mouth." He nodded in Sadie's direction. "And you, Mr. Day, how *did* you think up such fitting nom de plumes? You may take your position behind that lovely rounded ass. I assume you know what to do."

Sadie felt cold all over as they arranged themselves in the positions Van Heusen had described. She forced herself to get on her hands and knees and tried hard not to let the terror and dread she was feeling show on her face. And yet, there was another emotion mixed in as well . . . desire. She could already feel the familiar, warm electric current beginning to flow between the three of them. Holt and Blakely hadn't even touched her yet. Just being between them was enough.

Oh, Goddess, I can't believe what I'm turning into. Can't believe this is actually turning me on. But it was. Sadie squeezed her thighs together tightly. Soon Holt would part her legs and push the black satin panties aside. Just the thought was almost more than she could bear.

She could feel the little voice getting ready to criticize some more and she ruthlessly switched it off. The only way to get through this experience, she understood instinctively, was to just go with it. Guilt and shame and fear couldn't help her now. She was supposed to be the perfect prostie-borg and she had to act the part—had to *be* the part. If Van Heusen found out what was really going on none of them would have a chance in hell of getting out of here alive. Anyway, she thought, trying to soothe herself, though the act they were about to engage in would strengthen the bond she had wanted to let die, it wouldn't bond them completely according to what Holt had told her. Wouldn't create a Life-bond.

She knelt on the rug between them, the heat from the fire licking along one side of her body, and felt the hesitance of both men to touch her. Holt was hovering over her arched back and uptilted ass without laying a hand on her. Blakely had released the thick, dark shaft of his cock from the tight pants he wore, but he made no move to bring it near her mouth. She could feel the longing, the need and desire coming off both of them in waves. They wanted to touch her, but didn't want to break their word. Sadie realized she would have to take the initiative and act like the prostie-borg Van Heusen thought she was.

"Master," she whispered, leaning forward to nuzzle her cheek along the hard length of Blakely's thick cock. The texture was like rose petals laid over hot iron. His spicy, musky scent, half sandalwood and half just aroused man rose to meet her and Sadie breathed him in. Remembering the difficulty she'd had in taking that wide cock in her mouth before, she decided to lick along the length first, tracing the pulsing vein that ran along the underside with her tongue until Blakely moaned with the intense sensation.

Deliberately, Sadie looked up at him, watching him watch her in the shifting shadows, the firelight turning his indigo eyes purple as she sucked the plum-shaped head between her lips. Blakely's hand, warm and large, came down to caress her cheek as she worked on him and she felt his thumb rubbing lightly along her bottom lip, feeling the place where he entered her. The place where they were joined.

"Your mouth is so hot, baby. So sweet," he murmured lovingly, heat shadowing his dark face.

Then she felt another pair of large hands resting on her hips and Holt was cupping the globes of her ass, his thumbs tracing very lightly over the satin panties where Sadie could feel her swollen cunt lips parting in need and desire. Sucking Blakely harder, exploring the weeping slit of his cock with her tongue, Sadie arched her back, thrusting her ass up in a mute invitation she knew Holt could not refuse.

With a low groan, he twisted the crotch of her satin panties in his hand and ripped the flimsy fabric away, throwing the shreds carelessly into the fire. Sadie cried out as well as she could at the urgency of his gesture. Holt needed to be inside her, filling her up, sharing her with his partner until they both came, Blakely in her willing mouth and Holt in her sweet, slippery sex. Sadie could feel their need in the warm, pulsing current that bound them into one and in the bond that was growing every instant they touched her together. She understood their need because it was her need as well.

She wanted to gasp and moan and cry, to beg Holt to take her, to complete the connection between the three of them like plugging the last conductor into an electrical circuit, but she couldn't spare any breath and Blakely's thick cock was filling her mouth completely.

She twisted with sensation as Holt parted her thighs and braced herself for the feeling of that long, hard cock driving into her. Instead, she felt a hot breath on her bare ass and then Holt was pressing his mouth between her legs, lapping hungrily at her honeyed slit, spreading the lips of her pussy wide so that he could shove his hot tongue into her tight entrance. Sadie closed her eyes and moaned around the pulsing shaft in her mouth. Holt's tongue was replaced with two long, strong fingers and she realized he was going to make her come before he took her. She was close already, the current of hot need that flowed over and around and through all three of them had her on the brink and the thrust of Holt's fingers into her tight sex as his tongue went back to lapping her sensitive flesh pushed her over the edge.

A quick but powerful orgasm raced through her, making her cunt contract around his fingers. Sadie squeezed her eyes tightly closed, panting around the thick shaft she still sucked.

"Is that what you need, baby?" Holt's voice was pitched low and seductive, not meant to carry much over the steady cracking of the fire. "You need to be fucked?"

"*Mmm,*" Sadie moaned, thrusting her ass back to him, begging mutely to be taken. She felt Holt spread her legs even wider and the wide head of his cock swiped over her swollen clit, forcing jolts of sensation into her belly and legs before it slowly breached her entrance.

If Sadie could have, she would have begged him to take her hard and fast, to fuck her senseless right there on the ridiculously expensive rug, but she couldn't say a thing, and Holt seemed to be determined to take his time penetrating her fully. Inch by thick inch she felt him slide into her tight, slippery channel, stretching her, filling her with himself.

The mushroom shaped head bottomed out inside her, kissing her cervix with its leaking tip, and she knew that Holt was fully seated inside her, that his cock was as deeply into her cunt as it could go. She had never made love in this position before, Gerald had said it was unnatural. She was surprised at how pleasurable it was. She was kneeling on the rug, her legs spread and her tender breasts brushing the coarse carpet through her gauzy dress, sucking Blakely's cock with her pussy being filled and fucked by Holt's, and she had never felt so good, so hot and wet and open in her life.

Holt drew back and surged inward, fucking almost roughly into her tight pussy as Blakely pressed between her lips, brushing the back of her throat with his own thick shaft. There was a sudden jolt of almost painful pleasure like an electrical surge in the current flowing around them. *Like a thunderstorm when lightning strikes,* Sadie thought, hazily, wondering if she could bear the intense sensation. Then they did it again and all rational thought was driven from her mind.

Goddess, oh, Goddess, she thought raggedly as she felt Holt's thumbs dig into her hips to hold her steady for his furious thrusts. In the back of her mind she could sense his pleasure glowing like a white-hot river of molten gold at the feel of her tight cunt sucking around his invading shaft. She became aware that Blakely had reached down and freed her breasts from the confines of her silky dress and he was rhythmically twisting her aching nipples in time to the thrusts of his cock into her mouth. He was a solid weight in her mind, rock-hard and hot, dark, and intense.

Holt pounded her endlessly while Blakely invaded her mouth more gently, but no less thoroughly, and Sadie felt a warm tide of ecstasy crawling up the base of her spine and electrifying her whole body. She became aware that she was going to come again. A deeper more powerful orgasm than her first was building inside her, threatening to overwhelm her with its force. She was going to come and take both her lovers with her.

As though hearing her disjointed thoughts, Holt reached in front of her and rubbed her throbbing clit hard with two fingers. "Come on, Sadie, come for us," he whispered, his voice filled with intensity. Blakely, past words, simply growled low in his throat and twisted her nipples harder.

She tipped over the edge and exploded. The slippery walls of her cunt trembled around the thick shaft of Holt's cock. Instinctively, she sucked even harder on Blakely's shaft and was rewarded by a thick blast of salty fluid at the back of her throat. Holt was coming, too, ramming his cock as deeply into her clenching pussy as he could and holding steady, filling her up with his cum. Sadie had never felt so wild and wanton, so purely sexual before than at that moment, having her mouth and cunt stretched and fucked and filled with the thick cocks and hot cum of her lovers.

At that moment, when all three of them were locked in an orgasm so fierce Sadie almost forgot to breathe, she had a strange sensation in the back of her mind, even stronger than the ones her body was currently experiencing. It was a feeling of *almost* connection—that was the best way she could put it. As though she had come within a micron of the most intense union possible in this or any other universe and had fallen short. *Oh, please . . . please, just a little bit more,* Sadie found herself thinking. She felt the bond between her and Blakely and Holt grow and stretch, reaching for that moment of ultimate connection, but falling inevitably, unspeakably short. *Is this how they feel every time they share a woman they can't bond with?* she wondered hazily. *Goddess, how do they stand it?*

Then the sensation ebbed away, along with the current of golden heat that had blanketed all three bodies as they coupled. Sadie felt first Holt and then Blakely withdraw from her body and she felt empty in a way she couldn't describe. She hurt. She let herself collapse into a softly panting ball on the bearskin rug, still tasting the strong, musky flavor of Blakely's cum on her tongue and feeling the warm trickle of Holt's running down the inside of one thigh.

Inside her mind the newly strengthened bond twisted like a thick rope, so tangible she could almost touch it. Goddess, what had she done?

17

"Well, that was quite a performance, I must say."

Sadie blinked wearily as the unfamiliar voice intruded into her consciousness. *Who?* she thought, her brain feeling muddled and unclear. Her body felt heavy, almost drugged with lethargy after the intense orgasm. Then she remembered—not only had she just performed an act that would make a whore blush—she had done it for an audience. She bit back a groan. *I had to—had to keep Van Heusen from suspecting the truth. Besides, he has a needler pointed at us,* she reminded herself, but it didn't help much. The disapproving little voice in her head that she had managed to shut off during their "demonstration" was back full force, making her cringe with shame.

"Satisfied?" Holt was staring at Van Heusen and his voice had a low, grating quality that spoke of intense rage.

"Not as much as you, I imagine." Van Heusen's voice was light and amused. "I must apologize for ever doubting your product, gentlemen. Clearly it *is* able to withstand rough treatment from time to time." Sadie saw Holt wince out of the corner of her eye at this, but Blakely's face remained stony.

"We did what you wanted, now show us the tanks," Blakely growled, zipping his pants with a quick, jerky motion.

"In good time, gentlemen. All in good time." Van Heusen eased out of the chair, unfolding his lanky form in stages carefully. "I'm not as young as I once was." He gestured to himself. "I have often thought of trading in this aging shell for a tank-grown body, but until I saw your lovely little prototype, I was reluctant. Now I am eager to be certain your conditioning formulas will work. Come." He gestured and then, appearing to notice he was still pointing the snub-nosed needler at them he shrugged apologetically and tucked it back into the satin smoking jacket he wore. "I'm sure there's no need for this now." He patted his pocket. The huge diamond he wore on his thumb flashed and glittered in the firelight. "No hard feelings, eh? I just had to be certain a prostie made with your processes could take a certain amount of abuse—if I use your techniques to grow myself a new body I have to be certain it's perfect in every respect, you see?"

He looked appealingly at both Blakely and Holt, and Sadie saw the men exchange a glance. There it was again, that nonverbal communication that spoke volumes. Only this time, she found she understood it, could sense it vaguely in the back of her mind like a murmur of half-heard voices. There were no words that she could understand, only vague glimpses of thoughts and emotions. Both men were angry and upset at Van Heusen, but they were obviously trying to control themselves and finish the job. Under the anger there was a current of regret at the broken promise, and sorrow that Sadie was so unhappy with what they had just done . . .

Wait a minute, if she could hear Holt and Blakely through the bond, could they hear her, too? Sadie sat up on the rug and wrapped her arms around her legs, squeezing her eyes tightly closed. This must be what it was like for Blakely and Holt all the time. Always being inside each other's heads and thoughts and emotions. Goddess, how did they manage?

Van Heusen was heading for the door, clearing expecting them to follow him. Sadie stood carefully, on shaky legs, still emotionally and physically drained. Without discussion, Holt and Blakely each took one of her arms, supporting her. Sadie felt a ghostly whisper of the warm current brush against her skin at the double contact and she pulled away, stumbled and nearly fell in the process. *No more*, she thought. *Can't take anymore of this.*

"Hey, wait a minute," Holt called, giving her a concerned glance. Van Heusen turned around, his hand still near the pocket that held the needler.

"Yes?" he said politely.

"Do you have a fresher cubicle anywhere around here?" Holt asked. "Our prototype needs to be cleaned up before we tour your tank-room."

"Oh, certainly. Third door on your left as we exit the lounge." He hit the main switch that caused the massive wooden door to slide aside for them. *Lounge*, Sadie thought. *If that's the lounge I'd hate to see the main living room.* They walked outside and back into the long, marble hall.

It was Blakely that took charge of her this time, taking her into the fresher and cleaning her gently with a damp cloth.

"You okay, kid?" he asked anxiously, gazing into her eyes as he spoke. Sadie felt his concern for her like a warm thermal blanket wrapped around her shoulders. She shrugged it off.

"Fine, I'm fine," she muttered, turning her face away from him.

"I can't tell you how sorry Holt and I are about what happened," Blakely said softly.

"After what we promised you, well . . . It's just . . ." He seemed unable to find the words he wanted.

"It's all right," Sadie said wearily. "You and Holt were just doing what you had to do. I was, too, I guess." *Not that it makes me feel any better about it,* she thought numbly. "We'd better get back to Holt and Van Heusen. After everything we've put into it, I'd hate to miss the bust."

"Okay, if you're sure." Blakely looked at her doubtfully.

"Sure I'm sure." Sadie attempted to brighten up some, knowing he could feel the guilt and despair in her mind. "Let's go."

18

The tank room was everything Holt had hoped for and more. Van Heusen had taken them down a long passage, secreted in the side of a wall behind a huge, antique Drusinian clock. A number of codes and passwords and a retinal scan were necessary to get in, and Holt had reflected that they never would have found the place or gotten into it without Van Heusen's cooperation. Holt had mixed feelings about that.

It made him glad, in a way. Glad to know that cooperating with Van Heusen had been a necessity. Even if the old man hadn't had a needler pointed at their heads or they'd somehow been able to call in their back-up without risking all their lives, the bust would have been a no-go without him. Without visual proof of the illegal flesh tanks they had nothing on Van Heusen and he would have gotten off Scot-free. He would probably have moved his base of operations to a more distant moon and continued buying black market brains, keeping the mind rapers in business and the colonists in danger forever. Why should he ever stop? With access to the flesh tanks he could keep growing himself new bodies forever. In the long run, it was a good thing he and Blakely had gone along with Van Heusen's commands in order to win his trust and ultimately, to nail his wrinkled hide to the wall.

That was part of what he was feeling. The other part, Holt admitted to himself as he surveyed the huge, subterranean room where they now stood, was guilt, pure and simple. Guilt that he and Blakely had both broken their promise to Sadie, and that they had enjoyed doing it. Even now he could feel her sorrow and self-loathing through their newly strengthened bond. The feelings were still vague, not nearly as clear as they would have been if she had been interested enough to forge a Life-bond with them, but they were clear enough for Holt to read. Sadie was ashamed of what they had done together and scared of the bond, scared of sensing Holt's and his partner's emotions in her head. Holt knew how she felt. Hell, it had taken him and Blakely a good six months to get used to the strange sensation when the T-link had first been established after their Tandem chips were implanted.

Sadie had only known them a couple of weeks and she had come along on this mission for a story, not a relationship with two guys she'd never met the month before. Holt knew they couldn't expect her to be overjoyed to find herself physically and emotionally committed to them via a semi-permanent bond. She was frightened and repulsed by her own newly awakened desires and responses to their link. Holt wished with all his heart he could change her mind, but he didn't think that was likely to happen. At any rate, what he needed to be thinking about now was how this bust was going to go down. Sighing, he tried to tune out the distracting new emotions coming from their unhappy "prototype prostie" and concentrate on the business at hand.

"Gentlemen, I think you'll find that I have an operation here to rival anything you'll find on Mars." Van Heusen's voice was proud, and he made a sweeping motion with his sticklike arm to indicate the vast room. It was, Holt thought, bigger than any Zero-G stadium he'd ever been in and it was stacked to the dimly lit ceiling with multiple rows of flesh tanks filled with murky liquids. He knew about how a body was grown, having studied the subject in preparation for this case, but it was still interesting to watch the process in action.

Each tank in a single vertical stack represented a different stage in the tissue growth process. The top tank in a stack would be filled with protein-rich emollients, high in iron and amino acids to nourish the scrap of DNA that would be placed in it, the blueprint of a newborn prostie made exactly to order. At a certain stage in the tank-gestation, an automatic sensor would inform the top tank that it was time to dump the lump of rapidly growing flesh into the cloudy green depths of the tank below it that contained calcium and other bone-strengthening agents. When the skeleton was strong enough to support weight, the second tank opened into a third, where the now adult-sized frame was encouraged to grow muscles, organs, and connective tissue in response to electrical stimulation constantly running through the reddish murk of the stem-cell–rich emollients it contained. The bottom or "finishing" tank was filled with a thick, clear gel that was the keratin-impregnated nutrient bath that encouraged the tank-grown body to form hair and an epidermis. It was this last stage that had never truly been perfected, which was the reason prosties had the brittle, latexlike tone to their skin.

The whole process from DNA to fully formed adult prostie took a little more than a week, which explained why the federal government of the Solar System regulated the ownership of flesh tanks so strenuously. If just anyone was allowed to own tanks, the known Universe might soon be overrun with an army of perfectly formed, empty-headed prosties.

"You must have enough tanks here to process a thousand prosties at a time." Blakely's voice interrupted Holt's train of thought.

"Two thousand, actually," Van Heusen said proudly, surveying the tank-filled room. "We aren't working at peak capacity just now because my, ah, suppliers—brain suppliers, that is—had a falling out. But I expect to be running at full capacity again within the solar month. Maybe just in time to implement your processes, eh, gentlemen?"

"Maybe," Holt muttered, noncommittally. "First I'd like to examine your tanks."

"Please." Van Heusen made an expansive gesture indicating that they should feel free to wander around the room. Actually, Holt was looking for a back entrance to the enormous room to bring the back-up squad through. He and Blakely made their way around the perimeter, being sure to keep Sadie safely in between them as they walked.

Workers in sterile white suits wandered around the vast space, seemingly at random, checking the pH balance of various tanks, but none of them appeared to be armed. A low beeping sound began emanating from a tank to Holt's right and a worker hurried over and pressed a series of buttons, causing the bottom tank to roll neatly out of position so that the worker could reach hands gloved in white up to the shoulder into the clear slime of the nutrient bath. A perfectly formed female body, its long blond hair and golden tan skin completely coated in clear, viscous slime rose to the top of the tank. Holt saw that its chest was rising and falling with shallow respiration, but there was no sign of any cognitive function whatsoever; the body just lay there, an inert lump. The worker rolled the corpse-like thing onto a nearby hover stretcher and trundled it off down the long row of tanks.

"Gotta 'nother Elise 2 ready for brain fitting," Holt heard

the man say into the visi-talk clipped to his collar as he went. He watched as the tank slid itself silently back into place. On its side was a bronze plaque he hadn't noticed before that said, "Elise Series 2." There was a muted "plopping" sound as the tank above the now empty bottom one released a mass of glistening, naked muscle tissue with a vaguely female form into the clear slime of the nutrient bath.

Circle of Life, Holt thought grimly. He felt Sadie shiver beside him and her revulsion was clear through the bond. Van Heusen had the place so automated that a hundred workers could easily turn out the two thousand prosties a week the tank room was capable of producing, providing they had brains to power them, of course. He doubted if even the Synthenex flesh tanks on Mars had the operation down to such a science.

"Hey, Holt." Blakely's voice drew his attention to a large white recessed panel at the far end of the room. Looking carefully, Holt could just make out the sign over the panel which said, DELIVERY. *Bingo!* Just what they had been looking for. Of course it made sense that Van Heusen would have to have a large entrance for shipping his product. Bringing the prosties through the main house would be much too obvious, even on the dark side of Iapetus.

Holt nodded at Blakely, signaling his partner to call in the back-up while he kept Van Heusen busy. If everything was done correctly, the old pimp would be safely in restraints before he knew anything was wrong, but Holt wanted to be nearby when it happened. Van Heusen had been prosecuted many times before but never convicted, mostly because the witnesses had a convenient way of dying and the evidence always somehow melted away. Holt didn't intend for that to happen this time. They had Van Heusen dead to rights with the largest collection of illegal tanks he or anyone else had ever seen, and he didn't want to give the old man a chance to start a countdown and blow the evidence and all the workers that knew about it sky-high while Van Heusen himself slipped out some secret entrance.

"Keep close and stay behind me," he murmured to Sadie, thinking of the deadly snub-nosed needler hidden in Van Heusen's smoking jacket. "Things are gonna go down fast and I don't want you hurt. Understand?"

"Got it," she replied, her lips barely moving. Holt could feel some of the emotional turmoil inside her mind turn to excitement as they walked back toward where Van Heusen was sitting easily in a floating air-cushion and smoking his pipe again while he waited for them to tour the room. Holt felt it pumping in his own veins as well—the thrill of a bust about to go down; it never failed to fill him with adrenaline.

"Well, well." Van Heusen got to his feet carefully and smiled. "And how do you find my equipment, Mr. Day? It's top of the line, you know."

"It's fine equipment all right," Holt agreed. Through the adrenaline-heightened T-link he heard Blakely directing the back-up squad through the back door and knew federal agents would be swarming down the long, tank-filled isles at any moment. He could feel his own version of Van Heusen's cold, sharklike grin spreading over his own face at the thought.

"I'm afraid I have some bad news, Mr. Van Heusen," he said to the anxiously waiting man.

"Your processes won't work with my equipment?" Van Heusen looked so upset it was almost comical.

"It's worse than that, I'm afraid." Holt moved in closer so that he could keep an eye on the old man's hands. "Not only is there no 'conditioning process,' but you're also under arrest for the possession of illegal flesh tanks and the use of black market brains."

Van Heusen made a move toward his jacket's inside pocket,

but this time Holt was too quick for him. He slapped a set of restraints he'd had hidden in his own inner pocket on the skinny, withered wrists and removed Van Heusen's needler in one motion.

Van Heusen looked at him angrily. "I suppose the girl isn't really a prostie at all," he said in disgust. "I should have known better than to think such marked improvements were possible."

"Got it in one," Holt said, grinning. "Although you have to admit if you really could make a prostie as attractive as my colleague here," he nodded at Sadie who stared back impassively. "You'd make a mint overnight."

"Agreed," Van Heusen said sourly. "Unfortunately, I was more interested in growing a new body for myself that was perfect in every respect than 'making a mint' as you put it. Money I have in abundance, but my youth is long behind me. You have greatly disappointed me, Mr. Day."

"It's Detective Holtstein, Old Earth Vice," Holt said. "Pleased to meet you, Van Heusen. My partner and I will be seeing you in court. Now, you have the right to remain silent," he began and then there was a sudden commotion behind him and all hell broke loose.

19

Later Sadie couldn't remember anything but a melee of yelling voices and colored uniforms. The workers, dressed all in white, were being herded into a loose group by the federal agents in orange and blue, but they weren't going quietly. She was trying to stay close to Holt, but somehow she got swept into the crowd, just another body in the rising tide of disorder.

Van Heusen's voice, surprisingly loud and clear, suddenly cut through the racket of babbling voices. "The girl—get the girl!" he shouted, and after one horrified moment Sadie realized he was talking about her. *Why me?* she had time to think and then a thick arm was locked around her neck, choking her, cutting off her air. She fought instinctively, kicking backward with the high-heeled shoes she had on, trying to connect with something solid. But all she felt was the soft give of the protective suit of the worker that held her, kicking and squirming, against his body.

"I'll do it, I swear I'll do it," he was shouting in her ear and Sadie felt the sharp pricking of a pointed instrument against the side of her neck. *Oh my Goddess, he has a knife!* The thought was barely a blip in the front of her mind and then someone knocked the man holding her flat and she was pinned beneath a bulky, male body, all the breath crushed immediately out of her lungs. The weapon he had been holding at her throat jogged upward as his arms came up instinctively to break his fall. Sadie felt a burning line of pain across her cheek and there was a silvery glint in the corner of one eye before the sharp, pointed thing skittered away into the confusion of shuffling feet.

Almost got my eye, she had time to think and then her forehead connected with the floor and everything was darkness.

"I think she's comin' out of it."

Sadie opened her eyes to a dimly lighted room that seemed familiar somehow. *Home?* she thought confusedly, thinking of her austere little bedroom at Aunt Minnie's house in Goshen where everything, including the walls and sheets, was a pure, blank white. Aunt Minnie had forbidden her to decorate the room, believing that Sadie would hang "devil posters" as she called the holo-vids of music stars most girls liked, on the walls of her guest room. Sadie supposed she might have, too, if there had been any way to see a concert in Goshen, but none of the bigger groups ever stopped there because the colony was too morally uptight for them to sell enough tickets to make it worth their while.

"Sadie?" She recognized the voice but couldn't place it. *Gerald?* But no, this voice was deeper than Gerald's whiny tenor; a soothing baritone she associated with warmth and comfort and safety and . . . love? That couldn't be right, though. Who had ever loved her, *truly* loved and wanted her since her parents had died in the shuttle crash when she was twelve?

"Sweetheart, don't try to move. The medi-tech had to give you somethin' for the pain and it knocked you out." Another deep, gentle voice, this one with a New Brooklyn accent. She knew someone from New Brooklyn, didn't she? But how could she? Old Earth was millions of miles from Io.

Sadie tried to sit up in bed and failed. She became aware of a dull throbbing pain behind her eyes, the remains of a really bad headache, she supposed, and then strong arms were lifting her into a semi-sitting position.

"Easy, honey," the first voice soothed.

"Weak as a kitten." It was the second voice again. Who were these people and why did the voices floating above her head provoke such a storm of emotion inside her?

Sadie blinked; everything was fuzzy and her head throbbed. She reached up, thinking to brush hair out of her face and found that the right side of her face was covered with something rigid and unyielding.

"Wha's wrong with my face?" The stiffness over her cheek caused her to slur her words. A vague, nameless fear was beginning to surface in her brain.

"You were cut," the first voice said again. "In the mess after we arrested Van Heusen. Another eighth of an inch to the left and you would've lost an eye."

"Holt, don't scare her. You're all right, sweetheart," the second voice said gently.

Van Heusen . . . wait a minute, the bust! The name brought everything rushing back and Sadie made a conscious effort to throw off the rest of the drug-induced drowsiness and come back to herself. She remembered Holt and Blakely, the plan to pretend she was a prototype prostie, the things they'd had to do to make Van Heusen believe, the bond between herself and the two detectives . . . *The bond. That must be why I can feel their emotions.* Sorrow, regret, worry, love, and an aching need filled her head before she made an effort to block it out.

She was getting better at that, she realized, better at ignoring the alien emotions in her head so that she could think clearly. Maybe in time she'd be able to use the bond like a vid-screen, tuning in and turning it up when she needed to know the emotional state of her men and turning it down to avoid mental confusion and strain when she didn't.

What am I thinking? Sadie realized she was thinking about the bond as though it was a permanent part of her life when she knew that could never be. She had to get away from Blakely and Holt, so far away that the bond lost all its power, thinned away to nothing, so that she could be on her own again. *But why? Why do I have to leave and get away? Blakely and Holt love me . . .* She pushed the thought away; it was obviously just the remains of the drug in her system talking anyway. Right now she had to ascertain how badly she was hurt.

She brought up a hand and felt the stiffness over her right cheek again. "How bad?" she croaked, struggling to focus her eyes on the two worried faces leaning over her on either side of the bed. In the dim light she could see a worried frown on Blakely's dark face and a grim expression on Holt's chiseled features.

"Not good," Holt said at last, apparently deciding to tell her the truth and get it over with. "You're going to need some reconstructive surgery, and even then there might be a scar."

"Holt!" Blakely hissed, shaking his head. The blond detective frowned at his partner.

"She needs to know, Blakely."

"Well didja have to just say it out like that?"

"I need to see." Sadie interrupted them. She struggled to sit up and swing her legs over the side of the bed, but couldn't quite manage it.

"Not right now, honey," Blakely said in an appeasing tone. "Why don't you try to get a little more rest?"

"No. I need to *see*," She insisted. She finally managed to get her feet on the floor, but the drug residue that lingered in her system made her feel like her legs were made of lead, and she wasn't completely sure they would support her. "Now," she added, tottering to her feet. For a moment she was sure she would make it to the fresher door, and then the world tilted and she felt herself collapse in slow motion. Strong arms caught her and Holt supported her on one side and Blakely on the other. Sadie was glad because her legs now seemed to be made out of rubber and she realized there was no way she was getting anywhere on them.

"Blake's right; you really don't want to see right now," Holt said in her ear. "Just wait a little while until the swelling goes down, Sadie."

"Don't want to wait," she said as forcefully as she could. "Please, Holt, just let me see. My face feels so *strange*."

Holt sighed deeply and she felt Blakely's arm tighten around her waist. "All right, fine," the blond man finally said. "But I'm afraid you're not going to like what you see."

"Anything's better than not knowing," she said, feeling that it must be true. Sadie had never been the kind of person who could wait patiently for bad news—she had to know the worst immediately. Borrowing trouble, her Aunt Minnie had called that particular character trait. Getting to the bottom of things, Sadie called it.

"C'mon, honey." It was Blakely in her other ear and together, he and Holt supported her into the fresher and stood her in front of the holo-viewer that hovered in front of the sink.

Sadie took a deep breath and looked at her own face in the viewer. Her hair was a wild, honey-colored bird's nest of tangles and there were dark, bruised-looking hollows beneath her matching eyes. A lump the size of an egg was rising from one side of her forehead and the entire right side of her face was covered in a stiff white flexi-seal that contrasted oddly with the screaming red prostie dress she still wore. Why hadn't Blakely and Holt gotten her into something more comfortable? *Probably didn't want to touch me without my permission,* she realized. Although after what the three of them had done together at Van Heusen's house, it seemed like a needless precaution. Just the thought of that, the memory of all three of them on their knees on the rug with the firelight playing over them while they moved together, touched each other, was enough to make Sadie's breath come short and her face turn red, the half of it she could see at least.

Putting the incident firmly out of her head, Sadie turned her attention back to the face in the viewer. Carefully, wincing as the adhesive that held the seal in place pulled at her skin, she moved the bulky white covering aside to look at her face. What she saw was worse than she could have imagined.

I will not cry, Sadie told herself grimly but despite her determination, the girl in the holo-viewer had tears leaking down her ravaged face and so Sadie supposed she must as well.

She had never thought of herself as a beauty queen, although she supposed she was pretty enough or she never could have passed as a prostie. Other than that she'd never given her looks much thought, had taken them for granted. Looking in the viewer, Sadie realized she'd never be able to take being pretty for granted again.

A jagged red line bisected her right cheek starting at the corner of her right eye and ending just below her ear. The wound was stitched together with neat little sutures that pulled the right side of her face into an ugly grimace when she tried to move her mouth. Holt was right, even with reconstructive surgery it was probably going to leave a hell of a scar. Sadie stared until the image in the viewer doubled and then trebled into a blur of tears and she couldn't see anymore.

Stumbling, she staggered away from the sink and would have fallen if Blakely hadn't caught her and pulled her close. Sadie buried the left side of her face against the side of his neck, feeling the rough brush of his dense curls against her hot skin and sobbed. Blakely held her close, one arm locked around her waist, the other stroking her back.

"Shh, honey, don't cry. It's not so bad," he whispered softly.

Sadie pulled away from him abruptly. "How can you say that?" she demanded. "I'm . . . I'm *disfigured* for life. How could it be any worse?"

"He was aiming for your throat," Holt said grimly. "If he hadn't missed you wouldn't be here right now. That would be a hell of a lot worse."

"You're not makin' this any easier for her, Holt." Blakely's voice was low and angry. He pulled Sadie close again, being careful of her injured face and resumed his soothing backrub. "I'm sorry we didn't get you fixed up better kid," he said to her. "But there weren't any reconstructive surgeons on Iapetus. I told the medi-tech we were takin' you back to Io though, and he said you oughta get somebody top of the line to see you once you got home, no problem."

"Back . . . back to Io?" Sadie pulled away again, looking doubtfully into the indigo depths of Blakely's black-fringed eyes.

"Sure, back to Io." Sadie turned her head to look at Holt as well. The blond detective was leaning against the sink platform in a pose of casual grace, but the set of his shoulders was tense and stiff. "The bust is over, Sadie, and you saw it all from the front line. You can write it up and send it out to the news-vids the minute we get to Io. It'll be breaking news and you'll have an eyewitness account."

"But," Sadie looked at the ice-blue eyes, confused. "I thought with the bond . . ."

"What didja think—we'd kidnap you 'n take you back to Old Earth?" Blakely asked gently.

"You made it pretty clear how you felt about everything, kid. We wouldn't do that to you."

"No . . . no, of course not." Sadie pulled away from him to

lean against the sink beside Holt, her back carefully to the holo-viewer. Of course they wouldn't force her to come with them if she didn't want to. They would drop her off on Io, leaving her to get on with her life while they got on with theirs, millions of miles away. She would probably never see them again. Sadie swallowed hard, wondering why there was suddenly such a lump in her throat.

"What . . . what about the bond?" she made herself ask. "What will happen when we get so far . . ." she swallowed again, "so far away from each other?"

Blakely cleared his throat. "We think it'll fade after a while, especially as Holt and I get farther and farther away from you." His deep voice had a hollow tone and Sadie could feel his regret and sorrow loud and clear at the back of her mind.

"Oh." She turned to go, where she wasn't sure, maybe back to bed or to look up reconstructive surgeons in the Io web-pages online. She knew exactly what Aunt Minnie would say when she saw her niece's horribly scarred face. She would say it was all Sadie's fault for going off on such a crazy, immoral mis-sion in the first place instead of staying home and marrying that nice Gerald. A large part of Sadie was inclined to agree with that; she was only getting what she deserved for the way she'd been acting lately.

"You don't deserve any of this." Holt's voice was a little ragged and he grabbed her arm to keep her from leaving the fresher "Sadie, please stop being so hard on yourself."

"How . . . ?" She looked at Holt blankly and then remem-bered the bond. They must be feeling her guilt and who knew what else through it.

"Besides," Holt continued roughly. "It doesn't have to be this way. You don't have to go back to Io by yourself. You can come with us to Old Earth . . ."

"Holt," she said as gently as she could. "You know I can't. I'm sorry."

Blakely let out a sigh. "Yeah, we know but Holt couldn't help askin', kid."

"At the very least, though, you don't have to go back with a scar," Holt persisted. He ran a large hand through his pale golden hair, making it into a nimbus of light around his head. "Let us . . . let us heal you, Sadie. One last time," he pleaded softly.

"Heal me?" For some reason it hadn't even occurred to her, although now that she thought about it, she knew it was possible.

"The wound's still fresh enough—Holt and I think we can fix it entirely." Blakely was suddenly at her other side, looking at her hopefully. "I wanted to do it earlier while you were asleep—wanted to spare you havin' to see that ugly cut at all, but Holt thought it was a bad idea. But now . . . the whole mess with reconstructive surgery . . . Why bother when we can make everything better so easily?"

"But . . ." Sadie knew what they were saying was true, knew instinctively deep in her bones and in the back of her mind in the place where she was bonded to them that what they were asking her to do was the right thing. The memory of what had happened in front of the fire at Van Heusen's house came back suddenly in a wave, washing over her with heat and light and wanting, and she was afraid. Afraid that if she started, if she let them start, that all three of them would be utterly incapable of stopping. If only her body didn't crave them so badly. If only she could *trust* herself.

"You don't have to worry about it going too far, Sadie," Holt said in a low voice. "We won't let it. We only want to heal you, to touch you one last time before we take you home and let the bond die forever."

"Well, I . . ." she began, thinking that she wanted it, too. Wanted to feel the warm, golden current flowing through all of them, binding them all together just one more time before she had to give it up forever. It scared her how much she wanted it.

"The, uh, bond can't get any stronger at this point unless we ... you know, at the same time," Blakely said, his dark face getting a little red. "And we're not gonna do that. It just makes sense to use it while we've got it."

"Just let me ... let me think about it, okay?" Sadie asked desperately, feeling their need mixing with her own until it was nearly overpowering. "Why don't you two let me take a shower—I feel disgusting right now and I just want to clean up."

She shooed them out and they left, a little reluctantly, Sadie thought. Trying not to look at the viewer, she stripped off the hateful red dress and stepped into the shower. But she already knew what she was going to do.

Later, it was that healing that Sadie remembered most, even more than the intense sex at Van Heusen's. She lay naked between the two muscular male bodies and gave herself up to sensation as Blakely and Holt kissed and caressed her body from top to bottom, summoning the healing energy that flowed between them. It itched along her hurt cheek like fire until the flesh knit together and became whole once more and then everything was pure pleasure.

Sadie closed her eyes, closed her mind to the nagging little voice of guilt and just let it happen. Hands on her breasts, her thighs, between her legs. Hot, slow kisses along her spine and belly, her hips and throat, and everywhere in between. They brought her to orgasm again and again so softly, so gently that she had barely stopped riding one crest before another one lifted her up and away.

Through it all was the most profound sense of love and need she had ever felt, flowing from Blakely and Holt into her and back to them, forming a closed connection of emotion and pleasure that blanketed them all in a golden glow. *Love you, Sadie, love you forever. Never forget this, the love we shared, the way we are now, together, forever for this moment that can never come again.*

The words seemed to sigh through her mind as first Holt and then Blakely mounted and entered her. One at a time but sweet, so sweet for all of that. Blakely cradled her gently, her back to his chest, whispering love and affection into her ear as Holt rose above her, piercing her sex with his shaft, pouring himself into her, loving her, healing her. When they had rested a little, Holt held her cheek against his chest so that Sadie could hear the steady thunder of his heart while Blakely took her gently from behind, thrusting deep to fill her completely with his hardness and his seed.

Never forget this, never, never forget this, she thought feeling the love and the need crest within her one last time before she fell into the darkness of an exhausted sleep.

20

"No, Gerald, I'm sorry but I'm not free on Sunday either. That's the day I leave."

His narrow, pinched face became tight with anger, a closed fist of emotion on the vid-screen.

"I get it, Sadie. Now that you're a big-shot reporter you don't have time for old friends anymore."

"Gerald, it's not like that and you know it." Sadie sighed. "Look, I have to go now. I'll call you later." She cut the connection before he could protest and sank back in her seat.

She supposed she should be grateful that Gerald wanted to talk to her at all. More than one old friend and neighbor had stopped speaking with her since she had shocked conservative Goshen with her eyewitness report of the prostie scandal. Even Aunt Minnie had disowned her after hearing where she had been and what she had been up to for the two-and-a-half months she'd been gone. Sadie had never been really close to her aunt, but the old lady *was* the nearest thing Sadie had to a parent and her rejection hurt more than she cared to think about. Hurt even more than the snide remarks and half-heard whispers behind her back when she walked down the streets of her old neighborhood.

It did no good whatsoever to explain that she had only gone undercover to get the story and had not actually serviced any clients in her role as a prostie-borg. People in Goshen were narrow-minded and disposed to believe the worst. Everywhere she went, Sadie felt like she ought to be wearing a scarlet letter tattooed on her forehead. It was funny, actually, that her fellow Goshenites were condemning her just for doing her job when she had done much worse things on her "two-and-a-half-month mission of depravity," as Aunt Minnie had called it, than wearing the skimpy prostie-outfits and spending time in a brothel. *If only they knew what I really did, I'd probably be run right out of the colony,* she thought more than once.

Despite rejection at home, her career was really taking off. As Holt had promised, she had the only eyewitness account of the whole scandal, and the news-vids had fallen all over each other to buy her story. It seemed like a dream, but she actually *had* been nominated for a Solar Pulitzer in journalism. Sadie had found out only the week before and she had wanted to tell *someone.* Calling Gerald, however, had turned out to be a bad mistake. He had somehow gotten it into his head that she wanted to get back together and all his talk of "old friends" aside, Sadie knew he was really angling for a date. In the past she might have gone out with him and given the relationship another shot, but not now. Not after all that had happened to her while she had been away.

It was ironic, Sadie thought, that all her professional dreams were coming true while her personal life crumbled away. She even had a job offer on the table to be a correspondent for the *New New York Times.* Because the *NNYT* was the most prestigious and respected news vid-mag in the System, Sadie felt extremely lucky. Accepting the job would mean leaving Io and relocating to Old Earth, of course, but she had decided to take it anyway. After all, what did she have to hold her to this narrow-minded, Goddess-forsaken moon anymore? Nothing, not a thing, Sadie told herself. And Old Earth was where all the power and money and opportunity was. That was where her future was now.

Of course, her decision had nothing to do with the fact that Blakely and Holt were stationed there. Nothing at all. In fact, she barely ever thought of them anymore and she was sure they never thought of her because they never bothered to call . . .

Don't think about it, she commanded herself. *It was months ago and now it's over—completely, irrevocably over.* The bond was gone, she was sure of that. She no longer felt any emotions but her own inside her head. No one else's pain hurt her, no one else's need filled her with longing, no one else's love surrounded her and made her feel safe and wanted . . . Sadie sighed and dragged herself out of the chair to finish packing her things. She had never thought she could be so damn lonely inside her own skin. Had never thought she could miss feeling someone else's emotions in the back of her mind.

She didn't have any romantic notions that she would "run into" Blakely or Holt when she moved to Old Earth. After all, it was a huge place, not a little backwater nothing of a colony like Goshen. She could probably live there in the big, dirty city of New New York and never see them once for the rest of her life. If one or both of them had called her, even once, she might have at least let them know she was coming. She had heard nothing from them in six months, not since they had dropped her off on Io with a final hug from each, so Sadie was forced to conclude that they considered the brief love affair to be over, too.

Of course, she had made no move to contact them either, but then, it was the man's, or in this case the *men's,* job to make contact; at least to her way of thinking. The ball was in their court and they had done nothing with it. It hurt her pride to admit it, but Sadie had begun to think that maybe she was just one of many. Maybe they picked up women everywhere they went. Maybe the whole story about having to have the right brain chemistry was just that—just a big story to make her feel special so she'd agree to be with them the way they wanted.

Sadie sighed again as she threw clothing haphazardly into a standard-sized compression cube that gobbled up whatever she gave it and compressed the article into a square-inch–sized parcel that could be easily packed. The cube had been expensive to rent, but it would save her money on transport fares in the long run. Sadie figured she could probably bring her entire wardrobe along in one small suit-pack. Her pictures and other personal items would be shipped on a carrier, which was cheaper than taking them along on the expensive star-freighter she herself was riding. The *NNYT* was paying for her passage, but her relocation costs were up to her.

Sure wish I had somebody to meet me at the port . . . Sadie nipped that thought in the bud. Despite their failure to call her, she had considered calling Blakely and Holt on the vid-screen and just letting them know that she would be in town. Seeing if they wanted to remain friends at least. A hundred times in the last six months she had punched in their number and then hit the cancel button. Because what if she placed the call and a woman answered the phone? What if they had only been using her to get what they wanted and now they had moved on? Sadie couldn't bear the thought.

Besides, even if there is no new girl and they did agree to be friends, I could never be just friends with those two. Not while she remembered so well the warm, electrical current, the golden fire that had flowed between the three of them. How could she ever be around Blakely and Holt and not long for that? Not wish for the utter total completion that had been so close each time she made love to one of them? There was no way she could withstand the temptation to form a Life-bond with them if they spent any significant amount of time together. *And that would be so bad, why?* She quashed the thought firmly as she did whenever it occurred to her, but it had been coming back more and more lately.

Once upon a time she had thought she was too moral, too purely Goshen, to think of the kind of lifestyle a Life-bond with Blakely and Holt would involve. It wasn't like she'd ever be able to take them home and show them off as her husbands. If she tried a thing like that . . . well, they still had stoning laws on the books in Goshen for extreme cases of immorality. Sadie had a feeling that flaunting a polygamous marriage might fall under that heading pretty easily. At the very least she knew they wouldn't be welcome in Aunt Minnie's house, the house where she had grown up from the age of twelve.

She was *already* a social outcast in Goshen. Aunt Minnie *already* wasn't talking to her. And Sadie was having a harder and harder time remembering why she had felt so shocked and horrified at what Blakely and Holt had proposed to her in the first place. *Because I'm not that kind of girl.* The little voice mocked her now. She obviously *was* that kind of girl or she wouldn't keep thinking about it.

It's been six months and you're moving to Old Earth to start an exciting new career, Sadie told herself sternly. *It's time to put the past behind you and move onward and upward.* She threw the last article of clothing into the compression cube and watched it shrink into an impossibly small shape. *New life, here I come!* And she was almost happy.

21

"Yes, dahling, your first assignment will be the trial. You've missed most of it I'm afraid, but the sentencing is today so you won't miss that at least."

Sadie looked at her new senior editor. Prissy De Tangelen was a wasp-waisted fortyish bleached blond with an old-fashioned pair of real glass spectacles perched on her knife-blade of a nose. She was wearing a tight, flesh-colored dress that became completely see-through at some angles. The daring dress made Sadie feel frumpy in her brand new cobalt-blue working-girl suit that she had purchased specially for her first day at the *Times*. But the see-through dress wasn't the most startling characteristic of her new editor. Behind the spectacles were a pair of poison green eyes, and her long blond hair rose three feet off her head and stood straight up on end, trembling gently in the passing air currents like seaweed under the ocean, making her look like a parody of a woman who'd had a terrible fright. It had taken Sadie a few minutes to realize that the jeweled choker Prissy wore was actually an anti-gravity collar. The senior editor told her they were all the rage in New New York at the moment.

"Better than a face-lift any day, dahling." She'd patted Sadie's cheek. "Not that you need to worry about such things yet."

Now she was looking at Sadie with an air of expectation. "I, um, where is the trial being held?" Sadie felt like an idiot. "I'm sorry it's just that I haven't been in the city for twenty-four hours yet so . . ."

"Not to worry, my sweet," Prissy De Tangelen said serenely. "It's being held at the downtown courthouse and it's a *complete* circus. Any hover-taxi can get you there so you don't have to worry about *that*. Now, as you may know we already have people covering the trial, have had from the moment they brought that old pimp Van Heusen in." Prissy paused for breath and patted her shimmering tower of hair absently. The writing stylus she'd been holding was caught in the anti-grav field and began orbiting her hair like a small, elliptical satellite.

"What the *Times* wants from *you*, is an eyewitness account written in the same style as your Pulitzer piece. It should have a start-to-finish kind of feeling. You saw the beginning and now you're seeing the end. You see? We're looking for a sense of *closure*, here, dahling. Can you do it?" Sadie opened her mouth but Prissy De Tangelen didn't give her a chance to answer. "What am I asking? Of *course* you can," she answered her own question with an expansive wave of her hand that sent her brassy blond hair into slow-motion ripples and caused the orbiting stylus to twirl lazily end over end. "So get to it, they're starting at nine."

"Thank you," Sadie said uncertainly, standing and gathering her things. She hadn't expected to be sent out on assignment quite so quickly; she didn't even have a desk yet. Or an apartment. She supposed she could stand to live in the cramped five by five mini-sleep cube a little longer. "You've been more than kind."

"And what else would I be to our newest Pulitzer nominee?" Prissy smiled a wide, white predatory grin bracketed by blood red lips that made Sadie distinctly nervous. "We at the *Times* just *loved* your little story, dahling. Positively ate it *up*. All the intrigue and danger and *especially* the sex angle. Sex sells like *nobody's* business. And it takes a real artist to get a Pulitzer nod out of tabloid material like prostie-borgs. Just keep up that level of writing and we'll keep you around. Remember, at the *Times* if you don't produce, you're out. Got it?"

"Got it," Sadie replied faintly through numb lips.

"Well then you'd better run, dahling. You don't want to miss the show. I'll expect the article on my desk before we go to press tomorrow. Oh, and here's your press pass. *Try* not to lose it." The editor tossed a small, leather wallet in Sadie's direction and she fumbled awkwardly, nearly dropping it before she could tuck it into the pocket of her cobalt suit.

"Absolutely, of course. I'll just . . . I'll let myself out." Sadie headed for the door and Prissy De Tangelen nodded absently, bending to look over some work scrolling across the front of her fiberoptic desk. Her hair seemed to be waving goodbye.

Van Heusen's trial, the very place Sadie had been hoping to avoid! She cursed under her breath as she settled carefully into the smoothly humming hover-taxi after typing in her destination. The blinking read-out informed her that her ride would cost three hundred credits and take thirty minutes. Sadie winced as she pressed her thumb over the red credit indicator and watched it read her print and deduct the credit from her account. The light turned green and the hover-taxi whooshed silently up into the air. She hoped the *Times* would give her some kind of expense account to cover this kind of thing in the future or she was going to be very broke very fast.

As the taxi ate up the miles, Sadie stared out of the window, wishing she was heading anywhere but the trial. She supposed she was lucky she hadn't had to be there for the whole thing.

She had narrowly missed being subpoenaed as a witness, but apparently her tell-all article had branded her as prejudicial in the eyes of Van Heusen's attorneys and they had worked hard to keep her from being called. Sadie had breathed a sigh of relief at the time, thinking that she surely would have run into Blakely and Holt if she showed at Van Heusen's trial. It would have been unavoidable. Now she was going there anyway and she just bet one or both of them would be there.

Sadie lifted her chin, feeling defiant. Well, if it happened, it happened. She would just put on her most professional manner and explain that she didn't have much time to talk because she had a deadline to meet.

Sooner than she would have liked the hover-taxi coasted down to a huge granite building that pierced the dirty sky of New New York like a gray, accusing finger. Sadie knew that Old Earth natives were proud that they lived on the only planet in the System that didn't need an atmosphere dome, but the polluted brown air currents that swept past her as she disembarked made her wonder what was so great about going dome-less. The air on Goshen had smelled dry and processed, but at least it didn't stink. Squaring her shoulders, she marched up the endless granite steps to the front of the courthouse. She supposed she'd get used to the stink along with everything else after a while.

Pushing through the endless crowds, she passed through three security checks with no problem, noticing as she went that most of the women and even some of the men were wearing the same see-through material that Prissy De Tangelen had been affecting. It made her feel frumpier than ever to glimpse the sleek, nearly naked bodies flashing past her in a constant hurry to get wherever it was they were going. Why hadn't she checked more closely into what the native New New Yorkers were wearing before she'd moved? Sadie supposed that as soon as she got her first paycheck she'd have to go out and get some new clothes, although, frankly, she would have almost been more comfortable in the prostie-outfits she'd worn on the mission. They covered far more than most of the weird, see-through dresses and suits she was seeing.

"Van Heusen trial?" asked the bored guard at the fourth security check and Sadie nodded wordlessly, producing her press pass. She started to walk past the man, but he stopped her with one arm across the chest.

"What's wrong?" Sadie asked anxiously. Did she look like a desperate criminal or something? The trial was starting in five minutes and she really had to get going.

"Visual check. Turn side to side, please," the guard said, in the same bored tone. Hesitantly, Sadie did as he asked, twisting from one side to the other, wondering what in the world he was looking for.

"Look," she said, still twisting. "The trial's about to start and I really need to get in there."

The guard gazed at her for a moment and then said, "You got the wrong kinda clothes on for this, lady. You're gonna hafta strip."

"*What*?" Sadie looked at him aghast. "What are you talking about?"

"I'm talkin' about gettin' outta them clothes so I can make the check and you can stop holdin' up my line," the guard said matter of factly. "This here's a restricted trial, lady. You shoulda wore somethin' made outta easy-vis if ya wanted to get in without takin' off your clothes." He gestured to the guard to one side of him who was scanning the people who passed by his desk after twisting to first one side and then the other, rendering the fabric of their suits and dresses see-through with the change of position before he let them past.

Sadie realized with a sick kind of dread the reason for all of the see-though clothing. Everywhere you went in NNYC there were multiple security checks. When you looked at it that way, it was certainly easier to wear the easy-vis outfits than to take off your clothes. People were beginning to pile up behind her. Some of them muttered, gave her disgusted looks and went to find a line that was moving. Sadie knew she was making people late, but the idea of stripping in public was less than appealing.

"Look," she said as reasonably as she could. "Can't you, I don't know, X-ray me or something? I'm new here and I didn't know . . ."

"No longer allowed ta use any kind of radiation on the general public for security checks. *People vs. the State of New York 2094*," the guard droned. "Look lady, you wanna get into the trial or not? It starts in five and Judge Cornwallis'll holdja in contempt if you come in late and disturb his court."

"Yes, all right, fine," Sadie said tersely. There was no way around it; she would have to undress. Gritting her teeth and trying not to catch anyone's eyes, she began stripping off the conservative cobalt blue suit, trying to pretend she was in the girl's locker room back in school on Io. She was down to her matching green bra and panties and was unhooking the front of the bra while the guard looked on with mild fascination when she heard a voice behind her.

"Sadie? Sadie, honey, is that you?"

"Oh *no*," she moaned under her breath. Turning around with her bra flapping open she saw Blakely standing behind her, that charming, lopsided grin she remembered so well stretched from ear to ear. "Blake!" she said blankly, all of her resolve to be calm and professional forgotten. "I . . . uh, didn't expect to see you here."

"And I didn't expect to see you either, sweetheart. Least not so *much* of you." Hot indigo eyes traveled over her chest reminding Sadie that her breasts were exposed for anyone to see, her nipples hardened from exposure to the chilly air. Blushing deeply, she clutched the bra shut, trying to hide herself and still her pounding heart. She noticed, a bit resentfully, that Blakely was wearing a dapper navy suit that set off his eyes to perfection. It was completely opaque, but no one was making *him* strip.

"I just got in last night and the *Times* sent me to cover the sentencing. I didn't know about the security checks," she babbled, feeling like a total idiot.

"Hey, take it easy, baby," Blakely said. Taking her elbow he turned toward the guard and said, "It's all right, Charlie. The lady's with me—I'll vouch for her."

"You say so, it's good enough for me, Detective," the guard said promptly. He shoved the pile of clothes she'd laid on his desk at Sadie who hurriedly began putting them on again. "She was holdin' up the line anyway," he added, beckoning for the next person to move forward.

"It's . . . it's so good to see you again," Sadie panted, hopping on one foot as she tried to replace her high-heeled shoes. Blakely obligingly slowed down and let her hold on to his elbow to perform this operation.

"Yeah, 'm glad I ran into you, kid. Holt and me figured we'd never hear from you again."

"Well all you had to do was pick up the vid-screen and call," Sadie said indignantly, hobbling in the uncomfortable heels as fast as she could down the marble hallway after him as he resumed walking.

Blakely gave her a piercing glance out of his deep blue eyes.

"We figured you didn't want to hear from us or you woulda called," he said quietly. "We've both been missin' you, Sadie. Missin' you a lot. Heard you got nominated for an S. P. Good work," he added quickly, not giving her time to remark on his last words.

But Sadie thought she felt a faint tickle of some emotion—sorrow, loss, hope?—in the back of her brain. Could it be that the bond wasn't completely gone after all? She supposed she would know for sure when she saw Holt.

Oh boy, here we go again, she thought. But strangely, the idea didn't upset her the way she would have expected it to.

"I'm working for the *Times* now." She smiled up at him a little shyly. "They called and offered me a job as correspondent after I got the nomination. I, uh, I never expected to run into you or Holt in the line of duty though. Where is he, anyway?"

"Saving me a seat. It's packed in there," Blakely said. "C'mon, let's see if we can squeeze you in."

Squeeze was the right word, Sadie thought, when they got settled in the long, benchlike seats that lined the courtroom. She was lucky to have run into Blakely, she thought, because there was no way she could've gotten such a good seat otherwise. People were actually standing three deep along the walls, craning their necks to see the front of the room, whereas she, Blakely, and Holt were in the second row of seats with a clear view of everything.

Holt had greeted her with more reservation, but no less warmth than his partner, and now she sat jammed between the two of them, her heart pounding and her breath coming faster than normal, trying to ignore the emotions she felt from both men and take notes on the court proceedings. The bond was still there all right; it was amazing how it had come to life as soon as she was sandwiched between the two of them again. It had flared like a smoldering ember that had been suddenly dowsed with lighter fluid, seemingly stronger than ever and apparently ready to pick up exactly where they had all left off.

Sadie wasn't sure how she felt about that. Being between them reminded her of how much she had missed them both, missed the closeness they had shared. The warm golden current that was buzzing through her nerve endings like a low-level electrical charge made her feel mildly drugged with her body's need for physical contact. How long since she had been touched? Since she had made love to anyone? Not since the night they had healed her for the last time. Sadie tried hard not to think about it.

She was wary of letting herself be sucked back into the seductively sexual relationship they had been involved in before she went back to Io. She also wondered at the way her body was reacting so strongly to the proximity of both men. It was like she had been starving for the last six months and suddenly someone had sat her down at an all-you-can-eat buffet and told her to dig in. Was she actually somehow physically addicted to them? Surely not . . . she crossed her legs uneasily, pressing her thighs together and trying to ignore the wet heat she felt building between them.

Sadie tried to keep her mind on the trial and wondered what Blakely and Holt thought. They kept exchanging those little half-glances over her head that spoke volumes without saying a word. She felt hope and need from both of them, although the hope was considerably stronger from the optimistic Blakely and fainter from Holt. If only she'd had a little more time to orient herself here in NNYC before she'd run into them! She was lonely and alone—a small-colony girl lost in the big city—and it made her feel vulnerable and needy. It didn't help any that she felt Holt and Blakely wanting to hold her close between them and ease her pain either. It would be so easy to let them . . . too easy, she thought warily, resisting an urge to squirm like a kid in her seat. Goddess, she could barely *breathe*.

The proceedings went fairly quickly, or at least Sadie supposed they were quick. She had never covered a trial before. Van Heusen had already been convicted of numerous crimes, including the ownership of illegal flesh tanks and the use of black market brains. He sat on the defendant's side of the room beside a small army of attorneys and legal aids, resplendent in a maroon synthi-silk suit with the huge diamond ring he had

been wearing the night they first met him flashing ostenta-
tiously from the thumb of his right hand. Sadie supposed he
had decided to go out in style, although she thought that
flaunting his wealth with the ring and the suit was a bad idea,
especially while the jury was settling punitive damages for the
colonists who had been wronged.

"Old bastard isn't givin' an inch," Blakely whispered low in
her ear giving her a little shiver. Sadie nodded, agreeing with
him. Van Heusen sat ramrod straight in the high-backed chair
as he listened to the judge levy fines in excess of a billion credits to cover the costs of growing new bodies and providing
emotional counseling for the colonists whose brains had been
stolen. The judge seized all his property in the name of the
court and sentenced him to three consecutive life sentences.

"Guess he should have grown himself a new body while he
had the chance," Holt whispered in her other ear. "Even if it
wasn't exactly perfect." Sadie nodded again, trying to ignore
the second little shiver that ran down her spine when his hot
breath blew across her ear, and concentrate on the proceedings.
Van Heusen had gambled and lost. There was no way he would
be able to fulfill his dream of immortality now. He would die in
prison long before he was able to get out and arrange to have a
new body grown for him. His fastidiousness and vanity over
the latexlike skin texture of a tank-grown body had been his
undoing.

At last it was over, and not a minute too soon to suit Sadie.
The entire time she'd been sitting between Blakely and Holt
she had felt herself becoming more and more aroused until
concentrating enough to take notes on the trial became a con-
test of wills between her conscience and her libido. *I have a
deadline. I have to pay attention to this!* she told herself sternly,
but her body was humming so loudly with sexual tension that
she could barely hear herself think.

". . . out for a drink?"

"Huh?" she asked, looking up to see both sets of blue eyes looking at her.

"I said Holt and me know a great little bar not far from here. How 'bout a drink?" Blakely ran a hand nervously through his dark curls.

Sadie thought about it—really thought hard. On the surface it sounded harmless, but if she went out for a drink with these two now she would, in all probability, wake up in their bed tomorrow once again full of remorse and guilt. She wished she could shake that kind of small-colony thinking right out of her head, but she couldn't. Love it or hate it, Goshen and everything she had learned there was part of her. She had come out here to start a new life and that was what she intended to do. *Even though you love them? Even though you need them the way they need you?* The little voice didn't sound like Gerald or Aunt Minnie or anybody else she knew, but it didn't sound like logic either. *I have a deadline,* Sadie reminded herself. *I have a brand new life and I don't want to blow it.*

"Guys . . . Blake, Holt, I'm really sorry," she said reluctantly, feeling like a jerk. "But, well . . . I've got a deadline to meet . . ."

"Sure, we understand, Sadie. That's okay. Some other time, maybe," Holt said quickly. The blond man's face was impassive, but Blakely had a harder time hiding his emotions.

"At least let us give you a lift home." Blakely reached out and took her hand. "We could catch up a little on the way and you'd get home in time to work on your story. Everybody wins. Huh, kid?"

"Well," Sadie felt herself wavering. She remembered how low on credit she was and how much taking another hover-taxi would cost. "All right," she said at last. "But you have to promise to take me straight home. I really have to work on this story—it's my big break and I don't want to blow it."

"Now where have we heard *that* before?" Holt rolled his eyes and Sadie couldn't help laughing. Blakely grinned and squeezed her hand and Sadie found herself thinking how good it felt to be with them ... how *right. It's not just sex with them ... it's everything.*

"Just let me gather my notes," she said.

"Detective Holtstein? Detective Blakely? Excuse me?" The courtroom had cleared out fairly well now and all three of them turned their heads to see whose voice was echoing in the nearly empty room.

Van Heusen was standing, surrounded by a phalanx of attorneys with a wider circle of guards around them and he was calling in his high, old man's voice and gesturing for them to come over, the overhead lights glittering on the huge diamond thumb ring he wore. Sadie saw Holt and Blakely exchange a brief glance. The blond detective frowned and shook his head slightly but Blakely shrugged and walked toward Van Heusen anyway. Looking like a thundercloud, Holt followed reluctantly.

Sadie trailed behind them, helpless to do otherwise.

"Gentlemen, I was hoping you'd consent to speak with me one last time." Van Heusen smiled genially, the wrinkles around his gray eyes crinkling with emotion.

"And?" Holt asked tersely. Sadie could see the tension in his broad shoulders and realized that even with all the security checks and guards around, the tall blond detective still didn't trust Van Heusen.

"And I just wanted to congratulate the men who finally caught me." Van Heusen beamed at them both as though they had played a particularly funny practical joke of which he had been the butt. "Do you gentlemen know, do you have any idea how many times I've been arrested, detained, accused, and arraigned? But you two were the only ones who could ever make it stick. You caught me—you and your lovely assistant there," he nodded at Sadie who looked silently back. "Seriously, detectives, congratulations are in order. Part of it, I must allow, was my own foolishness. But most of it was you, all you, and I for one would like to shake your hands. Would you allow me?"

He held out one thin, cadaverous hand and Sadie saw that it trembled ever so slightly, making the huge, glittering diamond on his thumb throw fractured sparkles of light from every angle.

Holt looked at the hand as though Van Heusen had offered him a dead rat. "I'm afraid I'm going to take a pass," was all he said.

"Ah, c'mon, Holt. What the hell. I'll shake with you, Van Heusen." Blakely extended his hand and Van Heusen clasped it firmly in both of his, the diamond winking at the sudden gesture. Sadie thought she saw the dark-haired detective wince, but he didn't say anything. When the shake was over, Van Heusen turned back to Holt.

"I'm more sorry than I can say that you wouldn't do me the honor of shaking hands, Detective Holtstein," he said gravely. "But perhaps I might be permitted to give you something else instead. Oh no," he shook his head, already reading the rejection in the set of Holt's square jaw. "No, it's nothing of any monetary value. My attorneys can vouch for that, so please, don't be alarmed, or think that I am trying to bribe you in any way. After all, what would be the point?" He gestured around the empty court room, indicating that everything was already over and done with and laughed heartily.

"No, it is simply a small communication reel I wish you to have. Feel free to play it for your own attorney if you have one. On it I have recorded some of my thoughts and feelings, the last mutterings, perhaps, of an old man who isn't long for this System. You've been worthy adversaries and since I haven't any friends to speak of, not that I haven't bought anyway," he nodded contemptuously at the men and women in expensively cut suits around him. "I would like you to have it. Burn it or destroy it or maybe just keep it for a time when you can find it in your heart to forgive an old charlatan for his sins. Will you do that for me?" he held out the fingernail-sized com-reel beseechingly. Grudgingly, Holt held out his hand and allowed Van Heusen to drop the reel into his palm which he slipped into the breast pocket of his well-tailored black suit. "Thank you," Van Heusen said, smiling at them both. "You've made an old man very happy today. I hope you both get the future that you deserve." And with that, he turned and was lost in the sea of attorneys and guards as they led him away.

"Well that was weird," Sadie remarked as they walked out past the security guards who waved them past without any trouble once they recognized Blakely and Holt.

"Nah, old guy just wanted to set things right. I wonder what's on that reel," Blakely said thoughtfully. "Ya know, he's got a hell of a grip for his age, nearly squeezed my hand off." He winced and shook the hand Van Heusen had clasped. "still kinda stings a little."

"That's what you get for shaking hands with the old pimp," Holt lectured.

"Ah, Holt, where's the harm?" Blakely shrugged. "C'mon, let's get this little lady home so she can get to work on the article for her next Pulitzer." He threw an arm around Sadie's waist and Holt copied his partner's motion and wrapped his own long arm around her shoulders.

"I haven't got the first one yet," she reminded them, finding herself falling automatically into step with them as they walked to the parking garage.

"Just give it time, honey," Holt told her comfortably. "Just give it time."

22

By the time they had reached their hovercraft, Blakely was feeling decidedly strange. He felt hot, then cold, then so hot he had to take off his jacket and unbutton the top two buttons of his shirt. His head had started to throb, too; probably, it was all because he had missed his morning caffeine-brew. Holt, who drank mostly herbal tea, had insisted that they had no time to stop at the Starbucks on the way, and Blakely just wasn't himself without his daily jolt of caffeine. Still, it didn't usually give him such an intense headache. He tried to shake it off and just concentrate on being with Sadie again. It was so damn good to see her, especially when he and Holt had figured she was out of their lives forever—her choice, not theirs. Several times in the past six months he had wanted to pick up the vid-screen and give her a call, but Holt had always vetoed the idea.

"We've gotta let her know we're still interested. Let her know we're thinkin' of her," Blakely had protested, but Holt always said the same thing: "We don't want to pressure her. If she comes to us it's got to be her choice."

The dark-haired detective didn't completely agree with that

point of view, but he was willing to defer to Holt's judgment—for a while. Actually, he had been on the point of deciding that when they got home from the trial he would call Sadie no matter what Holt said. He could tell her about Van Heusen's sentencing—it would be the perfect excuse to remind her of their history together and let her know they still cared. He had never been more shocked or excited in his life than when he'd rounded the corner looking for a caffeine-brew dispenser and saw her standing in the fourth security check line nearly naked and completely embarrassed.

She looked absolutely stunning, Blakely thought, stealing a glance in her direction as she and Holt talked. There were times in the past six months that he had wondered if he'd exaggerated her beauty in his memory, but if anything he had downplayed it. Her long silky, honey-colored hair swung around the shoulders of her cobalt suit, which emphasized all her luscious curves to perfection. The big, amber-brown eyes were as deep and beautiful as he remembered and just as easy in which to get lost.

Blakely knew that Holt thought Sadie's being here in New New York had everything to do with her new career move and nothing to do with them, but surely even his pessimistic partner couldn't ignore the way the three-way bond throbbed between them and how the T-link opened and poured out energy with an intensity that he had never felt before. Even with minimal contact they were generating enough energy to light up half the city, he thought.

"Blake, you driving?"

"Huh?" He blinked and realized the other two were looking at him expectantly. "Oh, sorry. Sure." He juggled the suit jacket he was carrying to his other arm and reached in his pocket to pull out the key card then fumbled it through suddenly clumsy fingers. "Oops," he mumbled dully.

Sadie bent to retrieve the card and held it out to him, looking concerned. "You all right, Blake?" she asked. "It's not like you to be clumsy. And you're sweating too."

"Just tired." He made an effort to stand up straight. And suddenly, he was. His arms and legs felt like they were all made of lead. "Maybe Holt c'n drive. I'm beat." He motioned for Sadie to hand his partner the key card instead.

"Now *I'm* worried," Holt said, frowning. "Since when do you ever let me drive? Especially in the city?"

Blakely shrugged as well as his new lead shoulders would let him. "Not feelin' so good is all." Holt opened the craft and he clambered awkwardly in and collapsed in the back seat, leaving Sadie and his partner to take the front.

As they drove, Holt kept glancing worriedly back at him until Blakely insisted he watch the road. By then even his tongue seemed to be dipped in lead and his words were coming out slightly slurred. Sadie and Holt were whispering in the front seat and Blakely caught the words "hospital" and "emergency room."

Making an effort to sit up he leaned forward to make himself heard. "Not gonna go to no damn hospital, Holt," he said, as clearly as he could. "Just tired 'cause you didn't let me have my caffeine today. Maybe comin' down with the flu. Drop me off at home 'n I'll be fine." Holt gave him a disapproving look and Sadie gave him a worried one, but his partner at last signaled and turned the craft in the direction of their apartment.

"Okay buddy, let's get you inside." Blakely was suddenly aware of a familiar pair of arms pulling him upright. Had he gotten drunk on a night on the town again? Damn, he knew how much Holt hated that.

"'M, sorry, Holt," he tried to say but his tongue didn't seem to want to work.

"I think he's trying to say something. Holt, I *really* don't like this." That soft, feminine growl would be Sadie. Damn she had a sexy voice. Blakely felt it all the way down to his balls every time she talked. Or he usually did, when his balls weren't made of lead, that was. Blakely wanted to say something to her, something about how glad he was that she had finally come back to them, but it was like someone had glued his tongue to the roof of his mouth—nothing was coming out.

"I don't like it either," he heard Holt say. "Come on, we'll get him to the med-chair and see what it says."

He tried to open his eyes and watch as they pulled him down the hall, but every time he tried it was a huge effort for nothing; the world was just one big colorful blur so why bother? Blakely shut his eyes and let himself be dragged. He was vaguely aware when they got him into the familiar apartment he and Holt had shared for the past six years and he could still hear his partner and Sadie talking, but all his other senses seemed to be fading in and out alarmingly.

"Here, give me a hand, would you? Grab his right arm and on the count of three . . ."

"Oh my Goddess, Holt. His hand . . . look at it!"

"What the hell?" Blakely felt his arm grabbed and cried out weakly. The rest of his body felt dull and lethargic, but suddenly the hand they were looking at was insisting that it *hurt*! That it was on *fire*!

It reminded him vaguely of the time he'd gone to visit his cousins on the old Mexi-Tex border and had stumbled into a nest of mutie lava ants. The thumb-sized, bright red insects had swarmed up his ankles, gouging fiercely with their serrated pinchers as they went, injecting their horrible, burning venom that felt like fire in his veins. If Uncle Vernon hadn't been right there and had the hose in his hand to spray Blakely off with he would've been a goner for sure. The ants were back now and this time they were in his arm.

"Water . . . wash 'em off," he tried to say but nothing but a strangled moan came out.

"Quick, help me take off his shirt and put him in the chair. It's linked to emergency services." He was pushed and pulled into position until he was reclining in the diagnostic med-chair that was a standard feature in every house and apartment since Old Earth had finally gotten standardized health care.

"Well, what does it say?" Sadie's voice was anxious, eager.

"It says . . . no, that can't be right."

"What? *What?*" Through a haze of pain he heard Sadie asking something but he couldn't understand what she wanted to know.

"It says . . . Sadie, it says he's dying." Holt's voice was low and ragged.

Not dyin'. Just get the ants off. But by now he couldn't even moan. The pain in his arm began to creep into his shoulder and chest and then everything went black.

23

"Dying? No, he can't be *dying*." Sadie sounded as frantic as Holt had ever heard her but he couldn't spare much thought for her feelings just then. "Call a doctor, call an ambulance . . . reset the chair and check it again. That *can't* be right."

Numbly, Holt did as she asked, resetting the med-chair and asking it to run a full diagnostic again. Slumped in its electrode-studded depths, his partner and best friend lay breathing shallowly, seemingly unconscious. Blakely's curls were plastered to his forehead by a thin film of sweat looking very black against his suddenly pallid face. His right hand and arm were swollen to twice the diameter of the left arm and there were evil-looking red streaks running up his wrist like some weird tattoo.

The machine beeped and Holt tugged the screen on its long, flexible arm around to read the results, already knowing what he would see. "It's true," he said dully. "I don't know how or why, but it's true."

"Let me see that," Sadie snapped, yanking the screen away from him and scanning it rapidly. "Holt, this can't be right.

According to the chair Blakely's in the last stages of Multiple Sclerosis. Has he been diagnosed with MS that you know of?"

"No," Holt said. "He's . . . he's always been healthy as a fucking ox."

"So then there must be something wrong with your med-chair. It says his nerves are deteriorating at an unbelievable rate. But there's no way . . . it must be the chair."

"There's nothing wrong with the chair," Holt said. He pinched the bridge of his nose and squeezed his eyes shut tightly. "Besides, I don't need the damn chair to tell me what's going on."

"How . . . ?"

"I can feel it here." Holt pressed the back of his neck where the Tandem chip was implanted. "If you'd stop denying your bond with us you'd feel it, too, Sadie. I don't know how or why, but the chair is right—Blake's dying."

"But . . . but . . ." Tears spilled out of her honey-brown eyes in a sudden flood. "I can't . . . we can't lose him like this. There must be something we can do. We have to *think*, Holt. It's like an allergic reaction, the way he's swelling up. Is he allergic to any insect stings? Something he ate?"

"No, no, nothing I know of." Holt forced himself to think past the dull despair that wanted to take over his brain. He could literally feel Blakely slipping away from him, from them, he realized, because Sadie had to be feeling it through the bond as well. *Think!* he commanded himself. If it was him lying there in that chair dying, he knew Blakely wouldn't have rested until he found the reason, had found the solution. But nothing came to mind.

Because he couldn't think of anything else to do, Holt pulled the screen out of Sadie's hands again and read the diagnostic results. MS . . . nerves deteriorating . . . a sudden memory was gnawing at the back of his brain, something about the latest in nerve-destruction . . . demylinization . . .

"Van Heusen!" he snapped, turning to Sadie. "Do you remember what he was saying, about the new drug the needles in his needler were dipped in when we were on Iapetus?"

Sadie's face got almost at pale as Blakely's and she brought a hand to her mouth, her amber eyes wide pools of shock. "Yes . . . he said it caused the nervous system to . . . to shred itself. Oh, Holt! The hand that's swelling up—it's the one he shook with when Van Heusen asked him to shake hands, isn't it? *Isn't* it?"

"Yeah, Blake's a lefty but of course he shakes with his right," Holt muttered. "Still, I don't see how . . ."

"The ring! That huge vulgar ring," Sadie exclaimed. "I thought I saw Blake wince when they shook and remember, he was saying how Van Heusen had a firm grip and his hand hurt? He must have pressed as hard as he could so Blake couldn't feel it when he was scratched."

It sounded too logical to deny. Carefully, Holt grasped his partner's wrist and turned it over to see the palm. On the underside of Blakely's thumb was what he had been looking for—a tiny smear of dried blood. He stared at it in disbelief and horror, remembering what Van Heusen had said about the drug being fatal and wondering how such a tiny thing, no bigger than a paper cut, could be robbing him of the best friend and partner any man could ever have.

After a moment, he became aware that Sadie was tugging at his sleeve.

". . . reel. The com-reel that Van Heusen gave you. Play it. Quick, Holt! Maybe there's some kind of hint or clue or something," she was saying urgently.

Numbly, Holt dug inside his jacket pocket and produced the fingernail-sized reel. He flicked the tiny indicator carefully to *view* and they watched as a Van Heusen's face popped into view in a holo-projection about the size of Holt's palm.

"If you're watching this, Detectives Holtstein or Blakely, then I have been successful," Van Heusen's tinny, old man's voice said. "If you're watching this then one or both of you is dying."

"Oh no!" Sadie's gasp was more like an intake of breath, but Holt shushed her anyway.

"I will be brief since you won't be able to give me your full and undivided attention for long; the process is much too painful for that." The grin on that narrow, wrinkled face was pure evil. Holt had a terrible urge to wrap his fingers around that scrawny throat and squeeze until the cold gray eyes bugged out, but Van Heusen was only with them in spirit and it wasn't possible. Instead, he had to go on listening to the message.

"How I wish I could see you scrambling around, trying to save yourselves. I tried to arrange for a camera in your apartment, but, alas, it was beyond even my means. So I must content myself with imagining, which isn't so bad—I have a wonderfully vivid imagination, that I can assure you. However, I digress.

"As I was saying, one or both of you will be writhing in pain by now, no doubt trying to reach the vid-screen and call for help." Van Heusen grinned, the cold, sharklike grin that made Holt feel like his heart had been dipped in ice. "Call all you like, gentlemen, there is no known cure. I repeat: *no known cure.* You won't believe me of course. You'll spend your last hours looking for answers that aren't there just as I will spend my last years rotting in prison. But at least mine will be a relatively *slow* death. I say relatively because by the time you finally breathe your last, you will be wishing I had used a much faster-acting agent. But I wanted you to have time to reflect . . . time to suffer." The grin widened even more and the room filled with the sound of Van Heusen's dry, sardonic chuckle.

"As you have taken my life from me, gentlemen, so I have taken yours from you. An eye for an eye, you might say." He looked thoughtful. "Actually, I rather hope only one of you is dying right now. You seem so close that I think the pain of losing your partner is a more fitting punishment than almost anything else, even death. As one of my favorite poets once said, 'Parting is all we know of Heaven and all we need of Hell.' I am quite sure that by the end of your little ordeal you will agree with that sentiment whole-heartedly.

"Gentlemen," the holo of Van Heusen's face nodded gravely. "I bid you a fond adieu. Someday I hope to see you both in Hell." There was a crackling flash that caused Holt to throw up an arm to shield his eyes and Sadie to cry out and take an involuntary step back and the com-reel shriveled to ashes.

24

Losing him, we're losing him. Holt's right, I can feel him slipping away . . . Sadie shook her head. No! There must be something they could do—some way to save Blakely, but Van Heusen's words kept ringing in her head: *no known cure.*

"Blake . . . Oh, Goddess . . ." The broken voice belonged to Holt. The tall, lanky body was slumped beside the med-chair now and he was holding his partner's left hand—the one that wasn't swollen and red—in his own left hand. Holt's right hand was pressed to the back of his neck, rubbing methodically, and he looked like a man who was suffering from the worst tension headache in his life. He rubbed harder and winced at the same time that the still unconscious Blakely moaned.

"Holt?" Sadie felt like someone had dumped a bucket of ice cubes into her belly. A cold fear, one she tried with all her might to push away and ignore, had begun growing there. "Holt, are you all right?" she asked anxiously.

"No, 'fraid not." Blakely moaned again and the blond winced as if in pain.

"What . . . how . . . ?" She couldn't even make herself form a logical question, but Holt seemed to understand her anyhow.

"Blake and I have been tandemized a long time, Sadie. We're too . . . too close. He's going and I think . . . think he's gonna take me with him when he does."

"Take you with him?" Sadie felt what could easily be the start of hysteria begin to build in the lift of her voice. "What are you talking about? Do you feel sick, too?"

Holt shook his head, the fine, blond hair glinting like gold in the apartment's soft lighting. "Not yet, but I will . . . I can tell it. Right now I just feel weak. Getting weaker all the time . . ."

Losing them both . . . Dear Goddess in Heaven please, no. No! I can't be losing them both . . . Sadie shook her head, feeling the words of denial bubbling up in her mind like a hysterical chant. She couldn't lose them, couldn't lose the only two men in her life she had ever really loved, who had ever really loved her. She thought of all the ridiculous reasons she had given herself as to why she couldn't be with them—immorality, fear, pain, her career—and they all melted away like fog when the sun comes out. She thought of that mean little voice inside her head, the one that sounded like Aunt Minnie and Gerald and Goshen all rolled into one . . . she had listened to that voice and thrown away her happiness with both hands.

For the last six months she had been wasting her life millions of miles away from Holt and Blakely, wasting precious time that she could have spent with them. They could have been loving each other, learning to live together, making memories that would last forever. Instead, she had been stuck on Io working on a career that now seemed pointless and trying to get people who never would to accept and love her, when all along Holt and Blakely were waiting for her, wanting to love her, protect her, cherish her. She had pushed them away and now it was too late, her time was up and she had wasted the most precious gift that had ever been offered to her, their love.

I guess this is what they call an epiphany, she thought dully. *I was too stupid to see love even when it was right under my nose and now I'm losing them. Losing them both.*

So what are you going to do about it? Sadie shook her head and looked around. Blakely was still passed out in the med-chair and Holt, looking weaker by the minute, was slumped beside him, still holding his hand. Do about it? What could she do about it? *You can stop feeling sorry for yourself for one thing. If you just stand here having a pity party you'll lose them for sure.* Sadie shook herself. Right. Standing there and crying wasn't helping the situation at all. She felt an icy blanket of calm descend over her nerves, the one that came over her when she felt truly threatened. Only this time it was her men that were in danger—she could feel them slipping away through her bond with them, could feel them growing weaker by the minute. *That's right—my men,* she told herself. *Now how am I going to save them, heal them? Wait a minute . . .*

Something nagged at the back of her brain. Images of herself pinned between the two of them being loved, supported, healed . . . but it was always Blakely and Holt that did the healing. Could the bond she had with them work the other way, too? *Only one way to find out!*

"Holt!" she said sharply. The blond man looked up at her, his sapphire eyes dull with pain and loss.

"He's going, Sadie. Blake's leaving me; I can *feel* it."

"He's not going anywhere," Sadie said grimly. "And neither are you. Come on—get on your feet and give me a hand."

Holt looked at her with glassy eyes, but did as she commanded, stumbling to his feet clumsily. He looked, Sadie thought, like she had felt a few minutes ago—so full of grief and loss that it was clouding his mind—making it impossible to think straight. Sadie thought it was entirely possible that even if the T-link hadn't been pulling him down, Holt would have died of grief when Blakely did. They were that close.

"Holt," she said again, sharply. "Holt, I need you to snap out of it and listen to me. I think I know a way to bring him back—to save him."

"But Van Heusen said there's no known cure," Holt protested. "What the hell do you think you're going to do, Sadie?"

She was glad to see some of the spark come back into the sapphire blue eyes and hear a little of the old, contrary Holt in his voice. Blakely was in bad shape, but his blond partner was more weak with grief than anything else, she was sure.

"Don't ask questions. Just help me undress him and get him to the bed. Where's the bedroom around here?"

"There's a king size bed through here," Holt motioned numbly and they hoisted Blakely between them, being careful not to touch the pulsing arm. Sadie noticed with apprehension that the red streaks that had started at his wrist had now marched halfway up his arm to encircle his bicep. *If it reaches his heart he's gone,* she thought, knowing it was true. *Haven't got much time.*

At last they had Blakely lying on the bed completely nude. There was a troubled expression on his face and Sadie thought that, except for the mat of crisp, dark curls covering his powerful chest, he looked like a tired, ill-used little boy having a bad dream.

"Now what?" Holt was panting, having done most of the lifting and carrying although Sadie had helped as much as she could. He no longer looked shell-shocked, however, for which she was relieved. The cool, light-blue eyes were alert and he was standing up straight.

"Now we heal him. Take off you clothes—all of them," Sadie said, beginning to strip herself. The red marks on Blakely's arm had advanced again, this time to his shoulder and she didn't like the look of them at all. He was beginning to moan and the dark fans of his eyelashes were fluttering against the high, dark cheek-bones. She remembered what Van Heusen had said about dying in terrible agony. They had to stop and reverse this process before the pain took over so completely that Blakely was unable to feel any pleasure. The pleasure was what would save Blakely and save them all.

"Heal him? What are you talking about?" Holt was protesting, but at least he was taking off his clothes, although considerably slower than Sadie would have liked.

"You and Blakely healed me, Holt. Three times. Once you brought me back from the brink of death, brought me back from where Blake is now." Sadie peeled out of her bra and panties with no shame whatsoever as she talked.

"But that was *us* healing *you*. Using the T-link to generate energy. I don't think . . ."

"You have a better idea?" Sadie snapped. She turned on Holt who was still fumbling with the snap on his suit pants while he talked. "Damn it, Holt, we have to try *something*. We have to fight for Blakely—we love him. *I* love him, love you both, and I'm not letting either one of you go without a fight. Now hurry up and *strip!*"

"Yes, *ma'am*," Holt muttered, speeding up his undressing process considerably and Sadie thought she saw a slight grin hovering around the corners of his full lips. Good, Holt believed they could do it. She was sure. "Now what?" he asked when he was completely nude, his long, golden body tense and waiting.

Sadie thought about it, thought of the way he and Blakely had always healed her. "Get behind him, support him on your lap," she directed. Without hesitation, Holt did as he was told, sliding behind his partner and cradling the darker man in his arms tenderly. Blakely moaned, his eyelashes fluttering half-way open.

"It's okay, buddy," Sadie heard Holt murmur soothingly. "Everything's going to be okay."

"Wha . . ." Blakely's voice was slurred and indistinct, but at least he was regaining consciousness.

Now! Sadie understood instinctively that she had to move fast, while Blakely was still on the edge between sleep and wakefulness, before the pain Van Heusen had predicted set in.

She climbed onto the bed between Blakely's legs on her hands and knees, feeling the brush of his coarse chest hair against her tender nipples as she pressed tight against him, putting him between herself and Holt. Blakely's dark head was leaned back against his partner's golden shoulder and Holt was leaning down, whispering encouragement into his ear. For just a moment, Sadie was transfixed by the sight of pure, masculine beauty, the dark and light heads close together while Holt's long, muscular arms encircled his partner's broad shoulders. Then she dipped her head and took Blakely's narrow, sensual mouth with her own in a heated but gentle kiss.

"Blake," she breathed against his mouth. "Come back to us. We need you—we love you."

She pulled back the tiniest bit to see the indigo eyes come all the way open. There was pain in their depths, but need and love as well. She knew Blakely understood her, and, like a tiny, flickering spark in the pit of her stomach, she felt the beginnings of the warm, golden energy that flowed between them when they all touched. *It's going to work! I know it!*

She bent her head again, rubbing herself wantonly against Blakely's naked chest, feeling her nipples stand to attention at the rough, delicious friction of her tender nubs against his curls. This time she put more into the kiss, parting Blakely's lips to slip her tongue between his white, even teeth, tasting him, letting him know how much he was wanted, was needed. The energy surged, but weakly, too weakly she was afraid.

When she pulled back this time Blakely was completely with them but the pain in his indigo eyes had grown along with his awareness.

"I love you too, kid," he managed to say. "Sorry . . . just hurts so much." Looking at his arm, Sadie saw that the evil red lines had advanced to his collar bone and were reaching for his neck.

"Oh, Blake," she whispered, feeling the start of tears in her eyes and pushing them ruthlessly down. She loved this man and she refused to give up without a fight.

More, need more somehow . . . Then more it would be.

"We're slowing it down but not stopping it." Holt's voice was strained as he stroked along the side of his partner's neck.

More, Sadie thought. She kissed Blakely again and then leaned upward to kiss Holt, pressing her full, naked breasts against the rough scratch of Blakely's cheek to do so. Again the power surged between them, but it was weaker now, dying. Frantically, Sadie kissed along the side of Blakely's strong throat, nipping and biting, licking and sucking as he had done to her the very first time they met. Marking him for her own. Making a mark on his skin the way he had made a mark on her heart. The way he and Holt both had.

"Sadie, sweetheart . . ." Blakely tried to say, but she shushed him with a finger to his lips.

"Don't try to talk, Blake. Just let yourself feel." Rubbing like a cat, she pressed her cheek against his chest, feeling the coarse curls rub her soft skin, drinking in the spicy, good, sandalwood musk of his body, loving him with everything that was in her. "I love you and Holt loves you. We love you so much, Blake. Please, please don't leave us," she murmured softly, continuing to rub her way down his body.

"Suck him, Sadie. Take him in your mouth," she heard Holt's voice urging her and she realized that she was between Blakely's legs and his dark, thick shaft, semi-erect and throbbing with need was right in front of her. Without hesitation, she took the dusky column of flesh in one hand and rubbed the rose petal soft head against her face.

Over her cheeks and forehead, lips and eyelids . . . the sandal-wood musk filled her senses and his cock hardened in her hand, velvet over hot iron, pulsing in time to the beat of his heart and hers.

"Blakely, I love you so much," she said again and then she lowered her head and ran her tongue lightly over the wide crown of his cock, savoring the musky, bitter, entirely male taste of him. Blakely moaned low in his throat and his hips jerked almost convulsively. The golden energy between them seemed to flex and grow, just a little.

"He needs more, Sadie." Holt's voice was hoarse, urgent.

"I know what he needs." She lowered her head. He was big, so big but she took him all the same. Lapping eagerly at the pearly drops forming on the broad head, she sucked the thick shaft into her mouth, taking him down her throat in a way she never would have dreamed was possible. She was only conscious of wanting to take her lover completely inside herself and hold him where he would be safe, and heal him there. Blakely moaned again, his hips bucking to press deep into her warm, willing mouth. Sadie felt another surge of the bright, golden energy around them, but it still wasn't strong enough. What was she doing wrong? She was doing what Blakely and Holt had done when they healed her. They had put her between them and pleasured her the same way she and Holt had put Blakely between them. An idea tickled the back of her brain.

Every other time the healing had occurred, she had been between the two men. She was the bridge, the connector, the conductor between them that allowed the T-link to open and pour its electrical healing magic through them all. Giving Blakely's thick shaft one last, loving suck, Sadie raised her head and looked at the two pairs of blue eyes staring back at her.

She knew what she had to do.

25

"We're doing this wrong. We're in the wrong position." She licked her lips, swollen with sucking Blakely's thick shaft. "Holt, prop Blake up on the pillows and come around behind me."

Neither man questioned her orders. Holt did as he was told, sliding out from behind his partner as gently as he could and made sure Blakely was comfortable on a stack of pillows before he came to kneel at the foot of the king-sized bed behind her.

"Now what?" his warm breath on the back of Sadie's neck and the heat of his golden chest so close to her own nakedness sent a shiver through her.

"Watch," she whispered. "Wait." Rising up on her knees, she crawled forward until she was straddling Blakely's groin and the broad, mushroom-shaped head of his cock was centered directly under her wet sex. "Blake," she whispered, lowering herself until she could feel his thickness brushing against the slippery, swollen bud of her clit. "Blake, I love you and I'm not letting you go. I'm not letting either one of you go." She let herself down, feeling his hardness breach her entrance and took his thick cock deep, so deep, all the way into her wet, hot cunt until she felt him pressing hard against the end of her channel.

"God, baby!" Blakely's voice sounded hoarse, strangled with need and love and Sadie felt another surge in the energy between them as she began to ride, rising up to feel the thick shaft slip almost all the way from her body and then lowering herself to take him deep again, feeling the exquisite pleasure that was more than half pain of having a man who was so large and thick stretching her cunt.

Sadie felt Holt hovering uncertainly behind her back and knew they had to make the circuit complete. "Touch me," she urged her other lover. "Love me, Holt. Get me ready."

"Ready for what, Sadie?" His voice was low and needful, almost a growl. He did as she asked, wrapping strong arms around her while she rode his partner and cupped her breasts in his large, warm hands. At the contact the energy surged again.

"Ready to take you," she whispered breathlessly. "I need . . . need you both inside me to make this work, Holt. Need you to take me, too."

"Sadie," he protested, nibbling softly along her neck. "You know what that means. You know what that would do to us. The Life-bond . . ."

"I don't care!" she gasped as Blakely thrust into her deeply, filling her to the limit and beyond. "Don't care anymore. I want it, Holt. Need it, need you both inside me at the same time. Making love to me, filling me, fucking me. Bonding with me. Please, Holt . . ."

He didn't answer with words, but she felt his large, warm hands on her back, pressing her lower so that she was leaning over Blakely with her breasts brushing softly against his face. Blakely turned and captured one of her nipples between his lips, sucking long and hard, making her groan as flames of pleasure licked along her sensitive flesh.

"Love you, baby," he whispered softly, releasing her nipple and then turning his attention to the other.

Blakely's hot mouth was so distracting that Sadie almost forgot what she had asked Holt to do until she felt something slippery and cold pressing between the cheeks of her bottom. She gasped in apprehension at first, feeling the immediate urge to clench herself closed and get away. *Never been touched there before. It's dirty, wrong . . . No!* With a huge mental effort, she pushed the mean little voice of guilt away and forced herself to relax and concentrate on what Holt was doing and saying to her.

"It's all right, sweetheart. Not gonna hurt you," he whispered low in her ear. He was massaging her gently and the cream he was using to help open her was warmer now, almost soothing. "I love you, Sadie," Holt said softly. "Love every part of you." Sadie gasped as he withdrew for a moment to lick a long, wet furrow up the groove of her spine as she crouched over Blakely. His fingers never stopped their gentle motion, working deeper and deeper into her body that already felt too full where she was pierced with Blakely's cock. "Lean over a little more, Sadie. Give me room to work," he whispered, his warm hand on her back urging her forward.

Sadie did as she was told, but inside she could feel panic rising, overwhelming the golden flood of energy she felt pouring from both men. The mean little voice was back, the voice of Aunt Minnie and Gerald and all of uptight Goshen. *Whore, slut, nice girls don't . . .* but what had that kind of thinking ever done for her? Why should she deny the love she felt, deny the men she loved just because there were two of them instead of one?

Closing her eyes, Sadie took a deep, trembling breath and turned away from that voice and all it represented for good. This was the life she had chosen, a life of laughter and caring and love. A life with Blakely and Holt. She would give herself to them, to both of them and never regret it. Never look back.

She bent forward and rubbed her face against Blakely's rough cheek, hearing his murmured words of endearment and love, the same sweet words Holt was uttering behind her. She was spread open, wider than she had ever been with one thick cock buried in her wet sex, about to be pierced with another from behind. She could feel the rise and fall of Blakely's chest, smell the hot scent of sex in the air as his sandalwood musk mixed with Holt's clean, sharp fragrance to create the aroma that was at once and entirely both of them. Her long hair trailed down her shoulders and Holt hovered over her, ready to pin her even more securely than she was already pinned to the bed, to his partner underneath her. Sadie breathed deeply and knew it was right.

"I love you both so much," she whispered. "Holt, I'm ready."

There were no words, but she felt his long fingers being replaced with a blunt, moist probe and she knew it was the head of his cock pressing against her entrance there. She could feel Holt's hot breath against her back as he panted, pressing up into her body, entering her slowly, trying not to hurt her if he could help it.

Hot tears pulsed behind her eyelids, and Sadie bit her lip and tried to hold them back. She knew Holt was trying not to hurt her, but she was already so filled with his partner's cock and the big blond man behind her was still only buried halfway in her body. *So full . . . Goddess, so full!* her mind whispered.

"Sadie, do you want me to stop?" she heard him whisper and she knew that he and Blakely had probably been exchanging one of those wordless glances over her shoulder and Blakely was warning his partner that this was becoming too much for her.

Sadie took another deep breath and tried to relax, tried to

feel the love pouring between them for her, tried to let the golden energy of their joining wash over her body and drown her in pleasure. Instinctively she understood that it would only hurt this first time. After both men had penetrated her completely and the Life-bond was fully forged there would never be pain in their joining again. There would be only the deep, fulfilling pleasure of baring her soul and opening her body to both her lovers at once. They were so *close* to that ultimate completion, she could feel it, throbbing beneath the surface of her skin, pulsing to get out and flow through them all, binding them irrevocably together. Did she want to stop?

"No." She arched her back on a gasp to force more of Holt's shaft inside her body, making all three of them cry out in wordless pain/pleasure. "No, Holt, I want you inside me. All the way inside me—*now!*"

Obeying her request without question, she felt Holt pull back a little and then sink his thick cock fully into her body until his hips were flush with her bottom, filling her completely, finishing what his partner had started, completing the circle.

They held still, all three of them motionless for a moment, feeling the warm electrical current flow between them as the T-link opened to its widest wavelength and bathed them all in a powerful pulse of sensation. Then, driven by instinct and need, Sadie felt both Blakely and Holt begin to move inside her, setting a rhythm between them that was almost more than she could bear.

Goddess . . . oh, Goddess, she moaned inside her head, feeling their pleasure as she did her own, the pleasure of plunging into her wet, willing flesh, the pleasure of riding her hard and deep as she accepted them both into her body and heart and soul. She had never felt so filled before, had never been so open or needed to be.

"Love you baby, love you so much . . ." It was Blakely beneath her, reaching between them to where they were joined to rub one callused finger over the soft, wet opening between her cunt lips, caressing the tender bud of her clit until she thought she might scream.

"Goddess, Sadie. Love to make love to you, love to fuck your sweet ass and cunt." That was Holt, gasping as he rose over her, wrapping his arms around her to pinch and twist her tender nipples as he thrust into her body. He was filling her completely as Blakely pulled almost all the way out and then reversing their positions as he pulled back and his partner plunged in all the way.

Sadie cried and moaned between them, a purely sexual creature, helpless to do anything but to give in to the overwhelming sensation of being filled utterly with two thick cocks at once. She could feel her orgasm coming, pulsing up from between her legs where she was pierced by their thick shafts, and she knew that the moment it took her their joining would be complete. When she came and felt them come as well, pulsing into her pussy and ass, filling her with their seed, the Life-bond would be forged forever. There would be no going back.

She didn't want to go back.

"Goddess!" she cried out loud. "More, I need *more*!" Blakely and Holt slowed for a moment and then there was a subtle shift in their rhythm. Sadie realized that they had changed the pattern of their strokes. Now, instead of Holt pulling out while Blakely pushed in and vice versa, they were both pulling out at the same time and both surging forward to fill her at once. They were fucking her in perfect tandem.

The shift in their rhythm and the feeling of being so completely filled and possessed by her two lovers at the exact same time was too much. Sadie felt herself tilt over the edge, falling into orgasm and taking them with her.

With a wordless cry her back arched in a spasm of pure ecstasy. Inner muscles clamped down hard, squeezing and milking the cocks inside her. A hoarse shout came from Blakely and a deep groan from Holt as both men thrust deep inside her body and pulsed into her. They filled her to overflowing with their cum and forged the unbreakable Life-bond forever.

"Hey, sweetheart, you okay?"

Sadie opened her eyes and realized that Blakely was talking to her. Had she been asleep? She stretched languorously, aware that she was lying on her side, sandwiched between two warm, slightly sweaty male bodies and that all three of them were naked. It seemed she could remember a similar awakening and she also remembered feeling horrified to find herself in such a position, but this time it seemed all right. After all, it was only Blakely and Holt holding her close between them. Their warmth gave her a feeling of peace and safety she had never felt before. Her men were with her, protecting her, loving her. Nothing could hurt them as long as they stayed together, she was sure about that.

"Is she okay?" The voice came from behind her. Holt.

"I'm fine." She wiggled a little to get more comfortable between them. "Why, what's wrong?"

"Nothin' except you kinda passed out there for a minute after we all ..." Blakely's voice trailed off a little, but he had said enough to jog Sadie's memory. Being pressed between them, the heat and pressure of two thick cocks filling her ... she should be sore, she supposed, but all she felt was a mild, delicious ache between her legs. She felt slippery and hot there, too, and realized she was probably leaking their cum everywhere, but she didn't seem to be able to make herself care. *Wow, it's like afterglow times ten,* she thought, wiggling some more to feel both hard bodies against her. A naughty little cat-that-got-the-cream—type smile spread over her face, and she was helpless to stop it. *Why should I try to stop it? I did get the cream ... all over me, inside me, everywhere.* That thought made her laugh out loud and she opened her eyes to see Blakely staring at her with an expression that was half puzzled, half worried in his indigo eyes. Turning her head to the side, she saw Holt leaning over her with the same look in his sapphire depths.

"Stop looking at me like that," she scolded, trying not to grin. "Can I help it if I just feel good? Anyway, it's not *me* you should be worried about. What about Blake's arm?" She twisted a little and half sat up in bed so that she could see the appendage in question. Blakely grinned and flexed the right arm, which was completely free of any red lines or swelling, making an impressive muscle for her to feel before she collapsed on his chest in a fit of giggles.

"What's gotten into her?" she heard him ask as he pulled her close and pressed a tender kiss in her messy hair.

"I think . . . I think she's a little bit drunk. Maybe from the bond. It *was* pretty intense, you know?"

"Mmm, ya don't haveta remind me," Blakely rumbled. "Never came so hard in my life."

"Me either," Holt admitted, leaning down to kiss the bare nape of Sadie's neck, making her giggle and squirm again.

"That makes three of us." Sadie rolled over so she could look at them both. She could feel the solid weight of Blakely in her mind and the shining thread that was Holt's consciousness as well. Through the Life-bond, a thick, unbreakable cable that bound them all together, she could feel the way she seemed to them as well, soft and beautiful and sweet as a single drop of honey on the tip of the tongue. Goddess, but she loved them both so much! If only there was a way to *show* them.

Looking up into the two pairs of blue eyes and feeling their gazes heat her skin as they roved over her soft, naked, newly opened body, Sadie began to have an idea. Arching her back to thrust her breasts, topped with already hardening nipples into the air, she purred, "Boys, I think I'm ready for round two."

Epilogue

It was a triple joining, at least Sadie *thought* you could call it that. Where Holt had found a priestess willing to perform such an unusual ceremony was beyond her, but she knew pretty well that the tall blond could talk almost anyone around when he wanted. Blakely pointed out that they shouldn't ask questions, but just be glad that Holt was such a silver-tongued bastard, to which she agreed.

It was a small, private ceremony, attended by a few of Holt and Blakely's fellow officers that knew about the Tandem chips and, surprisingly enough to Sadie, by Prissy De Tangelen. Her blond hair swayed gently overhead as she nodded to the solemn chords of the joining march, and Blakely did such an obvious double-take that Sadie had to elbow him sharply to keep him in line.

She had sent invitations back to Goshen, of course, not that she had much hope of any of her old friends and relations coming to see. Aunt Minnie didn't reply at all, but Gerald sent his invitation back with all three of their names circled. "Is this some kind of sick joke?" he had written in red marks-a-lot over the front.

It made Sadie sad that she had no one from her former life to share her joy, but any sorrow was completely forgotten when Blakely slipped a silver ring on her left hand and Holt slipped a gold band on her right and she heard the priestess say those magic words, "Ladies and gentlemen, may I now present to you Mr. and Mr. and Mrs. Blakely-Holtstein. You may now kiss the bride—both of you."

Two heads, one light and one dark ducked toward her, sharing the sweetest three-way kiss in history and Sadie felt like her heart might burst with happiness. She had finally found the men of her dreams—both of them—and she intended to live happily ever after.

Evangeline Anderson is an MRI tech who would rather be writing. She lives in Florida with three cats, one husband, and a college-age sister but no kids, because enough is enough already. She had been writing for a number of years before it occurred to her to share her ideas with the unsuspecting world. To her delight, it turned out that some people liked the weird way her brain worked. She has been writing science fiction and paranormal erotica ever since. Evangeline welcomes reader's comments. E-mail her at *vangiekitty@aol.com* or visit her website at *www.evangelineanderson.com*

Here's a sizzling look
at Jami Alden's DELICIOUS,
available now from Aphrodisia . . .

Suddenly a large, proprietary hand slid around Kit's hip to flatten across her stomach. She didn't even have to turn around to know it was Jake. Even in the crowded dance club, she could pick up his scent, soapy clean with a hint of his own special musk. Without a word he pulled her back against him. The rigid length of his erection grinding rhythmically against her ass let her know her dance floor antics had been effective.

What she hadn't counted on was her own swift response. Sure, he'd gotten the best of her in the wine cellar, but she'd written it off as a result of not having had sex since her last "friend with benefits" had done the unthinkable and actually wanted an exclusive relationship. She'd had to cut all ties and hadn't found a suitable replacement in the last six months.

Tonight, she'd only meant to tease and torment Jake, give him a taste of what he wanted but couldn't have. Now she wasn't so sure he'd be able to stick with that game plan. The memory of her gut wrenching orgasm pulsed through her, her nerve endings dancing along her skin with no more than his hand caressing her stomach and his cock grinding against her rear. His broad palm slid up until his long fingers brushed the undersides of her breasts, barely covered by the thin silk of her top.

She was vaguely aware of Sabrina raising a knowing eyebrow as she moved over to dance with one of the other groomsmen.

Without thinking she raised one arm, hooking it around his neck as she pressed back against the hard wall of his chest. Hot breath caressed her neck before his teeth latched gently on her earlobe. The throbbing beat of the music echoed between her legs, and she knew she wouldn't be able to hold him off, not when he was so good at noticing and exploiting her weakness.

"Let's go," he whispered gruffly, taking her hand and tugging her towards the edge of the floor.

She wasn't *that* easy. "What makes you think I want to go anywhere with you?" she replied, breaking his hold and shimmying away.

A mocking smile curved his full, sensuous mouth. "Wasn't that what your little show was all about? Driving me crazy until I take you home and prove to you exactly how good it could be between us?" To emphasize his point, he shoved his thigh between hers until the firm muscles pressed deliciously against her already wet sex. "What happened earlier was just a taste, Kit. Don't lie and tell me you don't want the whole feast."

She moaned as his mouth pressed hot and wet against her throat, wishing she had it in her to be a vindictive tease and leave him unsatisfied, aching for her body.

But her body wouldn't let her play games, and she was too smart to pass up an opportunity for what she instinctively knew would be the best sex of her life. Jake was right. She wanted him. Wanted to feel his hands and mouth all over her bare skin. Wanted to see if his cock was as long and thick and hard as she remembered. Wanted to see if he'd finally learned how to use it.

And why not? She was a practical, modern woman who believed in casual sex as long as her pleasure was assured and no strings were attached. What could be more string free than a hot vacation fling with a guy who lived on the opposite side of the country? And this time she'd have the satisfaction of leaving *him* without so much as a goodbye.

Decision made, she grabbed his hand and led him towards the door. "Let's hope you haven't oversold yourself, cowboy."

"Baby, I'm gonna give you the ride of your life."

Outside, downtown Cabo San Lucas rang with the sounds of traffic and boisterous tourists. Jake hustled her into a taxi van's back row and in rapid Spanish he gave the driver the villa's address and negotiated a rate.

Hidden by several rows of seats, Kit had no modesty when he pulled her into his arms, capturing her mouth in a rough, lusty kiss. Opening wide, she sucked him hard, sliding her tongue against his, exploring the hot moist recesses of his mouth. Her breath tightened in quick pants as he tugged her blouse aside and settled a hand over her bare breast, kneading, plumping the soft flesh before grazing his thumb over the rock hard tip.

Muffled sounds of pleasure stuck in her throat. She couldn't ever remember being so aroused, dying to feel his naked skin against her own, wanting to absorb every hard inch of him inside her. She unbuttoned his shirt with shaky hands, exploring the rippling muscles of his chest and abs. He was leaner now than he'd been at twenty-two, not as bulked up as he'd been when he played football for the UCLA. The sprinkling of dark hair had grown thicker as well, teasing and tickling her fingers, reminding her that the muscles that shifted and bulged under her hands belonged to a man, not a boy.

Speaking of which . . .

She nipped at his bottom lip and slid her hand lower, over his fly until her palm pressed flat against a rock hard column of flesh. The taxi took a sharp curve, sending them sliding across the bench seat until Kit lay halfway across Jake's chest. He took the opportunity to reach under her skirt and cup the bare cheeks of her ass, while she seized the chance to unzip his fly and reach greedily inside the waistband of his boxers.

Hot pulsing flesh filled her hand to overflowing. Her fingers closed around him, measuring him from root to tip and they exchanged soft groans in each others mouths. He was huge, long and so thick her fingers barely closed around him. It had hurt like a beast when he'd taken her virginity. But now she couldn't wait to feel his enormous cock sliding inside her stretching her walls, driving harder and deeper than any man ever had.

She traced her thumb over the ripe head, spreading the slippery beads of moisture forming at the tip. Her own sex wept in response. Unable to control herself, she reached down and pulled up her skirt, climbing fully onto his lap. She couldn't wait, her pussy aching for his invasion. God this was going to be good.

If anyone had told her twelve years ago that someday she'd be having sex with Jake Donovan in a Mexican taxicab, she would have called that person insane.

Pulling her thong aside, she slid herself over him, teasing his cock with the hot kiss of her body, letting the bulbous head slip and slide along her drenched slit. She eased over him until she held the very tip of him inside . . .

The taxi jerked abruptly to a stop, and Kit dazedly realized they'd reached the villa. With quick, efficient motions Jake straightened her skirt and shifted her off him, then gingerly tucked his mammoth erection back into his pants. With one last, hard kiss he helped her down from the van and paid the driver as though he hadn't been millimeters away from ramming nine thick inches into her pussy in the back of the man's cab.

Kit waited impatiently by the door, pretending not to see the driver's leer. Like they were the first couple to engage in hot and heavy foreplay. Jake strode over, pinning her against the door as he reached for the knob and turned.

And turned again. He swore softly.

"What is it?" Kit was busy licking and nibbling her way down the strip of flesh exposed by Jake's still unbuttoned shirt. He tasted insanely good, salty and warm.

"I don't suppose you have a key?"

She groaned and leaned her head back against the door. "I didn't take one." There were only four keys to the villa, and when they went out they all made sure they had designated male and female keyholders. Unfortunately tonight, Kit wasn't one of them, and apparently, neither was Jake. "What time does the housekeeper leave?"

Jake looked at his watch. "Two hours ago."

He bent over and picked up the welcome mat, then inspected all the potted plants placed around the entry for a hidden key. Watching the way his ass muscles flexed against the soft khaki fabric of his slacks, Kit knew she was mere seconds away from pushing him down and having him right here on the slate tiled patio.

He straightened, running a frustrated hand through his thick dark hair. Eyes glittering with frustrated lust, he muttered, "There has to be a way in here."

"Through the back," Kit said. All they had to do was scale the wall that surrounded the villa. The house had several sets of sliding glass doors leading out to the huge patio and pool area. One of them was bound to be unlocked.

With a little grunting and shoving, Jake managed to boost Kit over the six-foot wall before hoisting himself over. Holding hands and giggling like idiots, they ran across the patio. But Jake stopped her before she reached the first set of doors.

"Doesn't that look inviting?"

She turned to find him looking at the pool. Wisps of steam rose in curly tendrils off the surface. The patio lights were off, the only illumination generated from the nearly full moon bouncing its silver light off the dark water. A smile curved her mouth and renewed heat pulsed low in her belly. "I could get into a little water play."

He pulled her to the side of the pool and quickly stripped off her top. Kit arched her back and moaned up to the sky as he paused to suck each nipple as it peaked in the cool night air. Her legs trembled at the hot, wet pull of his lips, her vagina fluttering and contracting as it arched for more direct attention.

His hands settled at the snap of her skirt. "I like this thing," he said as he slid the zipper inch by agonizing inch. "Kinda reminds me of those sexy little shorts you wore that first time—"

Her whole body tensed. She didn't want to think of that night right now, didn't want to think about the last time she let uncontrollable desire get the best of her. Her fingers pressed against his lips. "I'd rather not revisit unpleasant memories."

She caught the quick hint of a frown across his features but he hid it quickly as he slid her skirt and thong off, leaving them to pool around her feet.

"In that case," he said as his shirt slid off his massive shoulders, "I better get down on creating some new ones."

Lyrical . . . mysterious . . . and dazzlingly erotic. Don't miss Noelle Mack's new story in THE HAREM, coming in December 2006 from Aphrodisia . . .

Yasmina sat down on the edge of the fountain, soothed by the rhythm of the bubbling water. She stared down, focusing on an elusive blue light in its depths that seemed to come and go. A minnow, she thought. With scales of a hue to match the twilight. The blue light vanished and the water grew calm. She drew in her breath. For two years she had come here and never in all that time had the water been still.

She saw a white rosebud reflected upon its mirrored surface, tiny and tightly furled, and so perfectly like a real one that she touched the water, thinking that it had fallen there. To her surprise, the bud opened, becoming a huge, full-blown rose under her fingertips. Its stem shot it above the water and an unusual fragrance filled the air. Yasmina drew back.

Come to me. The deep voice was male. It came from everywhere—and nowhere. Yasmina looked wildly about the shadowy garden and saw no one. If she were caught with an intruder, she would be killed with him, her throat swiftly cut. Or she would be tied into a sack and drowned in the indifferent sea, depending on the whim of the executioner. She had no friends within the harem, no wise woman to plead her innocence.

The huge rose sank back into the fountain and vanished by a magic beyond her understanding, yet its fragrance lingered. The air grew still and warm, oppressively sensual. Yasmina put her hand into the fountain, craving a few cool drops upon her forehead and her lips. Her mouth was suddenly parched.

A goblet made of ice rose from the depths of the fountain, brimming over with its water. Her hand clasped it and could not let go.

Drink, Yasmina. On a hot night, cold water is as intoxicating as wine.

Compelled by an unseen presence that seemed as male as the deep voice, she drank it dry. She closed her eyes, letting the enchanted water slide down her throat—and gasped when a man's hand covered her mouth. He was behind her. She could not see him and she dared not scream.

You must be quiet.

He took his hand off her mouth and she whispered a reply in her own language. "Who are you?"

Shall I reveal myself?

"Yes."

The intruder came around to stand before her. Clad in black rags, his body was outlined by the same bluish light that she had glimpsed in the fountain's depths. His eyes, blacker than midnight, held the unearthly light as well.

Yasmina was spellbound. Yet she could still hear the distant chatter of other women within the harem walls, and smell the smoke of the nargileh, the many-armed water pipe they shared to be sociable, drifting out into the air. Silent and lonely though she was, she would be missed. And she would be found with him.

His bold stance and the tight wrappings around his strong

legs, left her no doubt that he could easily overpower her. He was tall, far taller than any man she had ever seen, with the sensual grace of a panther and an air—a very odd air—of courteous menace.

Come with me.

"I cannot."

No one will see us. There is a door—a secret door. It leads to another garden.

"This garden is my refuge. I have walked here scores of times, in the sun and under the moon. There is no door."

For answer he reached out his hand to her. Yasmina took it, lifted to her feet with magical lightness.

You need not be afraid. The women inside will not miss you for a while longer. I have seen to that.

She followed him. She had no choice. The ragged man raised a dagger from his girdle of black rags and stabbed it into the stone wall. The stone gushed forth a river of blood that ran down to the roots of the white roses, which bent and sighed, filling with blood until they were crimson. A door appeared behind them, carved in an intricate pattern and inlaid with mosaic.

Now do you believe?

"Yes," she whispered. "But what is your name? What may I call you?"

Rustem. It is not my name but you may call me that. He took her hand and pushed aside the red roses. She glimpsed blood on his skin where he touched them and shuddered.

"I did not know that roses could bleed."

All living things bleed, Yasmina. But I do not.

He drew the tip of the dagger along his neck. A wound appeared and closed up again, quickly. She gave a little cry.

It is kind of you to feel pain for me. I cannot.

"Is there nothing that you feel?"

He pushed the climbing roses further away from the door. *Loneliness. And for a little while you and I shall keep that at bay. Enter.*

He drew her through the secret door into a garden she had never seen. It was much like the one in which she walked, though hers lay in shadow and this one shimmered with light. It boasted something that her garden did not: a small pavilion, strung with pierced lamps, in one corner. On its floor were cushions of silk. A young woman, naked, sat upon them and strummed an oud, singing melodies that hung in the air and repeated themselves. Yasmina came closer. The singer's flesh was transparent; her body as insubstantial as the notes of her song.

A ghost. She cannot see or hear you. But the music is pretty.

The transparent singer rose and floated to a different part of the hidden garden, where birds had begun to echo her melodies. They flew over the wall and she flew away with them, leaving the two mortals who had dared to intrude upon her music-making to themselves.

Yasmina sighed with relief. Her companion motioned her to sit beside him on the cushions, offering her more water in another goblet of ice, and unfamiliar fruit. She refused both.

The black-haired man shrugged and helped himself, eating with evident pleasure. His gaze traveled over her body, resting longest on her face. But the sight of her breasts, concealed not at all by the fine gauze that she worse, seemed to arouse him.

Are you a virgin, Yasmina?

The bold question surprised her. "N-no," she stammered, unable to lie. Like all the other women who entered the sultan's palace, her legs had been spread open and the most intimate parts of her body carefully inspected. She had been sold as a virgin and because of her youth, it had been assumed that she was. But she had not passed the shameful test, though her beauty had persuaded the kizlar agasi, the master of the girls, to keep her in the end.

Yasmina had been consigned to the lowest ranks of odalisques, forced to share a room with coarse, strapping young women who tried to rape her with a thick rod of ivory that they had stolen from somewhere. They'd bound Yasmina's wrists, clumsily. One had stripped naked and tied the rod to a string around her waist, letting it dangle in front of her as her companion tightened other strings at its base, running those through her buttocks and knotting it at the small of her back. That one had held Yasmina's legs apart, eager to watch the other violate a new and vulnerable member of the harem.

But Yasmina had bitten through the bonds around her wrist and fought them hard, twisting the heavy ivory rod from the strings that held it around her tormentor's waist and bruising her with no more mercy than she had been shown. In the years since then the two women had left her mostly alone, preferring to play their wicked games with each other, although they invited her to join in when they had drunk too much wine.

So you have known a man.

"A man knew me when I was far too young."

Ah. Then the experience was an exercise in cruelty, not tenderness.

"Yes."

Now I know why you seem afraid of me, although I have little more substance than your own dreams.

"I am not so sure of that," she said, trembling. She felt powerfully drawn to him, all too aware of the disparity between the sensual languor of his pose and the coiled strength that was hidden by his ragged clothes.

I will not hurt you, Yasmina. Undress me. I will let you go as far as you like and touch what you will. Allow yourself to know pleasure.

Unwilling but unable to refuse, she lifted her hand and stroked his face. Rustem closed his eyes, enjoying her tentative caress. Without her being quite aware of it happening, her hand drifted down and the black rags that bound him flew open to reveal a muscular chest. His skin was bronzed and gleaming, like soft, warm metal to the touch. But he had no heartbeat. She pulled her hand away, as if the increasing heat she sensed in his flesh would scorch her.

"What are you made of?"

I cannot explain it now. But I was once human. He took her hand and rested it between the juncture of his legs. *As you can see. Or should I say feel?* He smiled without showing his teeth, pushing his groin up slightly so that her hand pressed down. So. He was a man like any other. She could feel something she had felt before: a rigid shaft of hot flesh.

The black rags unwound from around his groin and he was fully revealed to her wide eyes. She could not look away any more than she had been able to stop herself from following him to this strange garden, from caressing his face and touching his chest. Under her gaze, his cock grew long and thick, the heavy head resting on the bare skin of his thigh at first and then rising as the shaft rose. The sight was mesmerizing. He was not a man like any other. He was made of pure gold.

Touch me. However you like. Your soft hand is soothing.

Yasmina clasped his cock. He cupped his balls as if he were offering himself to her. The rags that bound his legs stayed in place but she glimpsed his skin where there were openings. It was bronzed as his chest. he lay back in the cushions, moving just enough to do so but not so much that she lost her grip on the throbbing golden rod between his legs. The veins that curled around the shaft pulsed with a slow fire. Compelled to caress him again, she lay her white hand over the middle of his chest. Now she could feel, very faintly, the beating of a heart.

The sight of him, whatever he was, man or spirit, aroused her—and Yasmina had never been aroused. Everything that touched her skin excited a potent, animal desire. The delicate friction of the sheer silk over her breasts, bare beneath it, was unbearably stimulating. She let go of his cock with a soft cry and clasped her breasts, then her nipples, pinching them until the silk was torn to shreds. Her nipples were fully revealed by the ruined garment and she rubbed them frantically.

Ahh. Such sensitive breasts and such beautiful nipples.

Startled, Yasmina sat back on her thighs, ashamed that he had seen her fondle her own flesh so wantonly, and tried to draw the shreds of silk together. It was no use. She could not even cover her breasts with her hands, or the sensation of pure sexual excitement would overwhelm her again. No, she must sit before him in rags of her own making and be devoured by his hungry eyes.

Should she returned to the harem, she would be publicly punished, perhaps even whipped by order of the kizlar agasi, the master of the girls. The kizlar agasi decided which woman was brought to the sultan's bed at night; and if any were so bold as to forget that her body and the clothes that displayed it were his property, she would be corrected, forcibly if necessary. Though many odalisques indulged in private stimulation, alone or with each other, a woman of low rank could not be so willful as to rip her clothes in the throes of sexual pleasure, private or public.

She blushed furiously. Rustem sat up and caressed her hot cheeks.

Ah, pretty one. I enjoyed seeing you tear your clothes. Your bare flesh is much more beautiful than your finery. And your excitement is building more quickly than I thought. He put his mouth on hers and kissed her long and deeply. Yasmina moaned, helpless with lust for this strange man. If he was a man.

He picked her up as if she were a flower petal and placed her on his lap. *Such tender nipples,* he murmured into her ear. *And yet, how hard you pinch them. Sometimes pain is as irresistible as pleasure, and as sweet. Am I not right, Yasmina?* He grasped the sheer material and ripped the last of it away from her. *There. Your breasts are as bare as your soul.*

She cried out, knowing that he was right. He cupped her breasts in his golden hands and a sensation of warm fire shot through her. Able to curve around her with uncanny ease, he brought his head down to suckle her nipples and nip them until she cried out again.

Yasmina arched her back and her hair flowed loosely over the cushions. Her lover moved his body over hers, separating her legs, clad in billowing pantaloons sewn to a band about her narrow waist. He drew his dagger, holding the point precisely at the wet spot in the soft silk where her cunny had been enfolded by it. Her sexual arousal had been intense and uncontrollable.

She held still. He pressed the point of the dagger into the yielding place between her legs . . . but he cut only the cloth, in a deft slice that bared her from her navel to the soft double moons of her behind. Her cunny tightened when he bisected the silk and tossed the dagger aside. He spread the rich cloth and gazed upon her no longer hidden flesh. Yasmina tried to cover herself with her hands, but he pushed them gently away.

As I thought. Your cunny is beautiful, whether or not you are a virgin. As beautiful as life itself. And sweet and juicy as a plump little peach.

His eyes were burning with supernatural desire. She felt their odd radiance warm her most intimate flesh as he looked his fill, not touching.

You have to be nicely shaved. The hamam attendants take good care of the sultan's women.

Yasmina nodded. She had left the ritual bath late that afternoon, ignoring the gossiping women who drifted through the hamam, taking turns being scrubbed to perfect cleanliness, massaged and oiled. A silent slave had shaved and plucked her cunny, deftly removing every single hair as was the custom in the harem.

Was the slave young?

"Yes," she said, startled. Had this golden djinn seen her and the slave in the hamam? It was said supernatural beings lurked in water, and perhaps he had been there.

She was gentle with your tender skin. Sometimes the older women are not. But perhaps that is because they enjoy dominating the new ones.

"You know much about what goes on in a hamam," she said. "But no men may enter. It is forbidden."

Men have always found a way to watch such sport. The erotic games of frustrated women are highly arousing. Some men have died for risking a look, just one look.

Understanding opened her mind. "Oh," she said. "And were you such a man?"

Rustem sat back on his thighs, his erection subsiding. He rested his hands on her open thighs as if he were her lover, tenderly possessive, separating from her after prolonged and pleasurable intercourse. She was almost as wet as if he had climaxed inside her.

Yasmina wondered dreamily if his semen would be as golden as the rest of him, pouring forth from the little hole in the heavy cockhead like a hot river. She had watched the play of illicit lovers in the harem. Once. The culprit had been caught and castrated.

Yes. I looked often and long, and I loved a woman who was a sultan's favorite. I met death soon enough. And now I have met you. And I would taste life. He reached forward with one hand and spread her cunny lips with his finger and thumb. *Allow me to kiss you there, beautiful Yasmina.*

His mouth came down on the shaved, sensitive flesh between her legs and he wasted no time in thrusting his tongue in, tasting her fully. He was gentle but masterful, and his other-worldly skill gave her exquisite pleasure.

He quickly brought her to orgasm. Her first.

Wave after wave of sensation coursed through her shaking body. Hot tears rolled down her face as he continued his tender lovemaking, putting the tiny bud above her swollen cunny into his mouth and sucking it until she reached orgasm again, writhing, pushing helplessly against his soft lips, begging him for more. He stilled her with a hand upon her belly, stroking her there until the pleasure ebbed into a feeling of utter contentment.

He straightened and kissed the tears on her face away. *There. You remind me of the woman I loved . . . and died for.*

"How did you die?"

You will not like the answer.

"I must know."

The sultan immersed me in a vessel of molten gold. I am of royal blood and he could not kill me by ordinary means, though I had dared to love the most beautiful woman in his court. A jadi, a witch, betrayed us to the sultan and he saw to it that I did not die quickly. My skin burned away and became gold.

"And what happened to the woman you loved?"

He didn't answer for a long time. *You must be careful that you do not meet her fate.*

"Our fate is sealed at the moment of our birth," Yasmina said softly. "It is written on our foreheads."

Rustem nodded. *God can see such writing. And sometimes the dead can too. Which is why I came looking for you.*

GREAT BOOKS, GREAT SAVINGS!

When You Visit Our Website:
www.kensingtonbooks.com

You Can Save Money Off The Retail Price Of Any Book You Purchase!

- All Your Favorite Kensington Authors
- New Releases & Timeless Classics
- Overnight Shipping Available
- eBooks Available For Many Titles
- All Major Credit Cards Accepted

Visit Us Today To Start Saving!
www.kensingtonbooks.com

All Orders Are Subject To Availability.
Shipping and Handling Charges Apply.
Offers and Prices Subject To Change Without Notice

Is It Hot Enough For You?

DO YOU LIKE YOUR ROMANCE NOVELS EXTRA HOT?
Then Kensington has an offer you can't refuse.
We'll deliver our best-selling erotic romance novels right to your
doorstep, and the first set of books you receive are **FREE**,
you only pay $2.99 for shipping and handling!

APHRODISIA—

*redefining the word HOT! Not for the faint of heart, these trade paperback
novels don't just open the bedroom door, they blow the hinges off.*

Once you've enjoyed your **FREE** novels, we're sure you'll want to continue receiving the newest Aphrodisia erotic romances as soon as they're published each month. If you decide to keep the books, you'll pay the preferred book club member price (a savings of up to 40% off the cover price!), plus $2.99 for shipping and handling charges.

- You'll receive our **FREE** monthly newsletter featuring author chats, book excerpts and special members-only promotions.
- You'll always save up to 40% off the cover price.
- There's no obligation—you can cancel at anytime and there's no minimum number of books to buy.

SEND FOR YOUR FREE BOOKS TODAY!
Call toll free 1-800-770-1963 or use this coupon to order by mail.

YES! Please send me my FREE novels from the club selected below:

Aphrodisia – code BABA06

Name

Address

CityStateZipTelephone

Signature
(If under 18, parent or guardian must sign)

Send orders to: Romance Book Clubs, P.O. Box 5214, Clifton, NJ 07015.
Offer limited to one per household and not valid to current subscribers. All orders subject to approval.
Terms, offer and price subject to change without notice. Offer valid in the US only.

Visit our website at www.kensingtonbooks.com.

BOCA RATON PUBLIC LIBRARY, FLORIDA

3 3656 0435583 3

Anderson, Evangeline.
Take two /